The Christmas Cookie Club
is a reminder of deli...
that girlfriends help c...
and to celebrate the joy. . . . A ripple effect of delicious
nibbles in the darkest time of the year.
A ripple in our lives of the joy of one another.

Praise for Ann Pearlman and her debut novel
The Christmas Cookie Club

"Pearlman has delivered a passionate, heartfelt story of women's friendships and their importance with *The Christmas Cookie Club*. Her characters are personable, and their situations are those that most women have dealt with at some point in their lives. . . . *The Christmas Cookie Club* would be a perfect gift for girlfriends of all ages this holiday season." —*Las Vegas Review-Journal*

"Readers with large groups of friends will love this story of women who support each other through tough times." —*BookPage*

"The women love the gathering and find comfort in one another's company, but the book also relates the stresses and upheavals of their lives—marriage woes, financial meltdowns."
—*Ann Arbor Observer*

"*The Christmas Cookie Club* is exactly the kind of Christmas story I was looking for." —*SMS Book Reviews*

"Fans of literary sisterhood get their seasonal fix."
—*Ledger–Enquirer* (Columbus, GA)

"One notable feature of *The Christmas Cookie Club* is the inclusion of several detailed accounts of the history of various ingredients used in baking. I love it when interesting novels hide kernels of wisdom among their pages; it's such a delight!" —*AnnArbor.com*

"Ms. Pearlman has written a book filled with love, friendship, and heartache. Besides offering an entertaining storyline, the author also shares cookie recipes. A wonderful holiday book!"
—*The Romance Readers Connection*

**This title is also available from
Simon & Schuster Audio and as an ebook.**

ALSO BY ANN PEARLMAN

Keep the Home Fires Burning

Infidelity: A Love Story

Inside the Crips:
Life Inside L.A.'s Most Notorious Gang

the Christmas Cookie Club

Ann Pearlman

POCKET BOOKS

New York   London   Toronto   Sydney   New Delhi

The sale of this book without its cover is unauthorized. If you purchased this book without a cover, you should be aware that it was reported to the publisher as "unsold and destroyed." Neither the author nor the publisher has received payment for the sale of this "stripped book."

Pocket Books
A Division of Simon & Schuster, Inc.
1230 Avenue of the Americas
New York, NY 10020

This book is a work of fiction. Names, characters, places, and incidents either are products of the author's imagination or are used fictitiously. Any resemblance to actual events or locales or persons, living or dead, is entirely coincidental.

Copyright © 2009 by Ann Pearlman, LLC

All rights reserved, including the right to reproduce this book or portions thereof in any form whatsoever. For information address Atria Books Subsidiary Rights Department,
1230 Avenue of the Americas, New York, NY 10020.

First Pocket Books paperback edition November 2011

POCKET and colophon are trademarks of Simon & Schuster, Inc.

For information about special discounts for bulk purchases, please contact Simon & Schuster Special Sales at 1-866-506-1949 or business@simonandschuster.com.

The Simon & Schuster Speakers Bureau can bring authors to your live event. For more information or to book an event contact the Simon & Schuster Speakers Bureau at 1-866-248-3049 or visit our website at www.simonspeakers.com.

Cover design by Laywan Kwan, photo of girls by Image Source/Alamy, photo of apron by Image Source/Getty Images, photo of cookies by Rosemary Buffoni.

Manufactured in the United States of America

10   9   8   7   6   5   4   3   2   1

ISBN 978-1-4391-5941-5
ISBN 978-1-4391-6621-5 (ebook)

For my girlfriends
Thank you

PROLOGUE

We Gather Every Year

I AM THE HEAD COOKIE bitch and this is my party. The Christmas cookie club is always on the first Monday of December. Mark it on your calendar. Twelve of us gather with thirteen dozen cookies wrapped in packages. Homemade, of course. We each bring a dish to pass around and a bottle of wine. Sixteen years ago, when we first started, we'd drink the wine and then go dancing. Now we drink some and sit and talk at my house, or put on Al Green and dance. "Love and Happiness," that's our favorite. We take turns telling the story of the cookie we have made. Somehow each story is always emblematic of the year. We pass out our packages and donate the thirteenth dozen to our local hospice. We donated cookies from the beginning. The Christmas cookie club is about giving, not just the yummy morsels we share with our girlfriends and our families but also with people we don't know who are having a bleak time and might appreciate a wrapped sweet.

Because, believe me, in the midwest the depths of winter can be bleak. Gray skies. Cold. What daylight there is is often overcast. The bountiful lakes make summer glorious, but they hang clouds in the winter. You need to add light and joy. After all, isn't Christmas with its lights, and Hanukkah with its candle flames, about adding illumination to this dark time of year? We need to remind ourselves that the sun will eventually push the night to more reasonable margins. The Christmas cookie club, if it's anything, is a reminder of delight. And, of course, a reminder that girlfriends help one another to endure the grind and to celebrate the joy.

I have rules that have been devised over the years. Just so you know, if you want to form your own party, here they are:

1. No chocolate chip cookies. One year five of us made them.

2. No bars. They stick to each other and crumble.

3. No plates covered in saran wrap and bows. Just try carrying twelve paper plates wrapped in saran wrap. I used to be a waitress and even I can't do it. Plus, they're too limp to bestow to a charity. The containers have to hold the cookies and make an attractive gift. The added advantage is that we can use the containers later to wrap other presents.

4. No more than twelve women in the group. One year, there were fifteen of us and everyone complained that it was too difficult to make sixteen dozen cookies. I never got that three more dozen were such a big deal. But

I bowed to peer pressure. The group is only twelve. And we make a baker's dozen cookies. Besides, there's poetry to that.

5. You can't miss a year. If you can't come, send your cookies or you forfeit your place. There are other people who want to join the group. This rule resulted from the rule above.

6. After five years of coming to the party, you have tenure and aren't ever dropped unless you don't bring or send cookies.

7. It's always on the first Monday in December. Put it on your calendar and count on it.

8. Bring copies of the recipe for each of us.

Jackie falls in love, marries, and moves east and stops coming. Donna loves the party but hates making cookies. Janine has an affair with a colleague and divorces, and she and her lover move to Benton Harbor. Thus, positions open for cookie virgins. So the membership ebbs with the flow of our lives. Right after Thanksgiving, we bake, give delights to one another and the hospice, then pass the dozens of different cookies we've obtained to friends, family, neighbors, babysitters, and manicurists. They treat the guests of other Christmas and Hanukkah and Solstice gatherings. A ripple effect of delicious nibbles in the darkest time of year. A ripple in our lives of the joy of one another.

1

Marnie

Pecan Butter Balls

2 cups pecans
2 cups flour
1 cup melted butter
$\frac{1}{2}$ cup sugar
2 teaspoon vanilla
$\frac{1}{4}$ teaspoon salt
Confectioners' sugar

Preheat oven to 325 degrees.

Chop the pecans in a blender or food processor until you have two cups. Combine all of the ingredients except confectioners' sugar. Gather the dough into a ball. With floured hands, shape into one-inch balls and bake on ungreased cookie sheets. I line my cookie sheets with wax paper or parchment paper and spray them with Pam. Bake for 20 to 22 minutes. Pull the cookies and papers off the cookie sheet and onto a cooling rack and let them cool slightly; be sure they're still warm and then gently shake them in a bag with the confectioners' sugar. Place them back on the paper and add more confectioners' sugar while they cool. Makes 5 dozen

*M*Y DREAM FLUTTERS AWAY as I open my eyes. I stretch my arm out for Jim, but he is gone. Outside, the snow falls in tight crystals, almost like fog. Disney sits laughing beside my bed, his tongue lolling and his tail thumping the carpet. Today is a big and busy day and I had better start it. Reluctantly, I leave the remnants of the dream in the still warm bed and slide on my lavender fleece bathrobe, let Disney out, pour last night's coffee in a cup, and zap it in the microwave. I hug myself for warmth as Disney disappears behind the garage.

I didn't cut back the perennials and now snow clumps in the hollows. Should have mowed the lawn one last time. The microwave dings and I grab the coffee and continue staring absentmindedly out the window. Seven A.M. Only four in San Diego. I wonder if Sky is awake. She's supposed to get her results today . . . sometime this afternoon, her time. During the Christmas cookie party.

Disney bounds from behind the garage, black ears flopping, and sits at the sliding glass door. He runs in when I open it and shakes off the snow. "You doing a good job bringing in winter?" I ask him.

He wags his tail.

"Good boy." He has simple answers to all my questions.

I sip my coffee and scan the kitchen and dining room. The cookie party forces me to get decorated for Christmas. Mini bulbs are strung on the tree outside.

Chili pepper lights surround my kitchen window. Yesterday I trimmed my tree with the crocheted and macramé ornaments I used to sell at the town's art fair in my hippie days. A few wrapped presents and my collection of teddy bears cluster around the base. The one that Alex bought Sky for her first birthday lost an eye twenty years ago and Sky knitted him a lopsided red sweater when she was ten. A Steiff teddy I bought when I was in Germany with Stephen holds his arms open waiting for a hug. Tara's teddy bear sits in her perfection with a pink dress and a tiara. Pretty but unloved. I plug the tree lights in and it looks like Christmas.

After I turn up the thermostat, I make my bed, straighten the room, and slide on some jeans and a red T-shirt. Then I tie on my cookie bitch apron, the one Allie made with the stenciled cookie rules.

At first, the pecans clattering around in the Cuisinart sound angry until the nuts are sufficiently broken. This year, Sky and Tara will get an extra dozen of the pecan balls so the recipe is multiplied by three. I put the butter, a pound and a half of it, in a glass container and turn on the microwave. My mother's KitchenAid mixer is on the counter. I add in the measures of flour, sugar, vanilla, and salt. The microwave dings and I pour in the melted butter and turn on the mixer. While it stirs, I pull out cookie sheets and reach in the drawer for parchment paper. Then I scrape down the batter into the depths of the bowl and this batch is done. I turn my iPod to my rock playlist and Tina Turner wonders what's love got to do with it. Everything, I tell her. But I remember my dream and wonder if I had it because I love Jim or simply because I just want to recapture our great sex. Maybe both. I don't really like that I've fallen so in love with him.

Flour feathers my hands as they roll the balls and I dote on the methodical, rhythmical work. My hands place the morsels in rows of four across the top edge of the sheet. Three dozen on each sheet. The simplicity and beauty of the math and the routine reminds me of women spinning yarn with a drop spindle, kneading dough, harvesting berries, beading shoes, weaving, or grinding corn. I am connected to those ancient women, and to women around the world, as all of us, each of us, make food, clothes, tools for our families, our friends, ourselves. I place one sheet in the oven and start on the next. The easy part is done. For a few minutes I return to the peaceful rolling, and place the sheet in the oven, check the timer. Five more minutes.

I cover the dining-room table with sheets of parchment paper, fill a plastic bag with confectioners' sugar, and place potholders in the center of the table. The timer rings. I drag out a sheet and rest it on the table. The cookies are the brown of fall oak leaves; the aroma of cooked pecans fills the room. Seger sings about autumn rushing in and here it is winter. Already. How did it happen so quickly this year? I think about the revolving seasons and the motions we go through during each of them. I start rolling balls for the third sheet. And then slide the loaded parchment from the hot sheet onto the table, put the metal on the stove to cool, and gently place the balls in confectioners' sugar.

The work must be done quickly; the cookies can't be

too cool or the confectioners' sugar won't soak in. Too hot and fingers get burned. The second sheet is done and I go into the kitchen to retrieve it.

The phone rings.

I jerk around to reach the receiver lying on the counter next to the empty butter container and hit my cheek on the corner of an open upper cabinet. The door bangs closed, my cheek smarts, and the sting spreads.

"Mom?"

"You can't sleep, huh?"

I can't stop working, so I cradle the phone to my shoulder while my hands continue adding cookies to the sugar bag.

"Nope. Just tossing and turning. Afraid I'd wake up Troy." Sky's voice trembles slightly.

The cookies roll in the sugar. "I was worried about that."

"I figured you'd be up making cookies."

"You're right. I just took out the first sheet. I'm shaking them in confectioners' now."

"Ah. Nana's pecan balls."

"My favorite."

"Mine, too."

I didn't know that Sky and Troy were trying to get pregnant that first time three years ago. After all, they were both in law school and Sky plans her life to achieve her goals. But she called to brag that they had gotten pregnant on the very first try. The way she said it, "We got pregnant on our first try," and then giggled, it sounded almost as if they had never made love before.

I bought fabric to make my first grandchild a quilt,

was carrying it into the house, when she called, crying. She had lost the baby.

"Darling. I'm so sorry." My voice fell. "You'll be blue for a few months."

"That's what the doctor said. She said we could try again in six months. This is one helluva period." Sky sniffled and then tried to muster a laugh. "'It's not unusual to have a miscarriage. Especially for the first one,' she said."

"I'll come be with you."

"You don't have to." But her voice lilted with relief.

But then the next year she had a second miscarriage. Again she called to tell me, again I flew out to be with her. "I wish you were closer."

"Me, too."

When she was pregnant the third time, we held our breaths. I tried to wipe the tinge of concern from my voice when we talked. The pregnancy continued. "Maybe I should quit work," she wondered. "But they're monitoring this pregnancy." By the fourth month, I breathed again. Then in the eighth month, movement stopped. An ultrasound indicated the baby had died. The best thing for a future pregnancy was to wait and deliver the baby when contractions started.

"The baby is rotting inside me."

"I'll be there tomorrow."

"No, wait, wait till the labor starts. I'll need you with me then."

"How's Troy?"

"Scared. Confused. Like me." She sighed. "I'll just have to get through this next month. I guess I should remake the nursery into a guest room or office or something."

"Are you going to stop trying?" I imagined her pacing, holding the cordless phone to her ear and walking past the couch and the dining table, making a loop around the kitchen, and doing it again. It's what she does when she's upset. She moves.

"I don't know if I can go through this again."

"Plenty of time to decide that."

"I don't know if I can even do *this*. Live for a month with a dead deformed baby inside me."

"Deformed?"

"That's what they said when they did the ultrasound. There's something wrong with the baby. Probably why I've had those miscarriages."

"I don't get that. Why would something wrong with this baby account for former miscarriages?"

"It might be genetic. Troy and I may have a genetic problem."

I hunted for magic to console her. "They'll find out what went wrong now. Maybe they can help you. Both."

"Yeah. Right."

"You want to come home?"

"No. I want to pretend everything is okay and do my life. What I have of it."

I couldn't argue with her bitterness.

She called as soon as labor started. I flew out to her and arrived as she was entering transition. I held her hand. Troy paced. I wiped her brow. She clenched her eyes and panted. Grunted. She gripped my hand tight. Screamed. She endured all the agony of birth without the happy end. The pain didn't vanish with the baby's first cry. She squeezed out tears as she squeezed out the dead infant.

Blue. We saw the deformities the sonogram had hinted at. He had very short arms, a smashed-together face. Our glimpse was quick before they bundled the baby away for genetic testing and evaluation.

"At least that's over." She sank as though to fall through the operating table and disappear. "I didn't think I could do it."

"You did. And you came through like a champ." I squeezed her hand and kissed her forehead.

"Why didn't you warn me?" Her eyes were wide with shock, as though I had betrayed her, purposely kept important knowledge from her.

"Because you forget the pain as soon as you hold your baby."

She sniffed. "I guess I won't forget, then."

Troy kissed her. "I love you so much." Tears fell down his cheeks. "Our poor baby. You're so brave."

She sucked out a cry.

"Yes. Brave. Both of you." I held up water for her to drink. The doctor stitched her episiotomy. They gave her a shot to dry up her milk.

We didn't know what else to say. We simply cried under the blazing surgical lights, the doctor still sewing between her legs.

"We all lost the baby, didn't we?" Sky's gray eyes met ours, the pupils magnified by her tears.

I kissed her. "And we're all with you, darling."

Troy squeezed her hand and pulled away strands of hair stuck to her face with sweat.

We cried then and we cried together later on the phone when I returned home. Finally we went through a conversation without tears. And by that time Sky was pregnant again.

Now, four months along, she whispers as though she's apologizing, "All I ever wanted is to be a mom. I mean that's what's most important. You know?"

I place more cookies in the confectioners' sugar. "Yes." She tells me this often, as though if she says it enough then it'll happen, as though prayers are always answered.

She was the little girl who wanted baby dolls when her peers were collecting Barbies. She carried Matilda in her old Snugli, sang lullabies and slept with her. Even her Pound Puppy wore a diaper. I don't know if it stems from a longing for our closeness before Tara was born, or from some sort of reverse jealousy or competition because of Tara's birth. Or maybe it's from seeing my joy at being a mother. Or simply the drives of biology and loving Troy and wanting their love personified. But being a mother is the apex of Sky's sparky ambition. Maybe I need to accept that what is, just is.

I place the cookies in neat rows. Now six to a row. "There's lots of ways to be a mother."

"I just want it to be over. I want the test results. Four months of worrying has been enough. Now, other people know something crucial to my life and I just have to wait. Wish I could know first thing in the morning to start facing whatever's next."

"Or enjoy it, the pregnancy and the birth." I roll additional balls in the sugar. "I'm sure she'll call you as soon as she knows."

Sky is quiet. My cheek hurts, I should put some ice

on it, but I can't. Not now. After we finish talking. After this batch is done.

"I hope it doesn't ruin the cookie party."

"Ruin it? I'll have my friends to help me celebrate."

She hears my glimmer of optimism as tarnished hope. "Or console you."

"And you, too. They love you, too. You're not alone."

The confectioners' sugar is soft as feathers as I place the cookies in rows. The first sheet is almost done.

There's quiet. She stops walking. "I keep thinking, wondering why this has happened to us. So weird that Troy and I share this rare recessive gene when we're not even in the same ethnic group. . . . I mean, we're mostly German and he's Italian."

"They're very close, you know?"

"I know, but the doctor said it's like we're brother and sister, like from the same family."

"Maybe that's why you two are so good together. And don't forget, you've got a fifty percent chance that this one is okay. Each baby has a fifty percent chance. Maybe you've done the sad half and now you'll have three normal pregnancies."

"It doesn't work that way, Mom. It's fifty percent with each roll of the dice."

I know that. I tell her pretty fairy stories with happy conclusions as though they can erase the negative edge that haunts her. "Happy endings aren't impossible. Sometimes they actually happen," I say. The first sheet is finished. The cookies from the second are getting cool. I have to work quickly. "You have enormous strength. Even after the last time, you're trying again. Something inside you knows this will work out." I sweep a handful of cookies into the sugar and roll them from side to side in the bag. "So what are you going to do today?"

"How's Tara?"

"Fine." The truth is that her little sister, Tara, is eight months pregnant, eighteen, and unmarried. The father of her baby is a black ex-convict and aspiring rap star. This summer she voiced the irony that didn't escape any of us. Shaking her black hair chunked with blue, she'd said, "Damn, here I am in an unplanned pregnancy in what most would call a, like, insane relationship and you"— she tilted her head toward Sky—"who does everything in the supposed-to way, wants a baby so badly and . . ." Her voice trailed off; her eyes met Sky's fully. "Like they say, life ain't fair. It's . . . what do they call it? A mockery." Unspoken tension and competition dissipated with our laughter.

Now I say, "You never know how any of this is going to turn out. And each event is ours to interpret. You can see yourself and Troy as victims of peculiar biology, or see yourselves as even physical soul mates and this ordeal as strengthening." I place the sugared cookies in their row. "So what are you doing today?" I repeat.

"It's Monday. I have a trial to prepare for. I'm hoping other people's problems will be a relief."

"A distraction to make the time go quicker."

"I'm carrying my cell phone with me." She stops talking. "Hey. Troy's up. And calling me."

"Go to your husband. I'll be here all day. Call if you feel like talking. I love you." I blow her a kiss.

"I love you." The pop of her kiss vibrates in my ear as I finish shaking the cookies from the second sheet. More confectioners' sugar floats on the two sheets of cooling cookies. Six dozen cookies done.

I cover the baking sheet with fresh paper and turn to the bowl of batter, gather some dough, and begin rolling another series of balls.

Sky met Troy in the eighth grade right after the winter break. Troy's family had just moved to town and a teacher assigned Sky to escort him to his classes since their schedule was the same. "He's not cute, but he's nice," she reported. That night they talked on the phone. By the next month, he was in front of our TV watching *90210*; Sky sat next to him on the sofa. Tara sprawled in his lap. I popped popcorn.

"Troy's my best friend." Sky's shirt was cropped, her jeans low, her belly button revealed.

"You look cold." But I thought, No one, not even a thin girl, looks attractive dressed like that.

"It's the style, Mom." She squinched her face to express her exasperation.

"You sure are taking your responsibilities seriously. Introduce him to some guys."

"I did. We just like hanging out together." She grinned a quick smile but didn't change her clothes.

"Why don't you have a sleepover this Friday? Invite Marissa and Jennifer."

"Cool."

In the fall of ninth grade, her backpack slumped over one arm, her glasses sliding down her nose, wisps of hair strategically pulled from her ponytail, she said, "Mom." When she started like that, I knew she was setting an agenda for a serious conversation.

"What." I put down the workbook I was reading on health insurance and turned toward her. At that point, I was studying to pass my state test licensure exam. Now I'm licensed in life, health, and long-term care insurance and run my own small agency.

"Troy said he loves me."

"Loves you?"

"I said, 'I love you, too.' And he goes, 'No, I mean, I *love* you. Love you like that.' I had the remote to the TV, so I turned it up." An invisible remote was in her hand and she hit a button. "I didn't want to hear him. I just go, 'I love you, too. You're my best friend.' But he says, 'I want more.' So I pushed the sound again." She hits the imaginary button. "I didn't know what to say. He wants to be my boyfriend. He wants us to go together."

"Like steady?"

She shrugged and slid the backpack off. "It'll ruin the friendship. It always does," she said as though she had worlds of experience.

I wondered if she'd been eavesdropping on my conversations with my girlfriends. "How?"

"Well, our relationship will change. We'll never be able to go back to being just friends. And our friendship is perfect." She draped her coat on the back of the dining-room chair. This time I didn't scowl.

"Not for him," I pointed out. "It's not perfect."

She chewed on the inside of her lip. "I was just beginning to like Ryan."

My eyebrows rose. "Oh. So he's afraid he'll lose you to Ryan?"

"He can't lose me. He's my best friend." She popped

open a can of Diet Coke. "See what I mean? Already when you get that *love* stuff you fuss about losing someone or someone cheating."

"Do you think he's hot?"

"I never think of him like that. Well . . ." She bit her lip and slumped into a chair. "I just don't want to risk our friendship."

"Now that he's made it clear he feels this way about you, you can't pretend you're 'just friends' anyway." I used my fingers to place quote marks around the words.

"That's what he said. He said he can't help how he feels 'cause I'm so cute." Red crept up her face as though she'd crossed a boundary.

"He's right. You *are* cute." I laughed. "Beautiful. With unbelievably fascinating eyes."

She widened those gray eyes of hers, flecked with green, and said as though amazed at the coincidence, "That's just what he says."

Their friendship evolved into boyfriend and girlfriend and then at some point, I didn't know when, they became lovers. They went to college together, and by their sophomore year, shared an apartment. Graduated together, went to law school together.

"Too grown up, too early," I complained.

"It is what it is. It's happened and it's as good as it gets. Why would I throw away something so perfect just because of my age?"

"You two have such little experience in relationships." I worried if curiosity about other lovers might destroy them in a future mess of cheating and betrayal.

"Why would I throw away something so perfect just

because we were virgins when we met? Besides, I've watched you."

"Yes." I touched her cheek. Twenty years ago we had gone through her father Alex's illness, a lingering tiredness and chills that was diagnosed as acute leukemia. They hospitalized him and he dwindled before our eyes, each day a noticeable loss. He died in one week. I didn't have time to believe he was seriously ill before he was dead.

He was thirty-five years old.

Thirty-five. Just thirty-five.

Only now am I beginning to reconcile it.

Sky was seven. She watched as I started a relationship with Stephen, got married again, and had Tara. Stephen. His philandering raked me over burning coals. The flurries of sincere guarantees that I was the love of his life and promises that it would never happen again worked for a while.

But always, a few months later, I would face again the unexplained and inconvenient absences, hoping he'd been in an accident rather than what I anxiously suspected. Then the smell of another woman on him, credit-card bills for hotel rooms, suddenly minimized computer windows, whispered telephone calls, increased drinking — the clichéd paraphernalia of adultery. A divorce. Remaking my life again, now as the single mother of two daughters.

Troy was the most stable man in her life.

"I sure don't have the answers to relationships." Truth is, the absolute truth, after Stephen, the men I saw wanted a commitment, but I needed a guarantee of perfection, and people don't come that way. And my daughters came first. I wasn't sure what to do with my life when it fell off its anticipated track other than raise them.

Men want your attention. Don't forget this. They have problems sharing you with their own child, let alone another man's. Their needs must be paramount. One wanted me to send Tara to boarding school. Another wanted me to leave her in the house and come live with him. She was fourteen then. "I would have loved living alone when I was fourteen," he told me.

"Yeah, I bet. No way. No fucking way," I answered.

I met Jim at a party, the friend of a colleague's son. She hadn't invited him to meet me. He was simply there. Bald, with his cuddly potbelly, and his grin. His absolute friendly warmth.

"You're beautiful with that white hair. Shows off those bright blue eyes," he told me.

"You're my friend's son's friend!" I exclaimed, as though that made him a baby.

"Hey, I'm over twenty-one," he said with a laugh. "Legal." And he grabbed me to dance to Marvin Gaye, swaying into me and then spinning me away. "And like I said, you're beautiful and sexy as hell. And there's never any harm in dancing, is there?"

"Of course there isn't." I relaxed in his arms. "And you're good."

"I am at that." He held his head back and laughed as he twirled me under his arm.

So first there was that palpable electricity and then there was the curiosity we had about each other. After the party, he came over. He told me that he had primary custody of two teenage sons. And that they were his first priority. I used to caution men about my daughters with almost the same words. "I like that. Children do come first."

He leaned away from me. "Most women don't understand what that means. It means what with my job and taking care of them, I don't have much time for a relationship. Women want more time. So I haven't been looking." He sipped some wine and shrugged.

I guessed this would be a night's flirtation. I threw him a quick escape and easy out. "Listen, I have to trim my tree. I'm having a party on Monday night."

"Can't come on Monday. I'll be in Atlanta."

"You're not invited. It's women only. But I do have to trim my tree."

The tree was bolted in its stand. The lights were strung but unplugged. A green plastic ornament container rested beside it. He lit the tree and said, "That's better." Nodded at the box, then asked, "So are the ornaments in there?"

"Yep."

"Let's do it. I love trimming trees."

We trimmed the tree and then poured some more wine. "To a great holiday," he said as our glasses clinked. "To meeting you."

That was a year ago. The Saturday before the Christmas cookie party. By New Year's we were lovers and by Valentine's I was in love with him. But I didn't tell him. I've never said I love you to any man after Alex. Stephen first told me he loved me when I discovered him cheating. As though that would compensate for his adultery.

All it did was convince me that saying I love you was manipulative. When he proposed, he held my hands tight and looked into my eyes and said I was the most important person in his life. The world was empty without me. Love, he said, is just another word. So I didn't say it to him. And he was cheating on me by the time I was pregnant with Tara, so I didn't even tell him after she was born.

I've told Sky and Tara I love them. And my parents. Some of my girlfriends. But with a man, I'm not certain what those words mean. They're too much of a demand and a burden. They sound like you want something. Strings are attached. Obligations. Besides, how can we know what it means? I read somewhere that the color of our eyes impacts the hues that we actually see. If that's true, how do I know *love* means the same to me as *love* means to you? Especially since we don't even know if *red* is the same to both of us. Plus, isn't love supposed to be forever? And there's no forever with a man.

So that Valentine's Day, when Jim said, "I think I'm falling in love with you," I answered, "I'm infatuated with you, too."

He nodded.

Infatuation is safe. It lets you both off the hook. There's no weight of permanence; in fact, there's a promise of flightiness and transience that reassures.

That impermanence should be a relief to Jim as I'm parceled around his edges. He sells medical software to hospitals across the country, so he's often away working, and then he's home helping his sons with their homework, watching them play soccer, teaching them how to drive. My time, our time, happens when he's home and his kids are out. Or on a Friday or Saturday night before their curfew. Now I'm the one having to make allowances for a lover's attention to his children and his work. But it's what I respect and love most about him: he takes fatherhood seriously.

I haven't seen him alone for two weeks. We watched his son play indoor soccer on Saturday night. We were supposed to spend Friday night together, trimming the tree as an anniversary celebration, but his plane home was delayed and by the time he checked on his sons, it was too late. And then on Sunday the younger one twisted his ankle and they were in the ER. I went to the hospital to be with them. We haven't spent the night together, made love, for several weeks. That's partly the reason for the sexy dream.

The question remains: Is Jim another chance for intimacy, an attempt at a permanent relationship, or another dodge from commitment? To make matters more complicated, he's twelve years younger than I am. Forty-five. Just forty-five.

I pull the last sheet from the oven, slide off the cookie-laden parchment, and prepare to start rolling the last six dozen in sugar. Thank God for parchment paper. It makes baking cookies so much easier. I make some more coffee and let one of the finished balls melt in my mouth with its nut and butter and smooth vanilla flavors.

Disney runs to the door, tail wagging, bouncing. Snow dusts Jim's jean jacket.

"Why, hi! I didn't expect you."

"Thought I'd stop by on the way to the airport."

When he brushes my cheek with his lips, the dream returns with all its sensual details. In it, Jim kisses my eyebrows, traced around my eyelashes to the length of my nose. His kisses tasted of cinnamon. And I was all sensation, reception. I hesitated to savor this perfect join, this golden unite. The glow intensified to sharp waves filling me, washing me. The bliss woke me.

The luscious dream surprises me. When was the last time I've had a dream like that? It's been years. Decades. Maybe when Tara was a baby. I thought that squeeze of lust and obstinacy of satisfaction was finished, my desire dimmed by time and menopause. I don't see Jim enough. But now here he is, surprising me with a visit and kissing my cheek.

"Hmmmm. We can do better than that." He wraps his arms tight around me, one hand cupping my ass, and holds me close. I relax into him, savoring his slight cinnamon scent and the elements of the dream that are here with me now.

"Mmm, I've missed you," he moans.

He pulls away, checks his watch.

"Checking if you have time for a quickie?" I laugh.

"I wish." He parodies a sad face. "I have to be there in forty-five minutes."

"How 'bout a . . . cookie?" I glance at him sideways and lift an eyebrow.

"Yeah," he drawls, "I want one of your . . . cookies."

I hand him one and also my cup of coffee.

"These are fabulous. Hope you made extra for us."

Us. I don't know if there is an "us." When he says things that imply a future, I have too many feelings to pull apart. Fear, excitement, happiness, peace. I watch him enjoy the pecan ball. "Don't worry, I made several extra dozen. Besides, we'll have scads of cookies after the party."

"Oh, but these have got to be the best." Then he reveals a red-striped bag with green paper on top. "Ta da!" He bows and hands it to me. "I came by to bring you this. Figured you needed it for your tree." I riffle through the green tissue paper stuffed on top and pull out a caramel teddy bear wearing a sweater with Christmas trees trimmed with red hearts.

"Oh, Jim. Look at him. He's so dapper and he's smiling." I laugh and lean over to kiss him. "You're so sweet."

"It's all a manipulative ploy. I just wanted to see you because I'll miss you. But I didn't want you to know that."

"I love it when you flirt with me." Especially when I don't have any makeup on. I go into the living room and place the bear under the tree. "He fits right in with his new pals," I joke.

"I'm sorry I missed helping you trim the tree this year."

I consider saying, It was the anniversary of the first day we met, but I don't. Too presumptuous. Instead I say, "Well, he's perfect."

"Hey. What happened to your cheek?"

I forgot about it. When I touch it, it smarts.

"You look like someone tried to beat you up."

"Combat cooking." I laugh.

Jim grabs another cookie. He tries to watch his weight and bemoans his potbelly, but I find it cozy. "Put some ice on it or something." He checks his watch again. "Hey, I gotta go. I'll call you. See you Friday night."

"For sure?" I keep my voice light so he doesn't hear me as needy or nagging.

But he does. "Nothing but taxes is for sure. And death. Have to see what's up with the kids. I'll call."

"Have a great week," I say, kissing his cheek. He opens the door and I see snow crystals caught like motes in a sunbeam.

The door closes as though he sucks away all sound with his leaving. Then I hear my iPod playing and it's time to get back to work.

The music fills me as I roll the last of the dough. The tree's lights twinkle, the teddy bears beneath it. The one Jim brought looks like he's always been there. The secure implication of saying "us," I realize as I line up more completed cookies to cool, was immediately erased by his joke about death and taxes, his parry after my press for reassurance. Perhaps that's how the previous men felt about me, a seesaw, a push-me, pull-you. Was I always like this? Tentative about commitments? My relationships last only seven, eight years, not the long forty-five years my parents shared until my mother died. Maybe it's the bad luck of Alex's illness that set me on a path I never wanted to tread . . . the knowledge so young that life doesn't turn out the way you expect and that tragedy can be around the corner.

Just like great happiness, I remind myself.

I inhale the dissipating aroma of the cooling cookies and as I exhale I think of Sky and the wait for news about the viability of her pregnancy; Tara and the birth of my first grandchild, a son, she was told; and Jim, about to fly to Boston. My girlfriends are coming tonight to the party

laden with wrapped cookies. I know all their secrets. I
know the tensions between them. I have to remember
to try to seat Rosie away from Jeannie. They probably
haven't resolved their fight. Rosie will be all over Laurie
about her baby. I hope Taylor, or her husband, has found
a job by now. Both of them unemployed and their sev-
erance packages must be dwindling. And I wonder how
Sissy will fit in, meeting a bunch of women she doesn't
know.

Disney brings me his monkey, a squeaky toy that long
ago lost its voice. I reach down, pet him, and take the toy.
I say, "Thank you," and return it to him. I'm grateful for
the joys of life. No. Not just the joys. The richness of it.
The opportunity to experience it all. That's where I am.

The cookies are done. All they have to do is cool completely and I can pack them in their bags. Disney drops
the monkey and inspects the floor for fallen morsels.

It's still morning. I sauté onions and add chopped
tomatoes, chicken broth, and basil for soup. It simmers
on the stove. When it's reduced, I'll turn it off so the flavors will intensify. There'll be something warm when the
cookie bitches come in from the cold.

Three small pots of poinsettia add color to the bay
window over the sink. The living room is clean and
ready. The bedrooms and my office are straightened up.
I have a window of time, so I check my face and sure
enough there's a bloom of purple under my eye. I should
get some ice for it. But instead I get the holiday bandanna
I bought for Disney and tie it around his neck. I swear he
tilts his chin up and prances around like he thinks he's

extra handsome. I sit on the sofa with a new murder mystery, my feet propped on the coffee table. Disney jumps up and glides his head on my thigh. I read a few pages.

The phone rings.

"Hey. How're the cookies?"

"Cooling. How're you feeling, Tara? How's the baby?"

"Kicking the hell outta my bladder. I feel like I'm nothing but a ball with a head and tiny appendages."

I chuckle, because that's pretty much how she looks. All baby way out front and she has a month to go. "How's Aaron?" I remember to include him as though he's part of the family, though I'm not sure he'll be permanent. Maybe no one's permanent. But he'll always be the father of my first grandchild.

"We're in the recording studio. . . . He and Red are changing some lyrics, so I thought I'd call. I'm on break."

I picture Tara with her dyed black hair and blue chunks, sitting in the vestibule of a recording studio. In my image, there's a cigarette dangling from her fingers, but she quit when she found out she was pregnant, so I erase the cigarette. She became pregnant shortly before she graduated from high school. She told me in an off-handed way, as though she were telling me she was going to the movies. Her casualness was a way to diminish her concerns about my reaction or, perhaps, to encourage a nonchalant response from me.

"What in the world are you going to do?" I asked her. It's amazing to me that I have two such different daughters. Sky always told me everything. Tara said as little as possible. Sky sometimes hung out with me during high school. Tara wouldn't have been caught dead with me in public. Sky did what she was supposed to do, considering the future. Tara did what she thought of at the moment, living in the eternal now.

She blinked long light eyelashes at me and shrugged. Took a drag on a cigarette and snuffed it out. "Guess I'll have to stop."

"Have you decided?" I pressed the issue. I didn't know exactly how I felt. I didn't know exactly what I wanted her to do. It wasn't his race, but I didn't kid myself that racism was resolved. He'd been to a juvenile prison and seemed little able to support himself. And their dream of making it big as hip-hop musicians seemed like pie-in-the-sky. She composed the music and the backgrounds, played keyboard, and sang to his lyrics.

"We're excited about the baby, Mom."

"You're getting married?"

"Married?" She brought her brows together, huffed an explosion of air from her mouth, and shook her head. "Our love doesn't need legalities. Besides, what does being married promise?"

I didn't know how I felt about that, either. At least if it didn't work out, she wouldn't have to go through the hassle of divorce.

I hugged her then and at first she stood stiffly and then relaxed into my arms. "I'll give you a shower."

She pulled her head back and grinned. "Sure. Invite all your friends. I love them."

Now, she says breezily, "Hey. I'm driving Aaron's mom to the party."

"Sissy? You're bringing her?"

"I thought I'd see a friend while the party was going on and then drive Sissy home."

"Means I'll get to see you."

"Yeah, and Sissy doesn't know how to get there. Oh, Mom, she's excited about this party. She spent all yesterday cooking."

"She's the cookie virgin this year."

"Sissy thought that was a riot. A party making her a virgin at something, anything, again. And her about to be a grandma for the fourth time." In the background, the anger of electric guitar strings and then I hear Aaron, "Hey! Babe! You on."

"I gotta go."

"See you about six, then?"

"Between six and seven. Okay? Sissy's shift at the hospital isn't over until four and she'll have to get ready. And then the rush-hour traffic . . . and we're supposed to get a sleety mix this evening."

"Okay."

"So I'll just get to see you for a hot minute . . . Bye, Mom."

"Drive safe." She doesn't hear me; she's hung up.

I try to lose myself in the mystery I'm reading, but I can't concentrate. Maybe the cookies are cool enough. I start counting out twelve and put them in a Ziploc bag. When thirteen bags are filled with cookies, I retrieve the small makeup kits that I found at the dollar store in animal prints: leopard, snake, tiger. The bagged cookies go into their containers. I pull out ribbon and tie red and gold metallic strands around the handles of the kits and curl the ends. There's an extra bag for Tara to take. The remainder of the cookies, about three dozen, go in larger Ziploc bags and then into the freezer.

I wipe the table and sweep under the floor. The house is tidy. My cookies are done. The soup is simmering. Eartha Kitt purrs *so hurry down the chimney tonight.* Everything is perfect.

FLOUR

I take flour for granted. I don't wonder about it; it's always in my kitchen as it was in my mother's kitchen, part of my day-to-day life.

When Sky and Tara were small, they drew pictures in the flour I sifted on the counter after we cut out cookies or rolled pie shells. The flour we use as the base of almost all of our cookies is ground wheat. Wheat, a cereal grain, can be turned into bread, cakes, pasta, cookies, noodles, juice, breakfast cereal, and couscous. It's also fermented into beer, vodka, and alcohol.

I read somewhere that wheat was probably first cultivated in Turkey about ten thousand years ago. It was an ideal first crop because it self-pollinates, it's grown from seed, can be harvested in a few months, and is easily stored. The domestication of wheat allowed hunters and gatherers to settle. Villages grew.

Once we humans were able to count on a stable food source, we didn't need to travel to hunt and gather. As sufficient food became available, we traded with other groups and spread our knowledge and products around the world. Thus, wheat reached the Aegean about eighty five hundred years ago and India about six thousand years ago. Five thousand years ago it reached Great Britain, Ethiopia, and Spain, and a thousand years after that, China.

Three thousand years ago horse-drawn plows and seed drills increased grain production. Until recently, the 1800s, wheat was harvested as it had been in prehistoric times, with a sickle, then tied into bundles for threshing, where animals crushed the stalks or farmers beat out the grain. The grain was tossed into the air and the chaff blew away, leaving the important kernels. In 1834, Cyrus McCormick invented the reaping machine and industrialization changed food production, and our society.

The story of turning wheat into flour follows the history of machines. First, it was made by grinding with a pestle and mortar, which produced a gruel or pottage, not flour for bread. Saddle stones, which are two large stones, the top one of which is pushed by an operator, are seen in ancient Egypt. Water power was used to move the stones two thousand one hundred fifty years ago in Rome. Wind power was harnessed one thousand years ago. Then steam engines and electricity.

Flour is composed of carbohydrates, fat, and protein. Wheat contains more protein than rice or other cereals, and is the most nutritious of the common grains. Here's a baking tip: The percentage of protein, which ranges from 9 to 12 percent, determines how hard and chewy the food will be. Bread flour benefits from a higher percentage of protein while cookies are more delicious when made from flour with less protein. Softer flour, with less protein, is best for chemically risen products like cakes, cookies, and biscuits. Pastry flour is best to use for these, but if you don't have that, use all-purpose, and take a tablespoon out per cup.

Wheat is like air, we take it for granted. But for most of us, most of the time, grains really are the staff of life. Just think, the cultivation of wheat allowed the development of settlements and the first neighborhoods. So the next time you measure out some flour, consider its prime role in human civilization.

2

Charlene

Chocolate-Almond Bonbons

1 8-ounce can almond paste
1 12-ounce package (2 cups) semisweet chocolate pieces
1/4 cup butter
1 14-ounce can (1 1/4 cups) sweetened condensed milk
1 teaspoon vanilla
2 cups all-purpose flour

Preheat oven to 350 degrees.

Use a teaspoon and make tiny balls out of your almond paste. Do this prior to getting your chocolate ready. Set aside.

In a medium saucepan, combine the chocolate pieces and the butter. Cook and stir over low heat until melted and smooth. Stir in the sweetened condensed milk and the vanilla. Stir in the flour until well combined.

Once your dough and chocolate are ready, enrobe each almond paste ball with chocolate. Place your rounded chocolate-almond balls on an ungreased cookie sheet. Bake for 6 to 8 minutes. Transfer to a wire rack to cool.

Drizzle with glaze, or dust with powdered sugar. Makes 90 cookies

Almond Glaze

In a small bowl, stir together 1 cup sifted powdered sugar, ½ teaspoon almond extract, and enough milk (about 1 to 2 teaspoons) to make a thin glaze. You can tint it with food coloring.

Chocolate Glaze

In a small bowl, mix ½ cup sifted powdered sugar, 2 teaspoons cocoa powder, and enough milk (2 to 3 teaspoons) to make a thin glaze.

Powdered Sugar

In a large Ziploc bag, add the cooled cookies, 30 at a time, to 2 cups powdered sugar. Shake gently and remove with a large slotted spoon to remove excess sugar.

*S*HE COMES RIGHT IN without knocking or ringing the bell because Charlene knows that my house is her house. Disney greets her with his monkey. Last time I saw her, a little more than a month ago, her hair was a light brown, but since then she's highlighted it blond. She's trying to get back into life. Charlene lives in a town about an hour away and she's spending the night with me. Her purse and overnight bag are on her shoulders. She's dressed in black jeans and a decorated jean jacket. Charlene is still too thin. Still without the twenty or so pounds she's lost since Luke's death. "Fashionably thin at last," she had joked, "at way too great a price."

She places her overnight bag on the table along with her purse and hugs me. I feel her shoulders tremble as she relaxes in my arms and I hold her. "When I see you, my brave front drops away."

I just hold her.

"I keep telling myself that God is with me and Luke is with Him." Charlene pulls back and straightens up, sees the trimmed tree, the pot of soup, and the cookies in their containers. "You got it all done and it's only one o'clock."

"Woke up early today."

She shakes her head as though the very thought of so much activity exhausts her. "What happened to your cheek?" She leans away and squints red-rimmed eyes, then tilts her head slightly. "Jim didn't . . . ?"

Charlene's second husband beat her and she escaped him by entering a safe house with Luke and Adam, who was then an infant. She was living in L.A. then. To ensure her safety, she had eventually relocated to Michigan.

"Jim? No! I hit a kitchen cabinet while I was making the cookies. Couldn't stop to put ice on it."

She shakes her head. "That's fierce cooking." And musters a laugh.

"It's been a long time since I've heard you laugh."

She goes back to her car and brings in her bags of cookies, and a platter of cheeses and a box of crackers. Her cookies are in plastic bags. "I didn't have a chance to buy the boxes for them, so maybe we can run out and look for something together?"

"Good. I want to get some flowers, anyway." I place my containers of cookies in a Trader Joe's bag and take it to my office. We put the cheese platter in the refrigerator and Charlene's cookies on the counter. Disney almost trips her.

"I see you're all dressed for the party," she says to him, and he wags his tail, satisfied by the attention.

I met Charlene before Luke was born. More than a quarter of a century ago. She and I dated the same man, but rather than fight over him, we dumped him and started hanging out together. I got her a job at the Gandy Dancer restaurant where I was working. Then she met Luke's father and moved to California. Divorced him and married Adam's father. After Adam's father beat her, she returned with Adam and Luke. Adam is the same age as Sky. For two years, we lived together, pooling our resources and babysitting each other's kids. We both entered school; Charlene became a nurse, and I, with my degree in marketing, am the first person in my family to graduate with a four-year degree. She is Sky's second mother, I am Adam and Luke's second mother. Diane came with Charlene's third marriage, and a move across the state for her husband's job. But that one didn't work out, either, and she divorced for the third time. It's fast telling this, but it wasn't fast living it. In the telling, I can sum up a decade and a half in two sentences.

"Why do you have to marry them? Why don't you just live with them?"

"I do live with them. Then I marry them. It seems wrong to live with a man unmarried when there're children in the house."

"You're too beautiful for your own good," I told her then. Charlene has perfect features, Grace Kelly or Diane Lane with a toned body. No matter what she wears, she looks elegant with an extra flair, even now, even in the midst of tragedy, wearing black jeans and a T-shirt with her denim jacket. Yet she's unaware of her beauty. She wears it with no manipulation, no desire for gain. No flashy makeup. No sexy come-hither looks or coy batting of eyelashes. And men, who might shy away from a woman who's so beautiful, instead make passes at her. She piques their curiosity and then their lust, a lust that's founded more on the appreciation of the subtle than the blatant.

"I stupidly think that love solves all. Think I woulda learned different after Adam's father."

* * *

Then Luke died.

This is what happened:

Luke was a good-looking man, eyes the color of Charlene's deep brown mixed with his father's blue. Green eyes, long eyelashes, curly brown hair. Tall and muscular. A hunk. And he carried his handsomeness with the same indifference that Charlene carries her beauty. With no attention to it. He was an ironworker. A job with enough risk to maintain excitement and sufficient income to maintain the outdoor toys he loved. Motorcycles. Snowmobiles. Horses. Jet Skis. He turned twenty-seven the year he died, and he'd fallen in love with a slightly older woman, Jenny, with two little kids. They had rented an apartment together and were looking for a house and planning their wedding.

Luke was at work on a windy day in May — summer hadn't completely arrived, so remnants of winter coarsened the wind. He was building a new office building, walking on the scaffold, the rebar rods stretched to the sixth level. The rods rooted the cement, the drywall, the bricks, and the wood securely to the ground, providing the stable sheath for the structure. He had pride in his job, setting the rods. I wonder what he was thinking. I never asked Charlene this, not wanting to introduce a new anxiety or obsession. But this is one of mine: I imagine those last seconds before everything changed. Was he thinking about making love to Jenny? Was he thinking about waterskiing this summer? Was he slightly hung over from the beers he had had with his crew the night before? Or maybe it wasn't anything that I could imagine. Maybe he was thinking about setting the rod, carrying the rod across the scaffolding and welding it to its base. Maybe a glob of mayonnaise dropped from someone's sandwich. Maybe a sudden gust of wind swayed the scaffolding just as he took a step. Maybe someone called to him, "Hey, Luke, wanna grab some brew tonight?" Or "Did you catch that Tigers game?"

But he slipped.

He fell.

He was halted in his course by the tip of a rod honed by a furnace to the sharpness of a spear. The naked rod was two stories down.

It pierced his lower back, split his guts, missed his heart, penetrated his lungs, and exited his shoulder. Stopped his descent, so he hung there, above the ground, the rod piercing him. He hung there, completely conscious. To me, when I think of it, I think of him, dear Luke with his curly hair and obscenely long eyelashes. ("No boy deserves those lashes," I used to tease him.) I imagine him as Jesus, hanging impaled. Fixed by the metal rod and its fabrication instead of metal nails. A crucifixion by modern construction instead of Roman cruelty.

Luke hangs. He must see the rod, the ground four stories below him, people gathering and looking up at him. The tip of the rod splits his shoulder, maybe close enough for him to kiss it. His arms dangle away from his sides. He says, "Call Jenny. Call my mom."

First they call 911.

One of the men went to him. "Hey, Luke. We're here. We're all here. Going to cut you off this rod, dude."

It took twenty minutes to figure out how to cut the

rod and transfer him, with the rod still through him, to the ambulance. I get as far as wondering if the torch that cut the rod heated it throughout his body, or, if they used a saw, if he felt its vibrations. I consider those twenty minutes when he hung from that rod fully aware. I guess I imagine it so much that I'm with him; he's not alone.

Charlene called me on the way to the hospital. "Luke. He fell on a rod and they've just cut him down. He's still conscious."

"Slow down." I couldn't understand her. I didn't know if it was the connection or her gasps.

"One of those rebar rods. He's impaled on it, it's right through him. That's what the man said. They can't find Jenny."

"Where is he, where are you?"

"I'm on my way to St. Joe's. He's being transported there."

"I'll meet you."

WHEN I ARRIVED, Charlene was sitting in the waiting room clamping the arms of the chair. Her deep brown eyes darted in her pale face, her fingers tightened white on her chair. She clenched her eyes and shook her head.

"I just saw him. The doctors are trying to figure out how to remove the rod." Her words wheezed, and then she placed a hand at the base of her throat and inhaled and started again. This time with an even voice. "They'll take him to surgery. We can see him again. No one has been able to find Jenny." As though reminded, she pulled out her cell phone and pushed a speed-dial number. And then flipped her phone closed. "I think she forgot to pay the bill. I've called her mom, I left ten messages on her home phone. Maybe she's shopping. Maybe she's at work, but she wasn't supposed to work today." Charlene's voice was monotone.

"You've done what you could."

"I saw him. We talked." She turned to me, her eyes dark and shiny. "He said he wasn't in pain. It hurt at first, but it doesn't hurt now. He told me he was happy. That this was the best year of his life. This year with Jenny and the kids. Then he looked at me, closed his eyes, and said, 'You are a great mom.'" Charlene's eyes were full, and tears began to fill mine. When she told me this, I realized the gravity of the situation. Somehow the fact that he was conscious, that he was talking, that they had cut him down and he was in the hospital, made it seem redeemable. But Luke sensed his own peril.

The doctors came out, a group of five. A man with even teeth and hair graying at the front stepped forward. We walked toward them. "It's a testament to his strength and youth that he's alive." He nodded to Charlene. "We'll have to remove the rod. We considered sliding it out of him the way it went in but decided it's better to open him up to remove it. It will be a long and difficult surgery and we'll do the best we can. Luke is fully aware of the possible consequences and difficulties."

Charlene nodded, trying to comprehend what this meant, even though it was straightforward. "Will he be all right?" Her mind couldn't grasp the change that had just happened.

The doctor blinked. "If he survives the surgery, it'll be a long recovery and at this point we don't know what limits or disabilities he may have." He shifted his weight. "But your son is determined."

The doctor was accustomed to people seeking reassurance and positive outcomes that he couldn't promise. "We'll do the best we can, he's got his youth and strength in his favor, and we'll have to see what happens."

Charlene and I stood, swaying from one foot to the other, holding our purses.

"You can go in and see him now. We gave him something to keep him comfortable and we'll be taking him to the OR shortly." He checked his watch. His hair was cut very short and his scalp was pink. "In fifteen minutes."

Luke's face was so pale that his eyes appeared brightly green, almost like glass doll's eyes. When he saw us, he smiled. "Hi, Aunt Marn."

When I leaned to kiss him, his forehead was alarmingly cool but lacquered with sweat. He twitched a grin and then smiled at his mom. She grabbed his hand.

"Where's Jenny?"

"We haven't been able to reach her."

"Oh." He faded. Sheets draped his body, smoothing the edges into the white bed, which made him appear small and slender. I noticed then the rod poking from his shoulder. Terra-cotta red, rusty. Square. Its edges were black and the gauze wrapped close to his flesh was tinged with red.

"Did you see the doctors?"

"They're taking you to the OR in a few minutes. They said the surgery will be long."

He glanced at the rod exiting his shoulder. "It was just getting really good and now . . . One second. One split second and everything changes."

Charlene gasped.

"But don't worry. I'm going to fight. I survived it going in and I'll survive it coming out." He inhaled and closed his eyes.

Charlene rubbed his hand and then looked out the window to the blue sky streaked with clouds and the hospital parking lot filled with squares of pastel cars in allotted white rectangles painted on black tar. Endless rectangles in endless lines. She returned to her son. "We'll get you through this. You're a fighter."

"I'm so tired." He shifted his head to her slowly, as though his determination and anger had spent his energy. "This has been a good year. A gift year." He then turned to me and said, "You'll take care of her. Right?"

I met his eyes. I thought of saying something reassuring and optimistic, like, you'll take care of her, or she'll take care of herself, she always has, but I realized what he was asking. I nodded and said, "Of course, Luke. Of course. We'll take care of each other. And you."

But he knew what I meant and I knew what he asked.

He seemed to fall asleep as his breathing deepened. Charlene and I were on either side of his bed, each of us holding his hand. Tubes entered the one that Charlene held, connecting him to his IV. The light was very still. One of those moments when everything stops as though the very air is thick and motes quit dancing in their sunbeams and the world holds its breath.

Luke opened his eyes and said, "Tell Jenny that I love

her. And thank her for coming into my life. Maybe it's just as well she's not here. I don't want her to remember me like this. You either." He closed his eyes again and cleared his throat. "Tell her that if I don't make it, I'll be watching over her and for her to go on and make a happy life. A happy life for both of us." He swallows.

Charlene bowed her head, her hair covering her face, squeezing his hand.

"If I'm not going to be here to give you all the love I intended to give you, the joy, the fun, then you're going to have to do it yourself . . . you'll have to do it for me." Luke drew in air.

"Tell her. And tell yourself, Mom."

Charlene laid her head on his bed and I knew by the movement of her shoulders that she was crying and that she didn't want him to know, determined to maintain a semblance of strength and optimism. By force of will and mother-love, everything would be all right. He'd come out of surgery and return to work, to riding motorcycles and snowmobiles. This would be one of those nightmares that you endure with pounding chest, but once the dream is over, you return to ordinary life, the nightmare forgotten.

Tears ran down my cheeks. Sky had lost her baby just a few months prior and I thought of that birth, that horrible nonlife birth, and now this. Luke seemed peaceful. It was the morphine, I told myself. Luke lost consciousness or fell asleep. "I guess he's resting to gather his strength."

Charlene didn't respond. She kept her head on his bed, kissing his hand.

The nurses entered and said, "It's time to go."

Luke woke and put his hand on his mom's hair. She lifted her head and they looked at each other. The charge between them was palpable. "Love doesn't die. You know I'll always be with you. Right, Mom?"

"Yes, Luke." The end of the word caught in her throat and she sat there, hands empty, as they wheeled him out. "And I'll always be with you. You can't die."

He didn't die on the operating table.

He came through the surgery but did not regain consciousness. We waited. By then, Jenny sat with us as we shuffled between his room, the waiting room, and the cafeteria. That day, she had been called into work because a coworker was ill and, in her haste to get the kids to day care and herself to work, had left her phone at home. When her mom first called her at work, she had been at lunch. Jenny arrived at the hospital right before they wheeled him to surgery. She walked with the gurney, repeating over and over, "I love you."

After the surgery, Charlene sang him "Puff the Magic Dragon" and "Blackbird," the lullabies he loved.

Jenny read jokes she picked up from the Internet. Adam played his iPod for him. Diane read the novel he hadn't finished. We recalled the time when he and Sky got up early and decided to make us French toast. They weren't allowed to turn on the stove, so it was uncooked, soggy bread floating in cups of syrup.

Jenny laughed, but Luke didn't move.

For five days. Until it was apparent that the Luke in the hospital bed was his empty shell and that his spirit was gone.

"He's with me," Charlene whispered. "Just like he promised, I feel him."

Sky came for the funeral, another funeral too soon after her baby's death. Here we were, middle-aged and dealing with wrong deaths. It should be our parents, Charlene's mom was still alive, older friends. Not our children. Not our grandchildren. The world had turned upside down.

Charlene told me a month or so after Luke's death that she went to the site. She went on a Sunday when no one would be there. Luke's love for the outdoors was one of the reasons he became an ironworker. She had to see his last view. The day she went was one of those sunny June days with the birds madly singing and the air warm and moist, but not yet the sticky heat of full-blown summer. She dragged a ladder up the stairs to the floor he had been working on and propped it against the steel. The height, the still naked sides of the building, made her dizzy. But she didn't care that much if she fell. She inhaled and closed her eyes. Her fear was swamped by her drive to be with him, to experience his last moments as though he would not have endured them alone and they would be together.

The second step from the top, she had purchased his view. She was where he was when he hung impaled on the rod. A field stretched toward trees off in the distance. A breeze ruffled the grass. A few innocent daisies nodded their heads. He had seen a fresh field rather than the skeleton of the building he was erecting. You saw God's hand on the earth, she thought as she climbed down the ladder, acknowledging whatever spirit of Luke still floated among the rods he had affixed, the scaffolding he had climbed, the ledge he had sat on to eat lunch.

She returned to her car.

That was seven months ago. Now we're in my kitchen and the Christmas cookie club will start in five hours. "What kind of cookies did you make?"

"Those chocolate truffle things. I didn't want to try a new recipe."

"Everyone loves them."

"I couldn't miss the party, I'd lose my spot."

"You're one of the original members. I'd make your cookies and pretend they're yours."

"I'm trying to just move through my life as though it's normal. Like it used to be."

"How is Adam? And Diane?"

"Diane's busy being a teenage girl as though that would make everything okay again. And Adam?" She purses her lips together. "He's less depressed. He finally got a job training horses."

"You hungry? Want something before we go shopping?"

Charlene wrinkles her nose and shakes her head. "I'm never hungry." And then she jerks as though she's forgotten something. "How's Sky? Isn't today the day she gets her results?"

"Not until late this afternoon. Her time. Probably during the party."

She inhales. "I hope this one's okay."

"Neither one of us could sleep. She called me at four A.M. her time."

"I've been praying for her. For you, too."

"We could use some good news. Both of us. All of us," I added as an afterthought.

"What's she doing today?"

"Working. Carrying her cell phone with her constantly and jumping every time it rings. Trying to get her mind off the test results."

"She'll be okay, you know? Sky will."

"But *she* doesn't know that yet. And she'll be okay in a different way."

She nods. "There's lots of ways to be a mother."

"They haven't given up on the customary way." I check my watch. "We should get going."

When Disney sees me putting my jacket on, he looks at me from under his lids, his head down. "Nope. You can't come with me. Not this time. Besides, you have a job to do. Keep the dust from falling, Disney," I tell him, and he wags his tail. "That dog does the best guilt trip ever."

The snow has stopped and the sun peeks through a curdled sky. I hold my face up to receive its glow. "Gotta savor that sun," I say more to myself than Charlene.

Charlene's Honda backs to the powdered street. "Where should we go first?"

"Let's go around the corner."

Around the corner is a half-mile away. We drive through trees arching beneath their burden of snow and turn right into the strip mall. "Wanna try the dollar store?"

"Sure," Charlene says.

We roam the aisles and she considers shiny red bags

and then finds canisters that are blue with snowmen dancing among pine trees. There're only seven boxes and so she picks six that are rimmed with brightly decorated trees.

She wheels her full cart to the cashier while I grab assorted paper plates and napkins.

The cashier picks up the containers decorated with the dancing snowmen. "These are too cute," she gushes. Her nails are curved and painted with black and gold stripes. They click against the boxes. "I want some for my mom."

"I got the last ones. But there're plenty of the trees."

She picks up one decorated with trees and shrugs. Clicks her nails on the register to open the cash drawer.

The purchases are in her trunk and Charlene says, "Where next?" She checks her watch. "You think we have time enough for Crazy Wisdom?"

"Sure."

Monday afternoon isn't busy, and we find a parking spot on Main Street. Downtown is decorated for the holiday. An artist has painted sprays of white holly leaves and delicate red berries in storefront windows. The trees' lights glow under snow frosting. Wreaths hang around the streetlights. The window of Crazy Wisdom announces "Material Treasures and Ethereal Pleasures." The aroma of incense and perfumed candles surrounds the books and jewelry and assorted small objects. Since Luke's death, Charlene comes here seeking something: hope of eternity, the limitless suggestions of gods, the promise of salvation through Buddhism, Christianity, crystals, paganism, kabbalah, I Ching.

She picks up a statuette of Genesh, his trunk waving with his arms, and then Iemanja, the African mermaid goddess. A rack spins with charms of runes, Chinese birth years, zodiacs, animal spirits.

She opens a book and reads, her head tilted to one side. " 'Death is the passing of life. And life is the stringing together of so many little passages.' Whaddya think?"

"Life is more."

She squints her eyes. "Sometimes pebbles of joy." Shuts the book. "See, I still remember happiness is possible."

She moves to the incense, picks up one called rain, and smells it. "At first, I meditated to find Luke. As though he'd reach out to me and implant a message and I'd have him again." Returning the incense to its place, she sniffs a pine-scented candle. "Now I meditate to find peace." She turns toward me. "To escape this world, perhaps, or forget myself. Or just to exist in the endless now without a past or future." She spins away and walks to another section, grabs a book with a picture of the moon on it, opens it, and says, "Hey, Marnie."

I'm looking at a box of beautifully drawn animal-spirit cards.

"Listen to this one. 'The life of sensation is the life of greed; it requires more and more. The life of spirit requires less and less; time is ample and its passage sweet.'" She closes the book and repeats, "Time is ample and its passage sweet."

"It doesn't warn that the life of the spirit is difficult. So much to ignore and so much focus and concentration."

"It's all difficult." Charlene's shoulders slump as she wedges the book back in its place.

"Maybe it's an issue of balance: spirit, greed, love, and fun." I stop a minute and then add, "And don't forget to exercise regularly and floss your teeth."

She laughs.

I find a deck of cards displaying sexual positions and flip through them, wondering if there're any Jim and I haven't done. Charlene peers over my shoulder at a drawing of the woman's legs clamped around the man's back, his hands cupping her ass to hold her up. I shake my head. "Lord. I haven't done that since Stephen."

Charlene laughs. "Me, either."

I widen my eyes.

"I mean when you were with him. You and Jim could have fun with that."

"Or simultaneous heart attacks." But I consider wine and candlelight and crazy music and a game we could play, he and I, that takes us to the edge of the world. Choosing cards and letting them dictate until the playful sex becomes focused on making love and exchanging feelings and adult acceptance. I remember the dream of this morning. "Yeah. Think this could be one of his Christmas presents along with promises to carry out some of these suggestions."

She stands closer to me. "I've never seen you so in love."

"Yeah. We're okay." Then I add to my blithe answer, "I don't see him enough. Everything conspires against us." I touch a finger for each obstacle on my list. "The plane's delayed, his son gets sick, the basement floods, he has an emergency meeting in Denver." And then I spread my open palms. "We miss our window of opportunity. And that can happen two weeks in a row."

I jam the cards back in their box. "I know he wants to see me. But I feel way down on his list. After the kids, his job, his house . . . all his obligations. I don't see him enough. But I don't want to be nagging or demanding."

"It's kind of amazing, isn't it? Now you're feeling the same neglect as the men you dated after Stephen."

"I've told myself that a million times. Maybe it's my fear of closeness. First I use my obligations as an excuse, and when they're gone, I pick a man who has the same ones. Is it a trick of life or my own psyche?"

"Have you told him?"

"Not really. Our alone time is limited by his stage in life."

"Have you told him you love him yet?"

"Love him?"

Charlene knows I haven't said that since Alex. "You do, you know." She gives me a hug. "Don't be so scared." She puts down the pine-scented candle she's been carrying. "Look what we all go through even if we don't take risks."

"Ah, but love is the biggest risk of all."

"I'm going to go upstairs while you buy those cards."

At the cashier, there's a celadon bowl filled with angel cards. I close my eyes and pick one that says "expectancy" and then meander up the winding staircase banked with statues of Buddha and Isis to the tearoom. The menu lists a bewildering assortment of teas, daily homemade soups, sandwiches, and pastries. A sign announcing the folk singers, storytellers, tarot card readers, and psychics that will perform at the tearoom is on the wall along with a schedule of discussion groups and meetings. A slender man with gray hair hunches over a newspaper at a table in front of the window.

Charlene and I order Clouds and Mist tea and I ask for a vegan Ding Dong.

The waiter has bleached white hair and plugs in his ears. When he brings the tea, he says, "Don't let it steep too long or it will get bitter." The tea floats in a hand-tied bag. I point at the chocolate Ding Dong. "I know you're going to help me with this."

"You're just trying to get me to eat."

"Caught me," I confess as I taste it.

Charlene picks up the other fork and begins eating.

"You laugh occasionally. You're getting through it."

She tilts her head and narrows her eyes slightly. "I didn't realize. There're moments now, split seconds, when I don't think of him. When I don't imagine him hanging on the rod or remember the look in his eyes when he said I was a good mom. And Adam, well, he's been so difficult with his depression and insisting it should have been him and his drinking that I'm worn out." She stirs her tea. "He may have turned a corner, though. He likes this new therapist and he's attending AA meetings. And he loves being with horses."

"It's only been seven months. Not even a year."

"I dread this Christmas and New Year's. And his birthday in February."

"Don't pretend nothing is different. Talk about him."

"We can't help it." She stabs another bite of cake but

forgets to eat it. "I thought I'd light a candle that represents him so we acknowledge his spirit is with us."

I nod. "Want me to come for some of it? Depending on whether Tara's baby obeys his due date, I could come on Christmas Eve. Drive home in the morning."

"Would you?"

"If I can . . . Not sure yet when Sky and Troy will be here, either."

"I can't cry with my kids, it scares them as though they've lost both Luke and me. As though I'll be crying forever." She chews on the inside of her lip and her eyes fill. "Diane is determined to enjoy everything teenagers are supposed to, parties, dates, football games. Most of the time she's off with her friends. I guess that's her way to handle it. Once when I was crying, Adam asked me if I wanted to go be with Luke. 'Not yet. Not now,' I told him, but I wonder if his depression is his way to be with Luke. Or his way to keep me here."

"You're not going anywhere."

"There's nothing for me to do but plod on through. Somehow." She stops and closes her lips and sits there as though listening to the flute music playing in the background. Baskets of philodendron hang in the window from macramé holders.

"Shit. I don't know how to help you, either."

"You sit with me and listen to me and cry with me. It's all there is. It's love."

I think, like I have a million times, how Charlene is going through every mother's worst fear. It scares me and I am reminded of my blessings each time.

"Sometimes I think God wanted Luke to be with

Him. That thought comforts." Her eyes are on mine as though waiting for an answer or a question. Then she continues. "People say to me, Too bad he didn't get to live his full life. You know, marry Jenny, maybe have children together, grow old together. All that. But now I wonder why we insist that a full life lasts eighty years and anything less is a cheat. That was *his* life. Those twenty-seven years. It was *his* full life."

"I've never thought of it like that. Time doesn't make a full life. Living your life to the fullest makes it full." I drink the tea. "You remember Doobie?"

"That fat gray cat?"

"Yeah. She lived twenty-two years. A long life for a cat. But all she did was sleep. In the winter she moved from one register to another. She had twenty years of sleeping and two years of living." I shrug. "But, hey, that's what she wanted to do. Who's to judge?"

The piece of cake still rests on her fork, still in her hand, and she eats it. "At least I can sleep. And work is a relief. And making those cookies." She laughs. "Even though it took all yesterday." Then she stops and shakes her head and places her hand on mine. "I'm so glad I have you." Her eyes are slightly moist.

I squeeze her hand. "Me, too. We're like soul friends or something through the years. You get a few of them. You, Allie, Juliet, Tracy. People who are there and I can tell everything, anything to."

The man crinkles his newspaper closed and walks past us. His movement reminds me of the day ahead. "Hey. We better get the flowers," I say. "Almost forgot them." On the way out of the store, Charlene retrieves the book and buys it.

At Fresh Seasons, a clerk wheels a cart of roses and jams them in buckets of water. Carnations, irises, baby's breath, sprays of holly, ginger flowers stand in buckets of water on the floor. I pull out a ginger flower and sprays of miniature red roses and white carnations. I buy an additional bottle of Chardonnay. The cashier wraps the flowers in green paper and ties them with raffia after tucking in an envelope of Floralife.

WE FOLD CHARLENE'S cookies in tissue and place them in the snowmen and tree canisters, then bags, and take them into my office. A burgundy cloth protects the table and the ginger flower in a slender vase is the centerpiece. Roses and carnations go in a bulbous red vase on the coffee table, except for a few that I place in a stem holder on my bedside table. One rose is now in a bud vase in the bathroom.

It's time for me to take a shower. When I'm dressed, Charlene is curled up on the sofa reading. "Here's your paper."

The headline is about corruption among public officials. Spending was lighter on cyber Monday. Blame and finger-pointing continues between the workers and the CEOs.

"I went to the drugstore. I know how to get rid of bruises." Charlene rolls her eyes and I realize she's talking about the years when she was abused. "Yellow covers blue, green covers red. So that's blue." She points to my cheek.

I'd forgotten about it.

I look at it for the first time in the makeup lights over my bathroom mirror. It does look like someone punched me. "It matches my eyes and enhances the color of my white hair."

"You don't want to answer questions about this all night."

A brush with the yellow dabs my face.

"See. And then cover it with concealer." Charlene adds light beige. "Voilà! No bruise. Look."

The bruise is less obvious.

"You should have put ice on it."

"I was making cookies, talking to Sky. My cheek wasn't important." I spread makeup with a sponge. "It doesn't hurt. Not really."

"Sometimes put yourself first."

"Yeah. Right."

I LEAN OVER to dust on some eye shadow, line my lower lids, and apply mascara, jiggling the wand so it won't clump. Black pants and a new red T-shirt with black abstract strokes and a few sequins and beads will be perfect for tonight. Fluffing my hair, I check my teeth, my nails, and place silver earrings in my lobes. My white hair does bring out the blue in my eyes. Think I'll let it grow longer. Maybe get Laurie to add a few more platinum highlights.

I dial Sky's cell. "How's it going?"

"She still hasn't called."

"Oh."

"I hoped you were her."

"Sorry. Nope, just calling to see how your day is going."

"I just keep hoping 'this afternoon' means closer to noon than 6 P.M."

I hear someone in the background say, "Here's that citation you wanted." And Sky's muffled "Thanks."

"Sounds like you're busy."

"Trying to be . . . and it's mostly working. Staying distracted and getting things done."

"Charlene's here and we're just getting dressed for the party."

"Oh, can I say hello?"

"She's taking a shower. I'll let you take care of that citation. Call me when you hear, okay?"

"Of course."

"Promise?"

"Yes, Mom."

After lighting cranberry-scented candles on the kitchen counter and in the living room, I put my iPod on shuffle and position it in its stereo dock. A beat kicks in and I twirl around the kitchen pretending Jim is swinging me as I retrieve wineglasses and a small dish with stem ornaments so people can use the same glass all night. I puree the soup in the food processor, return it to its pot, light a low fire, and sprinkle it with chopped basil. I set the table for the buffet with bowls next to the tomato basil soup.

Every year, after everything is arranged and I'm waiting for my friends to arrive, there's a sense of agitated eagerness. I'm ready. The house waits for my guests with a potpourri of smells: cookies, soup, cranberry, and roses. The bed waits for the tumble of coats, scarves, and hats. My office has room for many bags inflated with cookies. The tree announces Christmas, gaiety, cheer. Outside, snow floats in thumb-size flakes.

The stage is set.

My friends will arrive one at a time and the nestled quiet will dissipate. Some arrive freshly dressed from home, some straight from work. Some will stop at a store to pick up appetizers or wine. A few will enter with the cookies and wine chilled from a day in the car. But each brings a flurry of expectation and enthusiasm. And ease, for we are ourselves with one another. We've known one another too long and have been through too much to maintain reserve or caution. We've watched our children grow, relationships dissolve and evolve into new configurations, job promotions and career changes, illnesses and surgeries, wrinkles and spreading tummies and breasts. We've dealt with betrayals and fights. Though this year there's additional tension, and I'm not sure how Jeannie and Rosie will cope.

The shower stops and Charlene rustles in the bathroom, smoothing on body lotion, combing her hair, and then the blow dryer starts humming. She comes out a few minutes later wearing a black outfit and a leopard jacket. "You look great in spite of it."

"Huh?"

"The bruise on your cheek."

My hand flies to my face. "Thanks. So do you. In spite of it."

She tilts her face and presses her lips together . . . a gesture that acknowledges the incredible in spite of it to which I refer.

I pour her a glass of wine and one for myself. I put a snowman ornament on the base of my glass. We sit on the sofa side by side, our feet propped on the coffee table. "To us," I say. Disney jumps up beside me and eases his chin on my thigh. I stroke his soft ears.

"To friendship," she adds. We clink our glasses together and drink.

ALMONDS

Charlene's older brother fought in Vietnam. A few years ago he returned there and visited the prison we call the Hanoi Hilton. An almond tree struggled up from the cement in the courtyard. A sign next to it explained that prisoners used the tree's nuts as a source of food, the bark and leaves to cure dysentery, clean wounds, and soothe skin ulcers. The wood was used to make pipes and flutes. The tree provided shade from the sticky heat. While Charlene rolled balls of almond paste, she remembered her brother showing her a picture of the tree and the placard. She thought of the tree with its crusted bark and gentle leaves providing so much solace and comfort.

And for me, whether salted and roasted, or ground into paste, almonds are one of my favorite things to eat. As a little girl, I remember studying marzipan fruits painted with food colors and formed into oranges as a treat each Christmas. Later

I learned that the flavor in the center of cake roses was, if I were lucky, almond paste, and as an adult, I've loved decorating cakes with cut out leaves, or flowers fashioned of it.

Native to India and east to Syria and Turkey, almonds were one of our first cultivated fruit trees and its domestication proof of our ancestors' ingenuity. In the wild form, almonds contain cyanide. Early humans rid the nuts of their toxicity by roasting them. But domesticated almonds are not toxic. It's believed that a common mutation occurred and that by this happy accident humans have a nontoxic source of almonds. They were easy to grow because they produce fruit from the seed and grafting isn't necessary. Domesticated more than five thousand years ago, almonds were found in Tutankhamen's tomb in Egypt and mentioned in the Bible when Aaron's rod miraculously bore flowers and fruits.

Almonds are a fruit related to cherries, apricots, and plums. The "nut" we eat is the seed. The fleshy part of the fruit instead forms a hard hull around the seed. There are two forms of the plant. The one with pink flowers produces sweet almonds, and the one with white flowers produces bitter almonds. Bitter almonds retain the chemicals, including cyanide, of the pre-cultivated almond and are used for medicinal purposes. They can be deadly in large doses. It is the sweet almonds that we turn into salted roasted almonds, marzipan, baklava, meringues, cookies, pastries, and the scent used for aromatherapy. Almonds are ground into flour for people with celiac disease and wheat allergies. They are made into butter for people with peanut allergies, and used as a milk substitute for people who are lactose intolerant. Almonds are a rich source of vitamin E and, because they contain monounsaturated oil, help to rid the body of "bad" cholesterol while increasing HDLs or good cholesterol. They contain both magnesium, which is nature's own calcium channel blocker, and potassium. Both work to prevent arteriosclerosis and aid the proper working of the heart.

Almonds are grown in many of the countries that border the Mediterranean Sea and in the United States, which is now the world's largest producer, with half the production concentrated in California. Almonds are California's sixth-leading agricultural product and its top agricultural export. Almond trees were brought to California twice. Centuries ago, Spanish missionaries introduced them, but they were abandoned when the missions closed. Almond trees found their way back when they failed to thrive in New England because of the climate. Once again they were brought to California, where they now flourish.

3

Rosie

Star Cookie Trees

    1 cup (2 sticks) butter, or substitute ½
    with solid shortening
    1½ cups white sugar
    1 teaspoon vanilla
    2 eggs
    4 cups unbleached all-purpose flour
    1 teaspoon salt
    2 teaspoons baking powder
    ¼ cup milk

Cream the butter and sugar together until light. Add the vanilla and eggs and beat until the mixture becomes fluffy. In a separate bowl, thoroughly combine the flour, salt, and baking powder. Add about 1 cup to the butter mixture. Blend in the milk and then the remaining dry ingredients. Chill for 2 or 3 hours (or even overnight).

Preheat oven to 400 degrees.

Roll out the dough and cut into shapes. Cut the cookies into graduated-size stars. You can buy the stars or do what I did—make them out of cardboard. The largest is six inches across; the smallest is one. I made four different sizes, and since there are twelve cookies, I cut out three of each one.

Bake on parchment paper for about 8 to 10 minutes until the edges are crisp and slightly browned. Remove from the cookie sheet and place on a cooling rack.

When cool, stack together with decorator's icing.

Decorator's Icing

In a mixing bowl with electric beaters, beat 3 egg whites and $\frac{1}{4}$ teaspoon cream of tartar until foamy. Gradually add 1 pound (about 4 cups or 455 g) powdered sugar, continuing to beat the mixture at high speed 4 to 7 minutes or until it's of spreading consistency. (Note: If the mixture is too thick, add water, 1 tablespoon at a time, until the mixture is of desired consistency.) Keep the bowl covered with a damp cloth as icing will dry quickly.

To assemble the tree:

Place one of the largest stars on a serving platter. Begin stacking the remaining stars from largest to smallest, using a small dab of icing to secure in place; alternate position of points of each star as stacking continues to create the tree. Top the tree with a solid white star. Then, you can decorate it with more frosting and sprinkle with confectioners' or colored sugar. Whatever captures your fancy.

*D*ISNEY RUSHES WITH HIS monkey at the sound of a knock. I open the door and Rosie hurries in with a flurry of snow and a red-lipsticked smile, long black coat billowing. Her short hair throws iridescence as the light catches melting snow.

"Hi. Hi. Hi." She rustles her bags and kisses the air, placing her load on the table. "It's beginning to get nasty out there . . . icy snow. I'll be right back." The door slams as she rushes out again before I can ask if she needs help. She returns with more sacks. "So I didn't realize how much this would be. I could only get three in each one." And she's out the door again. I pick up two of her bags and take them into my office, and she returns with a bowl of Thai noodles in peanut sauce that she places on the table.

"There," she announces. "So. Now I can get my hugs." And grabs Charlene. "SOOOOO good to see you." She softens her voice, making the greeting a condolence as well as an expression of pleasure, and it's clear she wasn't sure Charlene was up to a party. Charlene plays it as though it's pure friendship without the tinge of concern and pity. Then Rosie clutches me as though she's home at last. "Ah, Marnie."

She smells of ylang-ylang and lime.

"You're looking well. How's Jim? How're the girls? Any word yet?"

"No." Now babies are the big issue for Rosie. She has a perfect life except for one flaw. Well, two. We'll get to the second one in a minute. She's happily married to a lawyer. She was a paralegal at the same firm just as he was getting divorced from his wife. I know, but I don't know if Kevin knows, that she was waiting for that marriage to end. She sensed it in his wife's disinterest in the firm, and she told me, more than ten years ago when she first started working with him, that she suspected he was having an affair.

We were both single and cruising for men, or at least dance partners, at the Top of the Park. We met at an early-morning jazzercise class, carrying coffee in with our gym bags. "At least I get to dance," I commented one morning, wiping off sweat with my towel.

"You like to dance? So. Let's go together," Rosie suggested.

"You're on." And we exchanged phone numbers.

That night at the Top of the Park, the band played classic rock and we met near the beer tent. Allie was with us. Rosie wore a flower haltered sundress that showed off her tan and her toned arms and shoulder bones. Her hair wasn't short then but hung down heavy and straight. She had a shine about her, such a blaze that every man who passed us did a double take.

"We look gorgeous tonight," I joked at their glances. "And Rosie, you look absolutely spectacular. What's with that? New man?"

And she blushed. That was a dead giveaway.

"Uh-oh." Allie saw it, too. "So. So. So! As you would say. Tell us."

"It's nothing. Not yet. But maybe."

"One of those secret crushes?"

"Well. He's married."

Allie and I both rolled our eyes.

"Don't roll your eyes. He's unhappy. I can tell. And I think maybe he's having an affair, or thinking about it, or just wanting one. Or just miserable at home. His wife's a bitch."

"How old is this dude? Where'd you meet him?"

Rosie gulped some of her Red Rock and said, "He's one of the lawyers at the firm and he's about twenty or so years older. In his late forties, early fifties."

I looked at her and she's glowing as though she's happiest when she's with him, and if not, then talking about him is almost as good.

"He's so lonely. He hangs around after work, we all go out for drinks — all of us — nothing inappropriate. But he blushes every time he sees me. It's soooo cute. And he's Puerto Rican, so the blush is subtle, only on his neck."

Allie straightened her shoulders and inhaled. "Why don't you pick something more difficult? One. He's older." She pulled down her index finger. "Two. He's sorta your boss. He's not supposed to fool around with the employees." She pulled down her ring finger, leaving her middle finger upright. "Three. He's married." She hissed the word. " 'Married' tips the scale."

"I know, but there's this special something."

A man came by, a tall man with curly hair and a carved look to his face, grabbed Rosie's hand, and pulled her to the dance floor. Allie and I followed them out to dance.

Later, I grabbed Rosie for a dance and said, "Who's the guy? He's cute. And no ring."

Rosie raised one eyebrow, a gesture I myself had mastered after seeing Vivian Leigh in *Gone With the Wind*. She actually did date him for a while, but without the glow that even thinking about Kevin created. And I watched in amazement as Kevin got divorced and Rosie patiently, sweetly, and sexily picked up the pieces and helped him reassemble them. She managed to tiptoe through potential land mines and emerge unscathed, untarnished, married, and prosperous.

Now, they're ensconced in the life they built. Her business and social skills blossomed when they opened a new practice and she began running it for him. She certainly isn't going to leave him alone to fantasize about ever younger women with even more perfect bodies without her watchful eye.

There is only one rub. We were having a glass of wine at a Friday happy hour. I was worrying about being involved with a younger man.

"So. At least you don't have the baby issue," she commented.

I sipped my wine.

"I mean. You both already have children."

"Yeah. We get to figure out how each set of kids will accept the other. And fit our time around his kids' needs."

"But that's doable. I would love to have a baby. But Kevin has BTDT. Doesn't want to do it again. He says now's the time for him to do *his* life." She laced her fingers together and placed them on the table. Her nails were French manicured and medium length. She raised her arm. A waiter slid by as she pointed to her empty glass. He nodded and added it to his tray.

"Yeah." I laughed a chuckle of sympathy.

"Sure. He always did what he was supposed to do. Everything for appearance. The law school, the marriage, the hard work to develop his reputation, the PTA and charity events . . . all that. Why he left was so he could do his thing." The waiter set a glass of ruby wine in front of her. She held the stem with two fingers and swirled the liquid. Then she shrugged. "So. I was, now am, part of his thing." She sipped the wine. "What about me? What about what I want?"

"You knew how he felt."

She tilted her chin down. "Yes." Rosie chewed one side of her lip and shook her head. "But I didn't know. I didn't know how I'd feel *now*. When we fell in love and started his practice, I thought all we had would be enough. It was all soo soo exciting. The vacations and then we learned scuba diving and then the thrill of making the practice profitable and building its reputation. Then we got the dogs. I thought that would be enough. But not having children seems selfish. So vacuous."

"Children are an irreconcilable difference. You can compromise on everything else, but children are too big a life focus. Too huge of a commitment. Parenthood swallows up your life and that gulp can be exhilarating or obliterating. Or both. Even when you want to do it."

"It would be different for him if it were ours. Our baby out of our love. His ex and he argued. They never agreed on anything. We agree on everything." She stopped a moment and glanced sideways. "Except this. But we would do it together, like the practice. It would work out."

Rosie's arms, toned from her work at the gym, crossed

on the table one on top of the other, her lips firm as she met my eyes.

I softened my voice and leaned toward her. "But maybe what he wants and needs is *all* your attention. Maybe he doesn't want to share you." I put it to her that way. Maybe his protest was a result of his clinginess, a desire to envelop.

But she was determined. "He shares me with the practice."

The waiter brought a plate of mussels in an herbed wine sauce. I opened a mussel, swished it in the sauce, and tried one more time. "The practice is *his* practice. Your, plural you, practice. He sees that as your loving *him*."

"My point exactly. So. Our kids would be the same."

I know when urges and needs veil examination of alternatives. I saw the steely determination in her. I didn't say, but wonder if I should have, "But you lock the door to the practice and go home. There's no locking the door to a kid . . . not even after eighteen years. It truly is forever."

This is something I question: When I see a friend heading down a difficult road, how much do I confront, and how much do I accept knowing I'll be there to pick up the pieces? How much am I the listening, loving friend and how much should I point out the danger? How much do I receive and how much do I warn? I see danger here. Kevin was clear from the beginning that he didn't want more children. Rosie is changing the basis of their contract. Is a baby worth a marriage? Maybe. Friends are going to do what they're driven to do regardless. And, regardless, I'll be there. I'm not in the business of change.

And Rosie seems to live a life that proves the unlikely is possible. It's how she thinks of herself. She looked away and then looked back at me and said, "If you were about to die, what would you say was the most important thing you've done?"

And I gave her the answer she anticipated. "My children."

She shrugged one shoulder.

I sipped on the wine and said, "Rosie, you always succeed at the difficult and make things work by the skin of your teeth. I hope you can skate through this, too." We all keep doing the things that worked for us, even when they quit working. Of course, we don't know that they don't work anymore until it's too late.

Now, eight months later, when Rosie asks if I've heard from Sky and how's Tara, I know that her question is laden with vicarious hope, fear, terror. And jealousy. And me, I'm reminded I have a potential for such riches . . . or such loss.

"Tara should be here any minute. She's bringing the cookie virgin and then visiting a friend. So you'll get to see her."

"Oh, I love it when we have new cookie bitches. . . . She's co-grandma, right?"

I chuckle. "Yep. Tara's bringing her from Detroit." I check my watch. "And Sky is hearing about her test anytime. I hoped she'd call by now."

Charlene places cutlery in symmetrical stacks. "How're you?"

"Incredibly busy. Our office Christmas party is next week and the caterer is fussing about the arrangements and the bar fund raiser is the next night and we're both on the board. So! I haven't had a moment to breathe." Rosie expands her lungs and exhales to accelerate the point. "And then," she continues almost as though she's forgotten, "it's Kevin's daughter's, my stepdaughter's, birthday right after Christmas and we're all supposed to go to Steamboat and hit the slopes. All good things. All soooo exciting and soooo busy and I don't know how I'll get it all done." Her layered tresses sway and shift and then she flashes a glossed grin that wipes away her show of exasperation.

"But you always do," Charlene says gently, absent irritation, but with only consideration for her sense of anxiety and panic.

"So. Is Jeannie coming?" Rosie's voice changes register, the anxiety breaking through.

"Yes."

She chews on her lip and scratches her jaw. Then she nods slowly. "I miss her. We were so close. The three of us."

"Maybe you two should talk."

"We tried. She is still furious at me, like I'm the one sleeping with her father." She grabs a cracker and a slice of cheese.

I place my hand on her arm.

The doorbell rings and there are Juliet and Laurie. Juliet is carrying huge shiny pink bags and a plate. I see snow floating through the cracked door and stray flakes bristle on curly blond hair that flies with static electricity. "I know what to do," Juliet yells, striding with long legs to the back of the house. Laurie comes in behind her. "I can't stay too long, I have to get back to the baby." She follows Juliet. Juliet returns, her cookies deposited in the office and her coat on my bed, to hug us all. She pulls the foil from her plate to reveal hummus dip surrounded by mounds of bright orange carrots, yellow and red tomatoes, and black olives, and then she says, "Ooops, I forgot," and rushes out coatless. She returns with a bag of whole wheat pita chips. She places them on a plate and heaves a sigh of relief.

Her chores are done. "Now PARRRRTTTTYYY time!" she trills. Juliet is tall, almost six feet when she wears her stilettos. Over the last few years, she has been taking belly-dancing classes. Now it's evident in her trim body that she shows off with a plunging neckline on a casual T-shirt and belted trousers. I know from her outfit that she's coming from her work in nursing administration. I recognize the hummus platter, too. She picked it up at Plum Market on the way here.

Laurie brings a bowl of cherry tomatoes and salted almonds. "Well, I figure we could always use some healthy snacks. And with the baby, the cookies were all I could make."

Rosie hurries to her, a glass of white wine in her hand, the stem of her glass decorated with one of my wineglass ornaments, a small Christmas ball. "So. How is she now? How long have you had her?"

"Three months and, well, she's just now beginning to sit up. She's twelve months." Laurie adopted a baby from China. "You wanna see the pictures?" she asks.

"Yeah!"

Laurie grabs Rosie's hand and pulls her into the bedroom to fish photos from her purse.

"How're you doing, I mean really, doing?" Juliet asks Charlene as she pours some red wine and chooses a Christmas tree as her glass ornament.

Juliet is my oldest friend. I met her in homeroom in ninth grade, the only girl I knew who loved Marvin Gaye and BB King when the Beatles and the Monkees swept the other kids. She's two months older than I am, but because of the oily skin that cursed her teen years with zits, her skin is unlined. We often joke that the plague of high school became her blessing after forty and my perfect poreless, translucent skin now reveals my character.

Before Charlene can answer, Rosie bursts from the bedroom shaking the pictures of Olivia, Laurie's baby. "Ohmigod. She's sooooo soooo cute, can't you just eat her up?" Olivia is in a car seat, almond eyes above fat cheeks and hair sticking out from a polka-dot pink and purple ribbon. Her mouth is open in one of those grins that express absolute joy. Laurie surprised her with a game of peekaboo to capture that moment. Rosie bites her lower lip with her teeth and shakes her head, her eyes fill with tears, and I know now that she believes a baby *is* worth risking her marriage for. And for a second the door is open to her future, just as the real door opens and Allie enters. No coat. Sunglasses on even though darkness has fallen. Arms wrapped around bags. She doesn't barge in but walks around us, tiptoeing around our conversation and into the office to drop off her cookies. Then she goes back out and reenters, this time with a coat slung over her arm, her sunglasses in her teeth, and a casserole covered in foil that she holds with both hands. "Entrées here?" she asks. I nod and she wedges her platter next to the Thai noodles and rips off the foil to reveal barbecued chicken. "Coats in the bedroom?"

Taylor is right behind her. Taylor, with dangling earrings and wrapped in a flowing scarf that she doesn't take off. Right now, in spite of the gorgeous scarf, black net with pink and white polka dots, she looks drab. She brings in chips and dip and her cookies and a bottle of wine all at once. The clothes are the remnants of her singing career.

I nod. I love this part of the evening, when my friends arrive bustling with excitement and armed with goodies. They bring warmth in spite of the cold and convey the season's thrill. Once again we feel a child's excitement for Christmas. I've set the stage, but they fill it with the action, the emotion, the event that is by its very nature best because of serendipity. Well, and the love we all have for one another. And our shared history. Every year, I can hardly wait for them to arrive, thrilled to see each one.

I met each of them on my own journey: in high school, as a hippie, as a young mother, as a divorcée, as a single mother, in the business world, with one man or another. Sometimes, when I think of my life, I think of the girl who met Juliet and the hippie who met Vera and the struggling woman who met Charlene and the business woman who met Allie. It's hard to put the different stages together as part of one woman's life.

Me. The wife betrayed by a man, the wife who was widowed young. And now. Now. Two pregnant daughters. This house filled with hand-painted and -decorated

•

walls of aubergine and beige and lavender and a decorated Christmas tree. Sometimes I can't get my mind
around the different versions of me, Marnie. And yet the
friends who met the other adaptations of me through the
decades are still part of my current life. It is as though
my friends give testimony to my history. Witnesses, when
we're all together, to my whole existence. I love them as
I love myself in all my varieties and aspects. And I love
them for the spectacular women they are, each in her
own way.

My eyes fill with emotion. And Allie, fresh lipstick on
her thin lips, narrows her eyes at me, wondering what's
going on. She notices then the slight blue on my cheek
still apparent under the yellow makeup. She tilts her
head and touches her own face. "You okay?"

"Yeah. Bashed into a kitchen cabinet. Kitchen fury."
And I hug her. "I love you. I love you guys."

I hear noises at the back door and Disney comes bar-
reling through, bouncing up and down with eagerness,
so excited he drops his monkey. Then there's Tara's voice.
"Here we are," she sings. "Hey, Disney. Cute scarf." And
then she says, softer, "We always come in through the
back door."

I am prepared to see Tara's black hair, shot with co-
balt, silver scattered over her face, but her hair is its original light red, no hoops, no makeup. "You look like you
used to, like my little girl." I laugh. "Took all the hardness
and armament away."

But Tara hasn't meant to cast away her street persona
and scowls. "Too much going on to bother with all that
stuff."

I lean toward her and kiss her. Clasp her to me as much as I can around the hard ball that will be my grandson. And she relaxes in my arms.

"I'm so happy to see you, honey."

"It was a time getting here in this blowy snow."

Sissy is right behind her, with short dreadlocks and a bright scarf keeping her neck warm. "Here. Where do I put the food?" She puts down a plate and then opens her arms and spreads that smile that welcomes me into her presence. "Gotta get some sugar." She kisses a loud smack on my cheek, then peels the cover off to reveal sushi.

"Sushi, I love it."

"You got to watch this sauce, though. It's serious spicy." Sissy's large eyes crinkle slightly with her smile. I introduce her to the other women, though she met Charlene this summer.

Charlene says to Tara, "I bought some perfume and a relaxation CD and a crystal to help you through the labor. You been practicing your breathing?"

"Oh, yeah. We're doing the whole Lamaze bit."

"Bet your sweet booty they are," Sissy adds.

Juliet says to Tara, "I love your hair. You like it?"

"It's my natural hair color. Or as close as I remember it. It's called Amber Sunrise. I went from Black Pearl to Amber Sunrise." Tara's hair is cut short, almost a buzz cut. "Then I figured I might as well do the nature thing all the way. So I took off the nose ring, the eyebrow ring, the seven earrings. So here I am. Just me. Without anything. Me and Smidgen,"—she pats her belly—"ready for our adventure."

Tara is at ease with my friends, who've known her since she was a baby, or in high school, as she advanced through her developmental phases.

"But I don't know. This pale red hair looks too bland. Maybe I'll put some platinum or fuchsia in it, after the baby's born. Whaddya think?"

She looks bare and fresh. When she blinks, I notice her eyelashes are two-toned, the light brown that was once mine and the red hair of Stephen as though our genes had a fight and no one won, so they agreed to exist side by side, making space for each other.

Tara looks at me and says, "You look great, Mom. I hope my hair turns your color, that shocking white, when I'm your age. That's the color I want my highlights to be."

"Thanks, honey." A few short years ago, she criticized everything about me.

"Looks like you're getting ready. You and Smidgen," Charlene says, staring at the bulge of her belly.

Rosie comes toward her. "You look beautiful. So, so . . ." She stops, hunting for the word, and then says, "Pregnant." And jerks her head as though making a pronouncement.

"Yeah, I'm humongous. Even here." She puts her hands over her breasts. "Size D! Can you believe it?"

"So that's what you do to get them. Get pregnant." Rosie laughs. "Now I know."

"Well, I gotta go to my friend's. I'm already late." Tara moves next to Sissy, already in a discussion with Juliet. "I'll be back at eleven?"

Sissy's brows come together. "Don't forget. Work for me at seven-thirty tomorrow morning. Okay, sugar?" She watches Tara leave, her bountiful smile revealing even white teeth.

The women cluster around the table nibbling chicken, dipping carrots into hummus, sushi into wasabi sauce, and bread into flavored olive oil, balancing wineglasses. Juliet talks with Sissy, probably about hospitals as they're both nurses. Rosie pumps Laurie about Olivia's naps and the process of adoption in China. Allie and Charlene huddle together over plates of Thai noodles. When I ladle a bowl of soup, I don't realize how hungry I am until I start eating. I flavored the soup with the perfect amount of basil, if I do say so myself. The sound of multiple conversations, laughter, and the clink of eating utensils fill the kitchen and dining area.

I check my watch. Sky should have called by now. I consider slipping into the bathroom and calling her but decide against it. Maybe too overbearing, maybe too intrusive. Let her control when she tells me. My cell phone is on vibrate and clamped to my hip.

Jeannie arrives dressed in an upscale tie-dyed T-shirt that shows off her cleavage, and Rosie huddles even closer to Laurie, stepping to the side so that her back is toward the entry. Jeannie brings a salad with oranges and walnuts and Taylor's chips and dip are tried. We roam around the table helping ourselves to food, holding our wine, each stem graced with a charm from the set that Juliet gave me as a birthday present some years ago. I glance at her and she laughs at something Sissy says. Rosie has relinquished Laurie and is talking with Charlene about the economy, while Allie, Jeannie, and Taylor discuss business opportunities for Taylor.

For a moment I watch my party, the enjoyment we have with one another and our effortless camaraderie year after year. The ginger flower surrounded by candles graces the table. Sissy takes some chicken and joins Charlene and Rosie while Juliet gets more wine, filling everyone's empty or almost empty glasses. The candles burn softly, the lights shine on the Christmas tree.

"Are we all here? Where's Tracy? And Alice?" Juliet asks me. "And Vera."

"They're not going to be able to make it. . . . Tracy's in Hawaii with Silver and you know Alice is in California." The plates are now stacked beside the sink.

Rosie stops her conversation with Charlene and asks, "Vera?"

"Vera'll be here. Unfortunately, she had to make an appointment this afternoon and she's coming, just late." I notice Sissy frown and check her watch. "We should start. She'll come and catch up." No one is eating anymore. At least for now, but I know they'll eat throughout the party.

"Uh-oh. What about the rules for Tracy and Alice?" Taylor asks. "We aren't gonna lose them, are we?"

I laugh. "No. I have their cookies already. Alice sent hers by FedEx and Tracy made them before she and Silver left."

"It won't be the same without them. They're such an important part," Jeannie says.

"We're all important. And they're here in spirit," I say. I meet Jeannie's eyes. "Hey, it's time to start."

We move into the living room. As though she needs the comfort and safety of its shelter, Charlene waits in an upholstered chair. You can smell the pine from the tree and cinnamon from the burning candles. My home-made peanut brittle, a family secret recipe I've never told anyone, and chocolate almonds grace each table. We crowd into the room sitting four on the sofa, one on each chair and ottoman. Juliet sits between Jeannie and Rosie. Well, at least they won't be staring at each other.

Disney slides under the coffee table. I've brought a chair from my office and then all nine of us are nestled in place, each with wine or water, each talking to her neighbor.

"Uh-oh, Juliet and Jeannie are sitting together," Charlene teases. "You know what happened when they did that last year." We laugh, remembering their talk and raucous laughter that disrupted the flow of cookies and the stories that accompanied them.

I hold up my finger and wag it at them as though I'm talking to two little kids. "Can you girls be good tonight?"

They joke back, "We promise. We promise. Allie will keep us cool."

"Yeah. Right." Allie rolls her eyes. We all know she's not controlling.

"Who wants to start?"

"I want to go last," Taylor says. Taylor has wedged a chair so she can sit next to Allie, who is on the sofa. The chair is jammed between Sissy and Allie.

"I'll start." Rosie stands up and goes to get her bags of cookies. She brings them in two bags at a time and everyone starts talking. My cell phone is still quiet. I turn down the music and then sit at the edge of the party, close to the kitchen. I sip some wine. Now I get to enjoy

the party. Charlene sits on one side of me, there's a space
for Vera when she arrives on the other side. Rosie has
returned with the last of her bags. The talking and laughing has escalated.

"How does this work?" Sissy's brows are twisted together. "What are we supposed to do?" Sissy has one
of those faces that easily express emotions so that each
movement she makes, raising her brows or smiling, resonates. Now, as she raises her brows, there's a hint of anxiety, the first time I've sensed any discomfort from her.

"We take turns passing out the cookies. The first year
we had it, everyone started exchanging simultaneously.
If you can picture twelve people passing out thirteen
batches of cookies, you can imagine the disaster. We
had to spend hours figuring out who had whose cookies.
Then we decided to exchange one at a time and, since
we had each spent time making thirteen dozen cookies,
to talk about that particular cookie. Our way to honor
each woman's effort. It makes the cookie and the work
entailed special. That I guess was the first rule. That and
no paper plates with saran wrap."

"How'd this start?" Sissy's brows are relaxed now and
the glimmering of uncertainty erased.

"Back when Charlene and I were living together, we
spent one night a year making six or eight different kinds
of cookies. We called it the night of cooking and stirring and drinking and laughing. We'd stay up all night
while the kids slept. Turned on a bunch of music and
drank way too much. We did that for years. And then
I was invited to a cookie exchange, and I decided to do
that. Took about five years to get it gelled. The first few

years we drank too much and partied too hard. I realized we needed food. So it's evolved. We add rules as we recognize the need for them."

Rosie stands by the end of the couch, her bags of goodies in front of her. "Okay, everyone," she starts, but no one hears her except Juliet, who stops talking to Jeannie. "So." Rosie says it louder and Taylor and Allie become quiet. But Laurie still giggles at something Allie said.

Rosie tries again. She puts her hand on her hip and scowls. Doesn't say a word, just looks at each of us with a schoolteacher's glare on her face and we shut up. It's her turn and she wants our attention. Her perfectly coiffed hair and manicured hand on her hip and the furrows between her brows, her height as she stands while we're all sitting, finally gets us quiet.

"Thank you," she says sweetly and cocks her head to the side. "So I want to tell you about my cookies. I spent all Saturday making them. I got the idea from the Internet. And I baked them all and carefully laid them out to cool before I assembled them, and soooooo that's allloooooottt of cookies." She inhales sharply, showing the great amount of work and difficulty. "You guys know how busy I've been with so so much to do . . . Ohmigod. And the cookies are always extra. Well, they were all over the dining-room table and all over the counter and so I had to put wax paper on the bed and put more there." She exhales. "So I start a load of laundry while they cool, 'cause after all I have to do the housewifey stuff, too, and just after I get the load in, Kevin calls. I'm considering putting some of the cookies on the washer and dryer next.

But Kevin needs me to check something on the computer about a case. 'I'm doing my cookies,' I tell him." Her voice changes to the sweet, cloying tone she purrs when talking to Kevin.

"'I know. I know it's cookie day. I hate to bother you.'" And now she deepens her voice.

"Boy, does she have him trained," Taylor jokes.

Jeannie says, "Yeah, my husband knows to stay away on cookie day, too. 'Don't interrupt the cookie bitch on cookie day,' he says."

"Ahem." Rosie brings the attention back to her. "So. I go into the office and fill out this quit-claim deed for him and it takes about fifteen minutes. All the time I'm thinking this is okay, the cookies'll be nice and cool. Then I email it to him." She punches an imaginary send button. "And call and tell him it's in his inbox and start back to my cookies." She has the invisible phone between her fingers. She leans over slightly. "But there's Thelma coming out of the bedroom with a guilty expression on her doggy face. I check the bedroom, and sure enough, she had jumped up on the bed and eaten half the cookies and messed up the other half." Rosie shakes her head annoyed. "That dog!" And shakes her head again. "That dog. I love her, but . . ." She exhales to show exasperation. "Then I check the dining room and she had pulled down one sheet of paper and eaten those. So I had to remake the cookies. And, you'll see, I had to figure out which ones she ate and that took almost an extra hour and then I had to redo them and let them cool."

We feel Rosie's annoyance at having to repeat work, an annoyance escalated into anxiety as she contemplated all the chores she had yet to do and now the ones she would have to do again. Jeannie's face is turned away and instead of watching Rosie she examines her engagement and wedding rings.

"I used to use that excuse in junior high. 'The dog ate it,'" Taylor says in a singsong voice.

Rosie ignores our laughter. "But it all got done. I swear dogs are more trouble than children. When Kevin gets home he goes, 'You still doin' cookies.' I must have glared at him because he slunk off to the family room to watch TV and didn't come out until I called him for dinner. Well. Here they are."

She pulls a foiled box out of one of the bags. The lid forms petals of a flower that open up. She reaches in and pulls out a tree about eight inches high formed of cookies shaped like stars. The icing is snow with soft red sprinkles.

"Ohmigod."

"How'd you do that?"

Now Rosie is in her glory. "It's twelve cookies — has to be twelve, right?" She glances at me. "Each one smaller, glued together with frosting. See how hard it was to figure out which ones were eaten?"

"It's too beautiful to eat. I'll use mine as a centerpiece at Christmas dinner," Juliet says.

Rosie beams with pride.

"Well, the rest of us might as well not even show our cookies. This one has got to be the most beautiful," Allie says.

"It's a simple sugar cookie recipe and I just designed the stars with cardboard and used them as a cutout.

There are actually several of each size stacked asymmetrically, so the stars end up looking like tree branches. I chose them because I needed something to be the centerpiece of my Christmas Eve dinner and thought this could be it."

"This is so cool. And the boxes are beautiful, too," I say.

She smiles at me. "Yeah, I had trouble trying to find those. So you can take out the cookies without ruining the design."

"Rosie, you may be busy and view yourself as frantic, but you always deliver. These are gorgeous," Charlene says. I've been watching her. She had seemed somber, sitting back in her chair and observing the party, so I'm relieved when she speaks.

Jeannie's face remains turned away from Rosie.

"Okay, so let's start passing them out." Rosie hands the box to Juliet, who hands it all the way around until it reaches Charlene. And Rosie keeps handing boxes to Juliet and each of us pass a box to the woman sitting on our left until that person already has one.

"Hey. Where's the bag for the hospice? Who's doing that?" Allie asks.

"I'll do it," Charlene says, and Rosie hands her a box, which she puts in one of Rosie's now empty bags.

"And I'll do Vera's till she gets here. And also Tracy's." I put an empty bag on the chair I'm saving for Vera, and another one between Charlene and me. "Who will do Alice's?"

Rosie says, "I will. I have room here for her bag." And she puts one of the boxes into the empty bag.

Allie stands up to get more wine. There isn't a pause so much as a reshuffling.

"Bring me some red, will you?" calls Jeannie.

I stand up and get a fresh bottle of white and bring in the red and place them on the coffee table. I know that there's a time after each of us tells our story and distributes the cookies when we go to the bathroom, get more to eat, talk and joke as the evening wears on. I feel the quiet cell phone on my hip and check my watch. I pull it out to see if I have somehow missed a call or if there is a message. Nada. No calls. No messages. I sink a little and refocus on the warm faces of the women laughing and talking. I pour myself more red wine and take some peanut brittle. I check on Sissy, but she's talking with Laurie, Taylor, and Allie. Allie says something, probably one of her double-entendre jokes that are absolutely obscene, and Taylor and Sissy burst out laughing. Just like I thought, Sissy is fine. Fits in with all these women. And then I think of my grandson about to be born and hope he fits in, too.

"Hey, Juliet, you're next."

LEAVENING AGENTS

I never used to understand the chemistry of baking. Practical science wasn't taught in my high school chemistry class, so I simply followed recipes, vaguely aware that I needed to add substances in order for the dough to turn into a bakery product. But baking soda, baking powder, and cream of tartar provide the magic for cookies to puff up in the oven. I'm comfortable improvising the amounts of spices and other ingredients I add when I'm cooking, but I never extemporize the chemistry of baking. Here's how they work:

Baking soda is sodium bicarbonate. The ancient Egyptians found natural deposits of it and used it as soap. Today it's used as an antacid, a tooth-whitening agent, to freshen the aroma of your refrigerator, and as a rug deodorizer if you sprinkle it on before vacuuming. When combined with moisture and an acidic ingredient—like yogurt, chocolate, lemon juice, vinegar, buttermilk, or honey—

bubbles of carbon dioxide form that expand with heat. The reaction starts as soon as the ingredients are mixed, so you need to bake recipes leavened only with soda immediately, or they'll fall flat!

Baking powder contains sodium bicarbonate, but the acidifying agent is included (cream of tartar), and also a drying agent (usually cornstarch). It's used instead of yeast because it's quick while yeast takes three hours. Modern baking powder is usually double-acting. With double-acting powder, some gas is released at room temperature when the powder is added to dough, but the majority of the gas is released when placed in the oven. That's why recipes instruct you to mix all of the dry ingredients together and then add the liquid. Also, recipes tell you to mix just until the ingredients are moistened, which minimizes the escape of the gas from the batter. If you stir too long, the reaction finishes and the bubbles will have escaped. You can make your own baking powder if you have baking soda and cream of tartar. Simply mix two parts cream of tartar with one part baking soda. Modern baking powder has replaced some of cream of tartar with a slower-acting substance such as acid sodium pyrophosophate. This hardly reacts at all at room temperature.

Some recipes require baking soda, while others call for baking powder. Which one is used depends on the other ingredients. Baking soda tastes bitter unless countered by the acidity of another substance such as buttermilk. Baking powder contains both an acid and a base and has an overall neutral effect in terms of taste. Recipes that call for baking powder often call for neutral-tasting ingredients such as milk. Baking powder is a common ingredient in cakes and biscuits.

Cream of tartar is made from the sediment of wine production. We know it best as it stabilizes beaten egg whites. Meringue, for example, is egg whites, cream of tartar, and sugar. It's the acidic ingredient in baking powder.

When Juliet's dunkers call for cream of tartar and baking soda, she's making her own baking powder. But every time any of us add baking soda, baking powder, or cream of tartar and then retrieve puffed cookies and baked goods from our ovens, we benefit from the magic of chemistry.

4

Juliet

Pennsylvania Dunkers

$1/2$ lb (2 sticks) softened butter
2 cups white sugar
1 cup brown sugar
2 large eggs, beaten
1 teaspoon vanilla
3 cups sifted flour
1 teaspoon baking soda
1 teaspoon cream of tartar
1 cup finely chopped pecans (Can use more.
I always toast mine.)

Mix together the butter, sugars, egg, and vanilla in a large bowl. Mix very well. In a separate bowl, mix together the dry ingredients and nuts. Slowly add the dry ingredients to the sugar mixture. Mix very well with your hands. Separate dough into four parts. Shape and pat each part into logs approximately 6 inches long, $2 1/2$ inches wide, and

1 inch thick. Wrap each log tightly in wax paper and freeze for three hours or overnight.

Preheat oven to 350 degrees.

To bake, slice thin, about $^1/_6$ inch, with a sharp knife. Bake for 8 to 12 minutes until just slightly browned at the edges. Watch closely, as they can get overbaked easily. Allow to cool a few minutes before removing from the pan. Each log makes about 25 to 30 cookies.

Cookies are very crisp and taste great dunked in coffee or milk. My favorite holiday breakfast and late-night snack!

*J*ULIET'S HIPS SWAY AS she sashays into my office to retrieve her bags. She towers above us, cascading curly blond hair.

"All that Pilates you're doing is really paying off," Allie comments.

Juliet reaches for a sip of wine and says, "I got the greatest compliment in my life. My daughter came home unexpectedly and I had just gotten out of the shower, dressed only in bra and panties, and she said, 'Wow, Mom. I hope when I'm your age I have a body half as good as yours. You look terrific.'"

"Well, you can see the difference. Like Wonder Woman," Laurie says.

Juliet brings her brows together and squints one eye, a perfect caricature expressing, *Oh yeah, right.* "The cellulite and wrinkly knees are under the clothes." She laughs.

I enter the kitchen for chips and dip, and Laurie follows. "Juliet's something else. Great husband, great career, great kids, grandkids. And to top it off she's beautiful."

The mention of grandkids immediately reminds me of Sky. My cell still hasn't rung.

"And in great shape." Laurie pours Diet Coke in her wineglass. "And lives in a terrific house! Well, I don't know how she does it. She makes it look effortless."

"We've all had our share of shit."

"But hers is invisible. She seems to float through everything. Even her cancer."

"She was scared. I was, too. Later, she led support groups for several years." A few days before her surgery, Juliet had talked to me about her fear. Breastless, what would happen to her marriage? Then she added, "Besides, so much of my erotic feelings are in my nipples."

I didn't know what to say. "Better to miss your nipples than your life."

"Exactly." And she looked away.

"Well, see? She turned lemons into lemonade," Laurie says.

"Yeah," I agree. I remember when I met her, the girl who sat next to me in homeroom complaining about curly hair she couldn't iron straight enough to meet the style of the day. So much is determined by whether our looks match the ideal of our teenage years. Her hair and her pimples and her height made her a giraffe among ponies.

"I hate hate hate my hair," she had said one day.

"I used to want hair just like that. Spent hours winding strands around my fingers trying to make ringlets."

"Used to." She spat back at me. "Back in elementary school."

"Who knows, maybe curly hair will be in again."

She smelled of Jean Naté. "I bet." She added white lipstick to her lips and stroked on eyeliner.

"At least you have long legs," I said.

She pulled down her miniskirt. "Yeah. And as a result my skirts are more than four inches above my knees. And I've been sent to the principal for having too-short skirts. Twice."

She wouldn't accept any positives. I think of her now

and her glow of confidence, her easy ability to weave her way through various roles and people. Beneath the smoothness and accomplishments she remains the insecure girl who lived in the Courtyard Trailer Park, fussing over her curly hair back then, fussing over her cellulite now.

Laurie says, "It seems so effortless. She's, well . . ." Laurie shrugs, looking for a word. "Always capable."

Then I realize what she's saying. "It's hard adjusting to being a new mom."

She flinches slightly, and when she turns to me, I see her eyes wide and motionless, a deer caught in headlights. "I'm thrilled with Olivia, but . . ." She snags a piece of chicken and pops it in her mouth. "I guess I feel like I'm just *her*. There's no *me* anymore. And I'm, well, tired. She still doesn't sleep through the night and I try to clean up the house while she takes her naps. And I can't make her happy."

My hand is on her shoulder. "She's been through a lot. Torn away from her roots and transplanted. She'll settle in." I wonder if the taking over of your body by the fetus prepares you for the taking over of your life by the baby. Adopting is a sudden wrenching. For both mother and baby. Not to mention the biological mother. I think about Sky and her test. If her pregnancy can't continue, then perhaps she'll adopt.

"Maybe that's why she cries so much."

"It's only been a few months. So many, many changes for both of you. For you, too. No matter how much you wanted her and how much you love her."

"Well, I guess that's obvious. It just doesn't seem obvious when it's you."

"It's like Juliet. She didn't learn to be the Juliet she is now all at once. It was one thing at a time."

And she's not exactly the Juliet she pretends to be. The trailer park left its scars. Not the place, but all that it entailed: being poorer than her peers, her single mom working nights to support three kids. Juliet had to figure out things on her own. Not until she got a job bagging groceries at Kroger did she get some of the things the rest of us took for granted, like school pictures. Oh, they snapped her photo, but she never received packets to take home. The rest of us exchanged wallet-size pictures signed on the back with sayings like "2 good 2 b 4gotten."

Once, she said she'd already given hers away and shrugged her shoulders. The next year she said her mom was forcing her to give them all to her cousins.

"You should've ordered more," said the girl sitting on the other side of her.

"That's what I told my mom." Juliet rolled her eyes with that universal exasperated look teenage girls perfect. I always gave her a wallet picture of me anyway. I was so dorky then, with my black glasses and bouffant hair. Once, I looked through her wallet and realized my picture and one of her mom and her brother and sister were all she had. The rest of the plastic sleeves were filled with notes and receipts. Then I understood the excuses she made. After that I visited her trailer.

Now her house, perfectly decorated in neutrals with only plants and cushions as spots of color, advertises her mobility. Inside, it is scrupulously neat and spotless. Outside, there is a garden of contained flowers, pruned trees, and a plane of smooth, even grass. So different from the cluttered two-bedroom trailer parked in a gravel yard and jammed with four people. She helped put her husband, Dan, through law school after she got her nursing degree. Her daughter is now a schoolteacher and her son is now in med school. Both are married. Her daughter has one child and her son's wife is pregnant. A Hallmark-card family in a Hallmark-card house. Safe. Prosperous. Happy.

She works to keep this image intact. But there's another side. I know partly because I happened to be there when it started. And partly because I always knew her. Juliet and Dan and Stephen and me were at a blues and jazz festival. It was a long time ago. Before things got squirrelly and awful with Stephen. When we all believed in monogamy, fidelity, loyalty, and that love could conquer all. Juliet and I had abandoned our husbands to their beers and chairs to get closer to Al Green. We were smashed in a group of other people, urging him on, but we were standing so close, when he held his hand down, Juliet reached up and touched it. Their eyes met.

She pumped her arm in the air and twisted her hips to his lyrics. His eyes traveled up and down her body, stopped for a moment at her thick lips and curly hair. He broke their gaze and scanned the crowd. A throng of dancing, thumping people packed under the bright sun. The crowd screamed over his blasting horns.

Juliet and I swayed in front of the stage, holding our arms up, singing with him.

And then it was over. It was his last encore.

"God, I gotta pee," Juliet whispered, and we walked toward the Porta-Potty and stood in line. Juliet stopped talking and stared at a woman exiting. She was attractive, about ten years older than us, and dressed in khakis, Dockers, a printed shirt, and a little scarf. When she saw Juliet, she came toward her and talked about the perfect weather for the concert when last year it had rained continually. "I have to get back to Tom. I'll see you at the next hospital party." Her lips were newly applied shiny red.

"Okay," Juliet had muttered, her face flushed, her arms hung close to her sides. She was the awkward high school girl complaining about her too curly hair and making excuses about not having portrait pictures.

"Who was that?"

"You don't want to know."

LATER THAT WEEK we went for a walk around Gallup Park. Tara was in day care and I had given myself a break from studying to spend an afternoon with my oldest friend. We passed the place where the festival had occurred, now empty of people, blankets, chairs, booths selling Indian, Italian, or deli food, beer, wine, and soda. Instead of Al Green's voice there was only quiet interrupted by an occasional squawking duck.

"Who was that woman?"

She instantly knew about whom I was asking. "Oh, God." She clenched her eyes and swallowed. "She's the wife of one of the doctors I work with."

"And you hate him?"

She snorted and then lengthened her stride, her hair

bouncing on her shoulders. "The opposite. We're good friends."

"You have a crush on him?"

"You might say that." She continued walking, her long legs pushing through the summer air, her voluptuous breasts bouncing with her steps. I had to trot to keep up.

"Hey. Slow down."

She slowed her stride. "Okay." We walked together past a bench and around a bend. "Oh, God."

"What's up?"

"Shit. I haven't even told myself yet." She turned to me. "Promise. No one. Not ever."

We stopped and faced each other. "Juliet. We've kept each other's secrets for years."

She nodded. "I . . . we've fallen in love, I guess."

"You're having an affair?"

"Well, no. We aren't doing anything except exchanging hot glances and talking in his office after work. And one afternoon we took off and went up to Hudson Mills and walked around the park and stopped for potatoes at Wendy's on the way home. And talked about how we felt about each other. Our obligations to our families. So nothing is happening."

"Oh." I inhaled.

"We've decided to ignore each other and we manage to do that for a few days and then he gives me one of those looks, one of those I-want-you-I-miss-you looks and I get goose bumps. And then he leaves a message on my pager: "I miss you." And a few hours later he pages me to his office. And I can't stop thinking about him and I review every conversation over and over and over."

"Like moths circling a flame."

"We don't want this. It's so wrong. Adultery." She shudders. "So wrong. I feel sick at myself. Sick at the thought of it. The lies. The secrets." Her hands hold her elbows across her chest as she walks.

"We all get feelings for other men."

"These seem . . . I don't know . . . compelling. Irresistible. I don't want to disrupt my children's lives. And I don't want to hurt Dan. But we kissed once and his lips stayed on mine, the sweet mint of his mouth, the texture of his tongue, I swear I felt him for hours and that night I had an amazing dream."

"And Dan?"

"He just asks why I'm up so early. I can't sleep. Wake up raring to go at four. I tell him something about so much to do and clean the house, do laundry, pack lunches. All that."

"What's with Dan? You and Dan?"

She looked down, examining her red-polished toes in her flip-flop sandals. I turned to her, but her eyes were closed. She had exchanged the Jean Naté for Charlie. "Nothing. There's no pizzazz anymore." She shrugged. "Maybe we can't expect sex to be great after fifteen years. It's product-oriented. It's just about the come. Not our feelings for each other. Not even about recreational sex. Just hurry up and come so we can go to sleep and get up and do the next day."

"Maybe you should go on a vacation. Just the two of you." We walked over the wooden bridge. A pair of swans floated side by side down the river.

"Remember? Paris last spring?"

"I thought you had fun!"

"I loved the trip. The museums and churches. Walking around the Latin Quarter and hanging out in cafés. The great food. Not lots of fun making love. Or even talking. It was the same as here. Busy, busy, busy."

I didn't know what to tell her. But if I could rewind that day, I don't know what I'd say differently. She couldn't or wouldn't make things better with Dan. Maybe she had already diminished him in her mind. That reversal in perception so the man is viewed as less, as a glass half empty. It's a spin on a dime that makes it impossible to see the person painted with the positivism of hope.

"He's just not exciting. He doesn't even see me anymore."

A flare of goose bumps prickle my arm. "What happened to the two of you?" The question comes from my desire for permanent love and an intact family. It's as if I already know that Stephen and I are condemned, although I didn't.

But she doesn't answer and we walk in silence. "You're right. I'm going to really try to make things better with Dan. Buy some sexy lingerie. New perfume. Give him an hour blow job and see if that switches things."

It only made things worse. Her attempts were not returned in kind. He simply rolled over exhausted and went to sleep, taking her attentions for granted. And the explosion occurred with Tom, the doctor.

"He understands me. He gets me. I mean, he comes from a—well, a poor family, too. His dad was an alcoholic and he only went to college because of a football scholarship. His dad thought college was a big waste of time." She blinked her eyes closed and shook her head. "Like my mom. 'Get a job.'" Juliet's voice picked up her mom's screechy tone. " 'What you gonna do with a college degree? Just walk around here with your nose in the air thinkin' you better than the rest of us.'"

We were having coffee at the farmers' market. "Look what he gave me." She ran her forefinger under a gold chain around her neck. "When I wear this, I'm reminded of him." Her eyes gleamed.

Two years later, after afternoon meetings in motels ringing the towns of Ann Arbor, afternoon gropes in the movie theater, and sudden meetings at the hospital, he rented an apartment. They furnished it together. She described the bed they bought and the Monet flowered quilt. A small couch and a TV. They even had pots and pans and plates and silverware.

"You furnished the kitchen? That wasn't what I imagined."

"Sometimes we cook for each other. But mostly we simply meet a few afternoons a week." She blushed. "Dan never picked out anything with me. He said I could do it however I wanted it. But, Marnie, it's so fun to do it with someone." She grinned.

That was twelve years ago. And the affair became part of her routine.

Last year we took another one of our walks. Once again at Gallup Park in late winter or early spring and we wound through the forest and nature path, striped with trails from cross-country skis. "We don't lie to ourselves or each other anymore. Tom and I. If we were going to leave to be together, we would have. Our kids are grown;

they can't be excuses anymore. Tom's wife has survived her mother's Alzheimer's and her parents' deaths. I have survived my breast cancer with Tom's help."

Tom visited following her mastectomy and sat with her during the chemo and radiation. When I came to be with her, he was there.

When she said Tom's name, her finger went to the gold necklace and slid under it, as though reassuring herself that he was with her. "And Dan survived his bypass surgery. Tom helped with that, too, from behind the scenes, but helped nonetheless. Tom and I have the same ridiculous arguments over and over that are never really resolved, just like any other couple. Just like Dan and me. Sometimes we don't even make love; we just sleep in each other's arms."

"Why do you continue?"

"Because we connect. We're both *with* each other. And it's my . . ." She shrugs, struggling to find the right word. "Life? I'm attached to him just like I'm attached to Dan. Each in his own little box. Neither one really experiencing me. And I thought Tom would be different. Remember? Neither one do I give all of me to." And then she turns to me and her pupils are very wide. "I guess you're the only one who has a clue."

Intimacy, I think. We all struggle so with being our authentic selves with anyone. Maybe Juliet couldn't relinquish the trailer park and had to keep a bit of tawdry to know herself. And since I knew her back then, visited her in that cramped space, she could tell me about her affair, too. Or maybe it's an escape hatch from the ideal of middle class perfection.

Charlene calls, "Hey, we're waiting."

I bring in the bowls of pita chips and spinach and crab dip and sit down. Juliet is standing. She grins.

"Okay. This is an old family recipe. My grandmother was from Pennsylvania and she used to make these cookies so my grandfather could dunk them in his coffee. As a kid, my grandfather would make me some—mostly warm milk with a drop or two of coffee—so I could join him. My grandmother always made these before Christmas and, when we went to visit them on Christmas morning, my grandfather and I would have our dunkers together." Juliet stops. Her eyes are shellacked with moisture. "Our Christmases weren't very plentiful. Clothes. Maybe one or two toys. And the dunkers. And the dunking ceremony was the only thing I really shared with my grandfather. It's absolutely my only memory of him." Her arms are crossed and her voice is even. "Every time I make these cookies, I dip the first one in coffee and think about my grandma's kitchen with the pattern worn off the linoleum in the spots where she stood and the kitty-cat salt and pepper shakers on the dinette table. The smell of my grandfather mixed with coffee and cookies. And of course the taste of the cookie. I don't know if it's the memory or if they're really so delicious. You guys tell me."

She stops again. Usually this is enough of a story about the origin of a cookie, but Juliet wets her lips. She blinks her eyes and swivels away from us and then turns back as though announcing that we're going to meet a different Juliet. "Now." Her voice has lowered and gathers a husky whisper. She sips on her wine and raises one finger. "You have to get to know your cookie. And my cookies have nuts in them. Be sure you have the exact amount." She raises her eyebrows. "And be tender with the nuts." Her gravelly voice tells us we're in a new arena and this is not about tree nuts at all. "Gentle because they're easily bruised. In this case I rock the knife when I chop. Rock it gently so the nuts split apart and are not smashed." She slides her hand, fingers pressed together, back and forth and sways her hips with the motion.

"Roast them slowly. At just"—she pauses and whispers—"the right temperature." She turns her head sideways and glances from the corners of her eyes. "Make sure they don't get too hot before you're ready to use them." She shakes her head slowly and whispers, "You definitely don't want them too hot."

Jeannie laughs loudly.

Laurie's eyes are fastened on Juliet.

Juliet waits and says, "Then you mix the dough. I mix it with my hands. Got to confess." She opens her lips and slowly wets them. "After I mix it, I lick the dough off my fingers." Sticking out her tongue, she places the tip at the base of her index finger. She slides the finger, slowly, very slowly, down her tongue. When she gets to the fingertip, she places it in her mouth and sucks. "Yuuummm. You got to make sure it's delicious. Tastes just right before the next step.

"Then." She places her hands on her hips and leans down. "You have to make the logs. First, you divide the dough into pieces." She gathers invisible dough between her palms and pats it toward us. "The logs have to be at least six inches long." Her hands separate about six inches apart. "At least six inches. Sometimes longer is better. Sometimes not. Depending on what *you* want."

"I want eight inches," Taylor shouts.

"Bigger is always better. I'll take ten," says Rosie.

"Then you'll use it all up in one log." Juliet turns toward her. "You can do it that way. But I want four or five."

"Four or five?" Taylor squeals. "Lord! One's all I can take."

"But you have to make it two inches wide." She spreads her thumb and forefinger about two inches apart and moves them back and forth over the sides of the invisible log. Back and forth.

"And don't forget to be tender with the nuts." By now we're laughing so hard we can hardly hear one another's comments.

"I can't wait to taste these nuts."

"You can keep the nuts. I want the dough. That six-inch log." Allie giggles.

Juliet reaches in the large shopping bag and brings out packages made of shiny scarlet paper and tied with a profusion of tightly curled pink iridescent ribbons.

The packages of cookies are passed around the circle.

Charlene sits next to me. She puts her package in her bag and leans back to watch the revelry.

Allie continues. "You ever think about what we're doing here? I mean the Freudian symbolism of it? He said what every woman wants for a present is a phallus. But we make one another something yummy and then wrap it pretty, very pretty, usually in some shade of red, and give it to one another. I always knew he was wrong."

I search out Sissy, wondering how she's doing, what she thinks of this ribald conversation, but she's smiling and joking with Allie.

Laurie opens the package and retrieves the recipe. "Then we have to put it in the freezer. A deep freeze. Well, I guess that's what I've been doing since we got Olivia."

"These are delicious. It wasn't just your memory. They're fabulous even without coffee."

The scarlet packages are passed out and I place one in the bag for Vera and another for Tracy. We all eagerly open them and taste a cookie, exclaiming how wonderful they are.

"Elegant and perfect," Laurie says. "Like you."

"Elegant? You think I'm elegant?" Juliet replies.

"Not just elegant. I didn't know you had it in you. You should do a TV show. Rachael Ray meets Dr. Ruth."

The group laughs.

Juliet gets up and goes to the kitchen. I catch a glimpse of her back, her head sagging, one shoulder down, and follow her.

"What's up?"

"I don't know. It's just . . . well, somehow making those cookies and thinking about my grandfather and Dan and Tom, and I don't know what it is about this year, but it weighs." Her words come out in quick whispers. "It all weighs so heavily," she says again, and her shoulders slope. "I miss him." She wets her lips, "But it's not him. It's the father I never had and the Dan I thought I was marrying, and the Tom I thought I might marry. And meanwhile it's just me and my kids and my parceled-out life. And you." She closes her eyes. "Always you. And my mom, of course, in assisted living. Still screeching at me." As she speaks, she rolls the gold chain between her fingers.

"Who knew back when we were at that concert that you'd be where you are now, that Tara would be pregnant and Sky would be going through what she's going through?" I check my watch. I was sure she would have called by now.

"That's right!" Juliet taps her forehead. "I'm just thinking about myself. Sky hears about her test today. Too much going on."

"Tonight you were a riot. On top of your game."

"Maybe that's what it all is. Just a game."

And then Rosie enters. "Game? What game?"

Juliet and I shoot each other a look and Rosie says, "Oh. I interrupted."

"We need to go back anyway. Who's next?"

"Jeannie." And then Rosie leaves.

I consider the irony of Jeannie going next and remember the raucous laughter that Juliet and Jeannie always share. Both are involved in triangles and neither one of them knows about the other's situation. At least I don't think that Jeannie has told Juliet. And I can't imagine Juliet telling Jeannie about Tom. I turn to Juliet: "Let's have dinner this week, or lunch? Just us. Maybe at the Roadhouse?"

"Of course." And Juliet hugs me. "I love you," she says.

"Me, too."

"I felt like such a shit when Stephen was cheating on you. I was concerned you'd quit being my friend."

"What? Quit being your friend?"

"That you'd start feeling, I don't know, weird, strange since I was doing to someone what Stephen was doing to you."

"It didn't feel the same. You weren't doing it to me. And Stephen was fucking the world. Maybe that's selfish, or egocentric, but that's the way it was. And that was so long ago."

"Marnie," Allie calls. "Juliet."

"And here we are. Here we still are." I grab a bottle of wine and sing as I walk back into the party, "Thought we needed more refreshment."

"Sounds like a plan."

And the party spirit fills me again.

NUTS

I confess a weakness for nuts of all kinds. They're my favorite snack, and since the discovery of their health benefits, it's easy for me to rationalize their consumption. Too easy! Cookies laden with nuts are guaranteed to be some of my favorites.

But as much as I love eating nuts, I must admit I find black walnuts a little suspect. Growing 130 feet tall with a spread of 75 feet, the American black walnut is often regarded as the national tree of the USA. I have several growing in my yard and they are feathery shade trees, but it's difficult, often impossible, to grow certain plants near them. Before I buy any plant, I research to learn if the plant can thrive. Redbuds and bleeding hearts flourish; lilacs and peonies expire. The nuts stain your hands, can be used as a dye, and the wood is quite valuable. The nut is smaller and has a tougher shell than the standard walnut, which grew wild over a broad area from southeast Europe through

Asia almost to China. Wild walnuts have been gathered and eaten since prehistoric times. The practice of pressing oil from them is mentioned in ancient Greece. Romans were prepared to pay high prices for good walnuts and had a tradition of throwing walnuts at weddings. Early settlers in New England brought the walnut here in spite of the fact that there were already several good native species. Walnuts are an excellent source of plant protein and also omega-3. Walnuts aid in the lowering of LDL cholesterol (the bad cholesterol) and the C-Reactive Protein (CRP), which is a marker for heart disease.

Pecans, named by the Algonquin Indians, and the most important nut indigenous to North America, come from a hickory tree related to walnuts. Both pecans and blueberries are native to North America and were major foods for Native Americans. The deciduous tree lives and bears fruit for up to three hundred years, growing as tall as 130 feet with a spread of 75 feet. Some old wild trees continue to produce nuts, but most are grown on cultivated trees. Antoine, an African American slave from Louisiana, propagated pecans by grafting a superior wild pecan to seedling pecan stocks. His clone won an award at the Philadelphia Centennial Exposition in 1876 and his tree stimulated the pecan industry. Pecans are an excellent source of protein and unsaturated fat, and lower cholesterol.

Peanuts were part of Sky's and Tara's favorite lunch in the form of peanut butter with homemade strawberry preserves. They're not nuts but a kind of bean or pea that thrust their flower stems into the ground after pollination so that the pods and seeds develop underground. First grown in pre-Inca times and probably domesticated in Argentina or Bolivia, it is one of the most important plants from the New World. Cultivation in North America was popularized by African Americans, who brought the Kikongo word *nguba*, which became *goober*. Peanuts spread rapidly, taken to Africa by the Portuguese. Now they are widely eaten as peanut butter, satay sauce, snacks, and in Chinese food. All of which I love. They're a major food crop vital to nutrition since they are 30 percent protein and are packages of good-for-you elements such as niacin, antioxidants, and coenzyme Q10. Unfortunately, many people are allergic to peanuts and have such fierce reactions that even the aroma may trigger life-threatening incidents. I read that the widespread peanut allergies in the United States have been traced to our habit of roasting the nut, using peanut oil in skin preparations, and the intake of soy products.

Most of us learned in school about George Washington Carver and his discovery of three hundred uses for peanuts, but the nut became widespread when the need for the oil escalated because of a shortage of other plant oils during World War I. The U.S. Congress has designated the peanut as one of our basic crops.

5

Laurie

Hermit Cookies

1 cup packed brown sugar

$^1/_4$ cup margarine, softened

$^1/_4$ cup shortening

$^1/_4$ cup cold coffee

1 egg

$^1/_2$ teaspoon baking soda

$^1/_2$ teaspoon salt

$^1/_2$ teaspoon ground cinnamon

$^1/_2$ teaspoon ground nutmeg

$1^3/_4$ cups all-purpose flour

$1^1/_4$ cups raisins or other dried fruit

$^3/_4$ cup chopped nuts

Preheat the oven to 375 degrees. Cream together the brown sugar, margarine, and shortening. Add the coffee, egg, baking soda, salt, cinnamon, and nutmeg. Stir in the remaining ingredients. Drop the dough by rounded teaspoonfuls about 2 inches apart onto an ungreased cookie sheet. Bake until almost no indentation remains when touched, 8 to 10 minutes. Immediately remove from the cookie sheet. Makes about 4 dozen cookies

WELL, I WANT TO go next," announces Laurie.

"It's supposed to be Jeannie's turn," Juliet says. "Hey, cookie bitch, can we switch like that instead of going in a circle?"

They love teasing me about the rules.

"Uh-oh. Are we gonna break the rules? No breaking a rule," Rosie taunts as she pours wine into empty glasses and stands, her hand on her hip.

See. The rules allow for more jokes.

But then Rosie asks who wants more wine and her eyes meet Jeannie's and Jeannie whips her head in a harsh no and then keeps her head turned away. Rosie doesn't get it. She doesn't accept responsibility and Jeannie finds it easier to blame her than her father.

"I'm going last, and I'm not sitting next to Rosie," Taylor reminds us.

"Olivia might need me, and, well, Brian might call." Laurie pats her waist, indicating her cell phone.

I can't help but touch mine. Still quiet. Still no call from Sky.

"And I really want to give everyone their cookies." The burgundy tunic Laurie wears echoes the reddish highlights in her hair. She wore that tunic last year.

"Brian'll be fine. You're missing your baby," Allie says, not dismissively but softly.

"I love this party so much. I love you guys and Ann Arbor," Laurie says. The tinge of nostalgia in her voice surprises me. Our eyes meet. "I don't want to miss a minute of it. This is the start of the entire exciting season." Her grin conveys her enthusiasm.

"Sure. You're up." I nod to Laurie.

Laurie retreats into my office and returns with her bags. Disney follows her, his tail turning in a circle and his eyes bright.

Laurie's my hairdresser. Vera started sporting a particularly sexy and sassy haircut about ten years ago and told me Laurie had cut it. I've been using her ever since. At that point, she was working her way through college, but she never quit hairdressing. Laurie helped me transition my hair from blond to what was increasingly becoming white gray. "It'll bring out the blue in your eyes. And give you more vibrancy."

"You sure it won't make me look old?"

"No. More flamboyant, if anything."

Slowly, we lightened the color I was using. Gradually, she increased the amount of white highlights. Now it's completely white. During one of those years, back when it was mostly blond, I brought her a couple dozen of our cookies. Brian loved them and she loved baking. I knew that Jackie was moving, so Laurie joined.

This year, after adopting Olivia, she cut her clientele to provide for her own maternity leave by working three afternoons a week instead of five. Her husband is a real estate agent. Their budget has gotten smaller, but Laurie never says a word. She doesn't meet us for shopping sprees or for dinner, but that could be because of Olivia. "Bring her with you," I say. "We'd love to see her."

There's silence on the phone and then she says, "Well, I better not."

"We're just going to split some appetizers at Zingerman's." I try to encourage her, but she still declines.

As she bustles back and forth gathering her bags and the women resume chatting to their neighbors, I think of all the years I heard about Brian's low sperm count. The shots, the drugs, even the operation they tried. But nothing worked.

"Maybe a miracle. It just takes one." Her hair was feathered then, and blond.

But the fast swimmer with stamina they needed never made it and they decided to adopt. I say that in one sentence, but it took them a decade to come to this point. A decade of expectations and tears and loss and tens of thousands of dollars. Then another few years to realize that the wait in the U.S. was five years and the wait in China shorter. A week before she left for China, Laurie showed me a photo of the baby with chubby cheeks and hair that stood straight up in every direction.

"I love her already," Laurie said, touching the picture as her eyes filled with a mixture of hope but also sorrow that she wouldn't be giving birth to her own daughter. There was a tentative tap of her finger on the picture. She closed her eyes and whispered, "I hope this'll be okay."

Sky and I had already crept through the death of her baby. I wondered if someday Sky would be where Laurie was. Would I anticipate a grandchild not born of my daughter?

"I mean, having children is hard enough even when

you have a sense of where they're coming from. From you. From your man. That's still scary. But, well, this." Her words trailed off as she bent her head down.

"It's a leap into the unknown."

Love grows from bonds, not biology. But I think the biological connection eases an immediate understanding of temperament and personality. Preferences, interests, and even penchants for colors and foods and hobbies are partly determined by genes. Characteristics we assume are learned when we believed personality was formed by nurture are in fact influenced by biology.

Take the ability to experience awe. Awe. Who would have thought that was biological? Who would have thought that a painting or a sunset or hearing beautiful music didn't transport everyone? Yet 35 percent of people never know that emotion. Allie told me that. She read it in a book on the biological basis for personality. She was as startled by that information as I was. As I felt overwhelmed by awe staring into Olivia's infinity eyes, I pondered these questions, pondered for Laurie and Olivia, and Sky and me. Preparing myself for whatever future I had in store. Mentally preparing myself for supporting Sky through the adoption of a baby, if the news about this pregnancy was sad.

"Yes. Scary sometimes. I hope I can love her enough."

"That bond, that rush of maternal love comes from caring." I knew that. Look how I loved Luke. "You're ready."

We both stared into Olivia's eyes. "It's always exciting and scary, both." I wanted her to understand that she was like any other mother. A different way of beginning, but for all intents and purposes, the love and fear is the same.

I didn't know if I was just telling us both a fairy story.

"Wouldn't it be wonderful, just wonderful, if we could turn conception on and off when we wanted it? Just think of the sorrow we could avoid."

We were standing so close that I smelled the lemon in her perfume.

She heaved a sigh of exasperated irony.

"There's no way to write insurance on any child, whether you give birth or adopt. It's a tossup." I think of Tara and the years when there was tension between us. "You and Olivia are going on a great adventure," I said. "An adventure across the customary boundaries." I held her hands. "Special." And then hugged her. "From one end of the world to another. And China! Who knows what Olivia will introduce you to."

Now I look around the room, at all these women, so many who have been part of my life for decades. Family, kinship, is what you build from the accidents of life; from different decades, different biologies, different countries, different races. Certainly that. I examine Sissy's features and imagine them mixed with mine. I wonder if the baby will have her astonishing smile, a smile that Aaron has. I wonder if he'll inherit her even teeth. The fine brows. Soon I'll see the features from the accident of Tara and Aaron, though really every conception is serendipity.

If things don't work out, a piece of Sky will always be sad that she couldn't give birth, couldn't see the love between her and Troy in the body of a baby, but she'll still form a family, somehow, one more diverse than hers would have been if she had given birth. If this embryo is deformed, I'll encourage her to adopt. But I know, once you're a parent, your safety net is full of holes. Any glorious or horrendous thing is possible.

After Laurie brought Olivia home, she called me. "You were right. I was ready. As soon as they handed her to me, in her little pink blanket with her teeny fingers, I fell in love with her. She looked at me and I was hers. Like her eyes swallowed me and claimed me as her mom."

Now, Laurie stands, a white baker's box in her hand with a cellophane window revealing its contents. It is tied with red and green ribbons, the ends furled. Laurie is one of the youngest cookie bitches. She and Taylor are in their late thirties. The rest of us span the forties and fifties. Me, I'm fifty-seven. Can hardly believe it myself it sounds so grown-up. In a few years, I'll be eligible for Social Security. Social Security! That sounds old. How did that happen? Vera is in her midforties. Allie's in her sixties. Or about to be. We stretch across all the decades of adulthood.

"This has been a big year for me. Well, you know, because of Olivia. And this party is the first time I've been away from her, except for work, since she was ours. And . . ." Laurie stops and looks at each of us.

I realize by the nervous hesitation of her speech that she's going to make an announcement. My heart picks up and I lean forward.

She presses her lips together and says, "Well, I love you guys." Her voice breaks. We all know now she is going to make an announcement and are quiet, our motions halted as we prepare for what she's going to say.

She snaps her fingers, inhales quickly, and says, "The cookies! Back to the cookies. These are standard fruit and nut cookies, hermits, but this year, well, I've been thinking about our planet and Olivia's healthy, long life . . . The health of all of us." She sweeps her hand around our circle and says softly, "I guess this sounds like a green ad about the future for our children, but I changed this recipe and made it more health-friendly. Used whole wheat flour. Added more walnuts; they're supposed to have lots of omega-3s. Used dried cherries instead of raisins or preserved citron and pineapple. But you can use whatever you want. Splurged on organic brown sugar. That's why I made this particular cookie this year. I've been thinking a lot about health."

She passes out the boxes. I drop a box in Vera's bag, the hospice bag, and take one for me.

"Healthy or not, they're yummy." Charlene has tasted one. "And I love dried cherries."

Laurie laughs. "Well, I thought about using dried blueberries since I read somewhere that blueberries and walnuts are extremely healthy together, but blueberries didn't seem like holiday time."

"I love dried fruit and nuts. Can't beat them." Allie flashes an enigmatic smile. "Healthy but fattening," she adds.

"They're all fattening." Taylor looks at Allie, her glance lingering.

Disney bounces to the door just before the doorbell rings. Vera's fur collar softens her face, which still looks freshly made-up. She doesn't join the group but tiptoes with her cookies to the back, goes out again and returns with a tray of cold cuts, which she places on the table, then removes her coat and sits down. Vera flashes a thumbs-up to me, and I know she made her sale. "Congrats," I mouth to her.

She frowns and touches a finger to her cheek where my bruise is.

The yellow concealer must have rubbed away. I shrug and mouth back, "It's nothing. The kitchen cabinet." It doesn't hurt anymore.

She's trying not to interrupt, but it doesn't work.

"Hey, Vera. How're the roads?"

She nods to Laurie, still standing, holding the last box of cookies.

"Wet, but not slippery. I think it's too warm to really freeze."

"We were missing you!" Jeannie says.

"Well, here I am. Late, but here." Vera wears a camel hair skirt with a fringe at the hem, high brown boots, and a multicolored blouse that sets off her platinum hair. I motion to her seat. "Here're your cookies."

"How was work?"

"Made my sale."

Rosie holds out her hand for a high-five across the coffee table.

"And now I get to hear at least part of Laurie's story." Vera's comment turns our eyes back to Laurie, who smiles appreciatively.

"Can't wait to hear about Olivia," Vera mouths.

"You got the cookies and heard the story. Though there's not much of a story about the cookie. Don't even know where I got the original recipe. Maybe some magazine. Well, I made the cookie while Olivia was napping. You know, one day I made the batter, the next I baked them. Luckily, you just drop them with a spoon . . . you don't have to slice or roll. I let them cool on the dining-room table, Olivia can't reach that, and finally I put them in the boxes the third day." She leans over and sips some water from her wineglass. "Brian helped taste them." She chuckles.

"Well." Laurie stops. Her eyes circle the room slowly. She studies each of us in the circle, our bags half full of cookie containers. Jeannie starting having Laurie cut and color her hair when she saw how mine looked. The first time Laurie came to the cookie party, she knew Vera and Jeannie would be there, too.

But I didn't know that she knew Allie. Allie had been her therapist when she and Brian discovered his low sperm count. Allie never said anything to me, but after her first cookie party, Laurie mentioned that she had seen Allie professionally. They had examined how much being a mother meant to Laurie, how much Brian meant to her, and what her options were. Now her eyes stop at Allie. Taylor is still staring at her, too, and Allie, the focus of attention, pulls a lock of hair behind an ear, a gesture indicating unease.

Laurie smiles at Allie and her eyes slide to Juliet, who has become her friend since they met at Laurie's first cookie party. What were Laurie's cookies when she was the cookie virgin? The same ones, I remembered. And I know what her announcement will be.

I inhale sharply and my eyes fill. She's coming full circle.

"Well." She tries again. "I have some news."

"So. You're pregnant," Rosie blurts out.

"No. Olivia is enough for me right now."

I know what she's going to say. I just don't know where she's going.

"You know, well, you all know because it's affected you, one way or another, how bad the economy has been. But particularly for us, particularly for a real estate sales-person. Houses are moving, but the prices are low, get-ting bank financing is harder than ever, and now plenty of people aren't even trying to sell their houses. Well, you can pick up foreclosures, but so often that's such a sad sit-uation, the people express their fury at an unfair system and their own gullibility and bad luck by wrecking the houses. Or they just leave the house and with it some of their furniture. When you go into the house, you see the love that people had for it, the window seats that are cov-ered with a child's favorite fabric, a desk painted with the family's handprints, printed curtains. Rose gardens gone to mold. And finding buyers is difficult." Laurie sounds like a teacher when she's anxious, the result of her mom, who taught high school. "Well"—she shrugs—"we need the money now. And"—she looks down—"you know I've cut back, partly because of Olivia, but truth-fully because people aren't going to the hairdressers as often. Fewer expensive highlights. Fewer cuts every six weeks."

Vera, Jeannie, and I glance at one another as though scolded.

She notices our expressions and says, "It's just the way it is, you know? Well, we've been thinking about this for a while . . . and Brian's sister is in North Carolina. We wouldn't have to go through winter again. Closer to my parents, since they're in Florida. It's one of the few places where the real estate market hasn't been hit hard." She counts the positives by pulling down her fingers. "Brian was able to connect with another broker. And his brother-in-law manufactures cabinets, so Brian can work there until things pick up. And I can get my license. And I guess"—Laurie swallows and shifts her weight—"well, this'll be my last cookie club party."

"What? You can't leave us!" Rosie says.

"Ohmigod." Vera's mouth is turned down.

"Oh, no." Charlene is dismayed.

"I'm so sorry. So sorry," Taylor says.

"You can still come back. Lynda did," Rosie says. "Or commute like Alice."

"I know. I've thought of all that. But I think I'll start a branch in Charlotte. Is that okay?" She looks at me.

"Of course."

"So when are you moving?" Rosie asks.

"We're going to take it in stages. After the holidays, Brian'll start selling our house. If it doesn't sell in three months, we'll look to rent it out. But he'll be in North Carolina starting his real estate business; he already has his license there. I'll stay here, hoping things are resolved." She crosses her index and middle fingers. "But regardless, I'll move down there in June."

Quiet settles over the group.

"I can't commute like Alice. Not with Olivia."

Several of us nod.

"We need to be a family. Not all stretched out."

I consider what Laurie's given up because of her love

for Brian. The adopted child, and now this move. But when you're a couple, you decide as a team. You sacrifice for your family.

"If worst comes to worst, we'll sell the house at auction. And there's some thought that Brian's agency will buy it and hold it until the market improves."

"Oh, Laurie," Jeannie says. "Leaving will be so hard. And what will we do without you?"

"What I'll miss most is you guys. My friends. I know I won't be able to find friends like you."

"Nope. No one's like us." We all laugh.

"But you'll find others."

"Different ones."

"But no one like us." More laughter.

"I've gone through so much with you." Laurie meets my eyes. "Well. I mean, you guys know my whole story. Other people'll just pick up with me as a mom."

"You'll make new friends." I look at Allie and she says, "Yeah, at Olivia's day care and kindergarten. I've met lifelong friends at day care. And kids' sports practices. Believe me, being a mom is a friend magnet."

Then Allie smiles at Laurie and her voice lowers. "It'll be hard for a while, but you'll do it and come up on top. You always do." Allie's voice locates the importance of the message.

Tears fill Laurie's eyes. "Well, I wanted to tell you. Didn't want to bring everybody down tonight, but that's really my cookie story. What I thought about was leaving you guys. Leaving Ann Arbor and the lights downtown and cross-country skiing, and Magic Mountain and the

Top of the Park, and the cafés in summer. The parks and art galleries. The salon and my clients. And, of course, this."

"How come you didn't choose Florida?" Jeannie asks. "My parents are there and I'd be able to visit you when I visit them."

"Since Mom and Dad moved, it's made it easier to leave and we considered Florida, but their real estate market is as bad as ours. No one wants to pay the enormous insurance rates." She stops abruptly and her eyes fill. "It's just that it'll be hard leaving these memories."

"Hey. You get to take the memories with you."

"But, well, it's like the Top of the Park. I know it's fun. I look forward to it every year. And the Townie Party. And this. And I'll have nothing to look forward to there."

Allie nods. "The anticipation is part of the fun. But you'll look forward to all the new discoveries."

"It's different even now. I'm always thinking. Will this be the last time I do this or see this person or shop here? As though I don't want to let any of it go, but I know . . . I know I'm going to a new adventure." She presses her lips together. "And this will be better for us, Brian, Olivia, and me."

"And you get to make new memories."

"North Carolina is a great state. The ocean, mountains."

"No snow!"

Sissy says, "I've lived in the same place all my life, down the block now from where I was born. My family's all there. Can't imagine leaving even though it's tumbled down around me. You don't change your friends because circumstances change." She shrugs. "Guess I stay to make it better."

"I couldn't leave no matter what, either," Jeannie says. "I've spent my entire life here. I'm a townie through and through. Don't know if I'd recognize myself if this wasn't my home." She smiles at Sissy.

"God. It's not like you're going to the North Pole in the eighteenth century or something. We have planes. And cars. And email. And cell phones. You can come back," Rosie says.

"Stay at our place," Juliet says, "we've got the room since the kids are gone. You gotta come for the art fair. What would it be without us browsing together?"

"Well, don't forget I'm not leaving yet. I'll be here, maybe, till June."

"Your house is so, so cute it'll probably sell and you'll move in February," Rosie complains playfully.

"Well, I hope." Laurie laughs.

"We all hope." I raise my glass. "To new adventures in new cities."

"We're all gonna drive down next year and pester you."

"Please do."

"Get away for a women's spring break."

"You're on."

"And, don't forget, I'm franchising your cookie club and forming one down there. Well." Laurie's eyes widen with delight. "I'll be the head cookie bitch."

"To cookie bitches everywhere," I say.

We click our glasses.

CINNAMON

My mom celebrated cinnamon by making us cinnamon toast: hot buttered toast coated with cinnamon and sugar. The heat melted the butter and turned the cinnamon and sugar mixture into the perfect treat on a cold winter morning. Now, I sprinkle cinnamon in my morning coffee. Its crisp aroma jump-starts my day with zest and focus. It is often considered the scent of Christmas and flavors much of our baking, its crisp sweet aroma perfuming our homes. I didn't know about the healing properties of this spice until recently. It helps prevent unwanted clumping of blood platelets and stops the growth of bacteria as well as fungi, including the problematic yeast, candida. Cinnamon's antimicrobial properties are so effective that this spice may be used as an alternative to traditional food preservatives.

Not only does consuming cinnamon improve the body's ability to utilize blood sugar, but smelling this sweet spice boosts brain activity! Specifically, cinnamon improves attention, virtual recognition memory, working memory, and visual-motor speed while working on a computer-based program. So chew cinnamon-flavored gum when taking tests.

Always considered precious, cinnamon has a history rife with jealously guarded monopolies motivating trade and exploration, including the discovery of the New World by the Europeans. Cinnamon is from the bark of a small evergreen tree, known from remote antiquity, native to Sri Lanka. Imported to Egypt from China four thousand years ago, it was used to embalm bodies. Moses was commanded to use cinnamon as a holy anointing oil, and in the Song of Solomon, cinnamon scents the beloved's garments. As a sign of remorse, Roman emperor Nero ordered a year's supply of cinnamon be burned after he murdered his wife.

Up to the Middle Ages, the source of cinnamon was a mystery to the Western world. Arabs established an early monopoly and managed to keep its origin a secret for hundreds of years. Indonesian rafts transported cinnamon to East Africa, and Arab traders brought the spice via overland trade routes to Alexandria in Egypt, where it was bought by Venetian traders from Italy who dominated the spice trade in Europe. The rise of other Mediterranean powers, such as the Mamluk Sultans and the Ottoman Empire, disrupted this trade and Europeans were forced to search for other routes to Asia. Thus, Columbus sailed to Asia and on the way discovered the New World!

Columbus thought he had found cinnamon in Cuba in 1492, but it was the West Indian wild cinnamon. In spite of that, his discovery was the rationalization for continued occupancy of the island. The Portuguese found wild cinnamon in Ceylon in the 1500s and the Dutch took over the island in 1636 and began to cultivate cinnamon. After the British conquest in 1796, the East India Company acquired domination and kept it until the 1800s. Then true cinnamon was grown in other places and cassia bark, which is difficult to distinguish from cinnamon when ground, became acceptable to consumers. Finally, the trade of cinnamon was freed from monopolies and secrets.

6

Alice

Buttery Pecan Rounds

    Pecan halves for top (untoasted)
    1 cup flour
    ½ teaspoon salt
    1 cup softened butter
    ¾ cup dark brown sugar
    1 large egg yolk
    ⅔ cup finely chopped pecans

Toast pecan halves at 350 degrees for 10 minutes, rotating every 3 minutes. Cool, then break or chop into small pieces.

Preheat oven to 325 degrees. Sift the flour and salt. Set aside. Cream the butter and sugar for 3 minutes. Mix in the yolk.

On low, mix in the flour until combined. Mix in the chopped pecans with an electric mixer. Chill for 1 hour.

Using a 1-inch ice cream scoop, drop the batter onto parchment paper-lined sheets, spacing 3 inches apart. Press a pecan half on top.

Bake for 12 to 14 minutes, rotating the sheets half-way through. Cool completely. Makes 3 dozen

$\mathcal{M}$Y PHONE VIBRATES AND my heart starts pounding. I bolt into the kitchen while pulling my cell from my pocket, and there's Alice's photo, snapped when we were drinking on Gratzi's patio last summer on a late Wednesday afternoon. The umbrella cast a shadow that highlighted her smile. My phone is set so that pictures of my friends appear when they call.

It's not Sky. Not yet.

"We were just talking about you." I haven't visited Alice yet, so I don't have an image of her setting. Her husband, Larry, found the perfect job in San Diego and so for right now Alice is working here and flying to California every other weekend. Some weekends, Larry comes here. They bought a condo a few blocks from the beach and she can see the Pacific when she stands in the corner of her balcony. When we talk, I imagine the sea sparkling behind her.

"How's the party?"

"Great. But we miss you. Laurie just handed out her cookies. She's moving to Charlotte, probably early summer."

"Oh, wow, that's big news." Her voice is eager, wanting to capture some of the cookie spirit. "I wish I could be there. Checked to see if there was a cheap flight, but no such luck. Besides, I'll be there in just a few weeks, in time for the Townie Party, and I'll see most of you there. Can't wait."

"You'll drop by here and we'll go together. You and Larry and Jim and me." That is, if Jim can get away.

"That's the plan," Alice says.

"Hey, everyone," I shout as I return to the living room, passing Vera on the way to the kitchen.

"Alice is on the phone," I say.

"Hi, Alice." Juliet is followed by a chorus. I hold the phone to the center of the room so that Alice can hear our love.

"We miss you!"

"We wish you were here."

Rosie holds out her hand. "Let me talk to her."

I hand her the phone. Taylor strolls into the kitchen, where Vera, Charlene, and Jeannie are making a second pass at the food. They're hitting Vera's salami and cheese. Sissy's sushi is finished and I remove the plate. Vera ladles some soup. She hasn't had dinner.

I sense the need to move around and recluster, to eat, pee, talk, and take a break from the cookie routine.

"Next year you'll be here?" Rosie says into the phone. "Hey, Laurie's moving. She's going to start a new branch."

I move empty plates from the table to the sink, then pull out a bowl of fruit and place it on the table. Then I open another container of chocolate almonds and pour them into a bowl and carry them into the living room.

Rosie hands the phone to Charlene and enters the kitchen.

I follow her back in. When I walk in Jeannie quickly turns from the table to stride into the living room, a plate in one hand and a glass in the other.

"Oh." Rosie halts in midstep, her back straight and

her shoulder blades kissing each other. "I almost bumped into you." She lifts her chin, but her tone trembles slightly.

Jeannie's face is flushed, her brows lifted. "Can't you watch where you're going?" She clenches her fingers around the stem of her glass, which is decorated with one of the charms. Her fingers are white with the exertion and I wonder if she'll snap the glass. "Are you aware of anyone else? Ever?" she hisses.

"Sorry." Now Rosie's tone is more belligerent than repentant. Sharp. And she narrows her eyes slightly. "Sorry for everything. Sorry for breathing." She's had enough of being Jeannie's scapegoat.

I snap my eyes shut and press my lips at the argument. Girlfriends fight. Jealousies and hurt feelings, concern about being left out or cast aside for a closer friend, evolve over time. They get resolved. Rosie and Jeannie had been so close, best friends. The three of them— Rosie and Jeannie and Sue—were the three musketeers. Whether out of guilt or awkwardness, Sue resigned from the club this year, leaving space for Sissy. I was relieved. I couldn't imagine the three of them in the same room. This is hard enough.

Now they stand, Jeannie holding a plate crammed with veggies and hummus, pita chips and barbecued chicken. The wine shakes in its glass.

Rosie holds her upright posture, her back ramrod straight, her eyes slits. "So. I don't see you running to tell your mom. See. You're just like me. You're making the same decision I did and blaming me for it."

Rosie is right.

Jeannie glares. She lifts her chin up. "I," she barks,

"didn't make this fucking mess." Jeannie tilts the plate. The food slides down to the edge.

I step toward her.

Charlene appears behind her. She, too, has watched this scene unfold. "Jeannie?" she says softly. "Jeannie?" She touches the cocked arm.

Jeannie turns.

Charlene's eyes are very still and dark, deep lines etched from her nostrils to the corners of her lips. Her sorrow dissolves Jeannie's anger for the moment. The death of Charlene's son trumps Jeannie's angst. Charlene motions with her head to a corner. "I haven't had a chance to talk with you all night," she says, as though nothing unusual is happening while placing her hand on Jeannie's shoulder, softly warm but firmly guiding her from Rosie. They turn their backs on the rest of us and huddle in conversation.

Rosie's face whitens except for two perfectly round circles on her cheeks that flush red.

When she pours herself wine, her hand shakes. She takes a large gulp and then squeezes her eyes shut. I reach my hand to touch her arm.

I love them both. I won't take sides. I wonder if they'll ever work their way back to each other.

"So. She's never going to get beyond this."

"Never's a long time."

"She made this all my fault. When I didn't do anything." Rosie swallows more wine. "And I miss her." She inhales, shaking her head. "The her I thought she was, anyway."

Allie enters the kitchen, holding the phone high. "Everyone have a chance?" She waves the phone back and forth. A chorus of yes's answers her.

There seems to be too much happening at once, but I have to talk with Alice, so I take the phone.

"I miss you," she says. "It doesn't seem like the real holiday season without the party."

"At least you'll have the cookies. You can fly them back with you."

"Yeah. This bicoastal shit is tough. My life parceled out in two different cities, two different houses, two different sets of friends. Well, one set of friends. When I'm here, it's just Larry and me. We hoped it would be an oasis. These weekends twice a month together."

"Right now I'd love time with nothing to do but play with Jim."

"This weekend the laptop got the play." Usually Alice puts on an optimistic front, ignoring or denying the stress of commuting between two cities, two time zones, two houses. Then she adds, "He had so much work I was lucky to get him away to watch TV. I might as well have stayed in Ann Arbor. Except at least we're together. And this crush in his job will slow by Wednesday. Next weekend should be all us. Normal." She chuckles. "Whatever our normal is. Maybe it's this craziness." She's quiet for a minute and I hear her inhale. "How's Sky?"

"I thought you were her."

"Sorry. Call me tomorrow, okay? Anytime. Middle of the night included. Promise?"

"I'll let you know."

I shut the phone and automatically check to see if I've missed any calls. I haven't. I consider using this break to call Sky but decide not to intrude. It's six now in California. She must know. Maybe her obstetrician had to deliver a baby and she and Troy are nervously picking at their dinners. I have to be patient, I remind myself. My worst, absolutely worst virtue.

Just then I hear laughter and turn toward it. Jeannie, Sissy, and Charlene are chortling together in front of the refrigerator. Jeannie says something and Sissy's merry laugh answers back.

No one is in the living room. I get Alice's cookies and put one on each person's chair. When she shipped them to me, they were in Ziploc bags along with twelve white bags decorated with silver swirls and trimmed with white fur. Now they wait for the party members to claim them.

I return to the kitchen and move toward the group in front of the refrigerator. "Jeannie, I think you're next."

Rosie walks into the living room with a plate. When she passes us, she looks down.

"That okay?" I ask Jeannie.

Her smile is overly quick, a nervous twitch. Then she says, "Yeah. I'll go next." She meets my eyes and nods.

BUTTER

Butter has a bad reputation. It's blamed for obesity and, because of its animal fat, for clogging arteries and increasing heart disease. Yet for thousands of years, it served as a preserved source of valuable protein and as a taste enhancer in sauces and baked items. For decades, I replaced butter with margarine only to find out recently that the trans fats in the substitute were more damaging.

In elementary school, Sky had an assignment to make butter from cream; we took turns shaking it in a glass until the butter "came." From her project I learned that churning fermented or fresh milk produces butter. It can be made from the milk of sheep, goat, and buffalo though we most commonly use cow's milk. Butter from different species tastes different and, in addition, the diet of the animal, especially if it includes aromatic herbs, affects the taste.

It takes between 2 to 3 gallons of milk to form one pound of butter. Butter

is churned agitated cream that has been
ripened by the action of lactic acid producing bacteria, which are present naturally
in nonpasturized cream. This type of milk
makes cultured butter. Sweet cream butter, which is the type in common usage in
the United States, is made from pasteur-
ized cream and then flavor compounds are
added.

Both types of butter are sold with
salt, which preserves it, or unsalted. Another way to preserve it is to clarify the
butter, which removes the water. Heat it
gently so that the emulsion breaks down
and fat rises to the top. If the water totally evaporates, you've made ghee. This
is what Allie uses in her Ramadan cookies.
In India, ghee was an offering to the gods.

Since even accidental agitation can
turn cream into butter, it's likely that its in-
vention dates from the beginning of dairy-
ing, perhaps in the Mesopotamian area
between ten thousand and eleven thousand
years ago. The earliest butter would have
been from sheep's or goat's milk since cat-
tle were not domesticated until a thousand
years later. An ancient method of buttermaking, still used today in parts of Africa
and the Near East, involves a goatskin half
filled with milk, then inflated with air before being sealed. The skin is then hung

with ropes on sticks and rocked until the butter comes.

Throughout the Middle Ages, especially in northern Europe, butter was considered a food for the peasants. It was also used as oil in lamps. In the British Isles, butter was wrapped in skin and buried in peat bogs for preservation. Buttermaking was considered women's work; perhaps all things to do with milk was the purview of women. It was "house work" while "land work," outside work, was considered men's work. Butter was made by hand until 1860. Then the manufacturing of cheese began and it was easy to also mechanize the production of butter. Suddenly, it was no longer women's work and the price rose. By the 1950s, more margarine than butter was sold as it was cheaper and considered healthier. Now, in dollar amounts, margarine and butter are about equal, but because it's cheaper, more pounds of margarine sell than butter. Interestingly, butter sales have stayed the same or inched up slightly, while margarine sales have decreased.

In a cooking class, I learned that butter is a great cooking medium because of its rich flavor and the attractive brown color it awards cooked foods. However, it doesn't withstand high heat as well as oils.

Cookie dough and some cake batters are partly leavened by creaming butter and sugar together, which establishes air bubbles in the butter. In the heat of baking, the trapped bubbles expand. Shortbread cookies have no other source of moisture but the water in the butter. In pie dough, solid fat becomes layered when the dough is rolled. In the oven, the fat melts, leaving a flaky texture. Because of its flavor, butter is a delicious fat in such a crust, but it is more difficult to work with than shortening because of its low melting point. I'd been making piecrusts for decades before this was explained to me. I simply followed what my mother had taught me. Now, I understand why it's helpful to chill all your ingredients and utensils when you're working with butter dough. Rosie, Juliet, and Taylor make cookies that require chilling the dough before baking.

7

Jeannie

Fortune Cookies

Fortunes

1 large egg white

$^1/_2$ teaspoon pure vanilla extract

$^1/_2$ teaspoon pure almond extract

$^1/_4$ cup all-purpose flour

$^1/_4$ cup sugar

Pinch of salt

2 tablespoons melted butter

Write fortunes on pieces of paper that are 3 $^1/_2$ inches long and $^1/_2$ inch wide. Preheat oven to 400 degrees. Grease 2 9 x 13-inch baking sheets.

In a medium bowl, lightly beat the egg white, vanilla extract, and almond extract until frothy but not stiff. Or, you can make these with only one flavoring, but don't forget to use an entire teaspoon.

Sift the flour, sugar, and salt into a separate bowl.

Add the dry ingredients into the egg white mixture, then the melted butter. Stir until you have a smooth batter. The batter should not be runny, but should drop easily off a wooden spoon. You may need to add water.

Note: if you want to dye the fortune cookies, add the food coloring at this point, stirring it into the batter. For example, I used $1/2$ teaspoon green food coloring to make green fortune cookies.

Place level tablespoons of batter onto the baking sheet, spacing them at least 3 inches apart. I have found that a cold baking sheets, sprayed with oil spray, works best. Gently tilt the baking sheet back and forth and from side to side so that each tablespoon of batter forms into a circle 4 inches in diameter. Try to keep the batter flat and even. I used a large circle cookie cutter to keep the edges round.

Bake until the outer $1/2$ inch of each cookie turns golden brown and they are easy to remove from the baking sheet with a spatula (5 to 6 minutes).

Remove from the oven and quickly remove each cookie with a wide spatula (you can spray it with cooking spray) and place upside down on a wooden board or clean oven mitt. Quickly place a fortune on the cookie near the middle and fold the cookie in half. Place the folded edge across the rim of a cup and pull the pointed edges down, one on the inside of the cup and one on the outside. This is to crease it and form the traditional shape. Then place the folded cookie

into the cup of a muffin tin or egg carton to hold
its shape until firm. You may leave the cookie sheet
in the oven with the door open to keep the unfolded
cookies warm.

Here are some of the fortunes I used:

The awakening happiness of one's own self is revealed.

I cast this from me like an empty shell.

I cannot control this now, but I can breathe through it.

We must live as gardeners, fertilizing the flowers and
appreciating the change of seasons.

May holiday lights illuminate your path.

You cannot predict the long-term consequences of any
event.

Exhale the past, inhale the present, imagine the future.

May I know the contentment that allows the totality of
my energies to come to full flower.

If that which you seek, you find not within yourself, you
will never find it without.

To every thing there is a season, and a time to every
purpose.

The wheel is turning. This is the dark time. What must
you gain from the night?

Feast on your life.

*J*EANNIE ASKS, "ALICE'S COOKIES?" and picks up the white bag.

"Yes," I answer.

She places her wineglass on the coffee table and pulls out a cookie. "These are fabulous. These pecan butter cookies are crispy and rich. She outdid herself."

"They're winners. I tasted one earlier."

Jeannie then retrieves her cookie bags from the office. As she leaves the living room, I notice her jeans are loose and that, when she returns carrying her bags, her shirt that just last year showed off her cleavage now hangs. She nestles into the sofa and for a minute we're alone in the room.

"Jeannie, you need to resolve this situation for your own sake. Something to make it better for you." I emphasize the word *you*.

"It's not about me. It's about them." When she shakes her head, the candle flame throws red sparkles in her hair.

"Rosie has a point."

She narrows her eyes at me, inhales. And then looks down.

"You both do," I say.

SO HERE'S THE story. Jeannie met Rosie at an open house that Rosie and her husband threw for their new office. Jeannie's husband, Mark, is also a lawyer, so they were invited. Jeannie and Mark have one daughter, Sara, who is now seven. Jeannie has worked since high school in her father's business, which was a Saturn car dealership. She was general sales manager before Sara was born. Even now she's there a few days a week working in floor sales. She assumes she'll take over the dealership when her father retires. At the party, Jeannie and Rosie immediately became friends. Sue and Rosie had been close since high school. BFF, as the kids today say. Sue and Rosie opened up their twosome and swallowed Jeannie. The three of them went shopping together and took jazzercise classes. Friday nights they met at the Earle for mussels and wine. Some of us joined when we could and knew they'd be sitting in the wine bar by five-thirty at the table you see first when you enter. They'd smile and wave all newcomers over. Together, they managed a fund-raiser for the local theater and formed a relief organization for Katrina. They even attended Sara's field hockey games. The three of them. Three hockey moms for the price of one!

Rosie's energy and organization complemented Jeannie's creativity and sense of service. And Sue, the complete saleswoman, could sell any idea that the other two dreamed up and gather support from her network. Jeannie said, Let's go scuba diving, the Cozumel reef is supposed to be beautiful, and Rosie researched dive shops and inclusive hotels, and Sue got the three of them a special deal. The rest of us watched as they charged through life, each enhancing the other.

Triangles are usually unstable configurations, but this

one seemed solid. No one seemed anxious or concerned about her position with the others. All of the usual negatives that plague women's friendships were absent. There was never a fight.

I have a picture of their feet after they got a pedicure. The angle of the shot was so evenly placed, it's impossible to know which one snapped the photo. I had to figure out which pair belonged to which woman. I mean, I don't look at feet much. One ankle has a silver link chain. I know that is Sue's. One set of toes is purple; I guess that's Jeannie. Even now her tie-dye T-shirt is in shades of purple and her hair has a burgundy cast to it. The little toe of each foot touches the big toe of a friend, making a foot circle. The new polish glistens in the sun. They stand on grass that must be Jeannie's because her garden is so precise we tease her that she cuts it with manicure scissors.

But Jeannie accidentally brought a snake to the garden and the snake was her own father.

Sue needed a job. And Jeannie's father, Jack, was looking to enlarge his sales force at the car dealership. Jeannie knew Sue's superb sales skills and suggested she apply at the dealership. She put in a good word with her dad and the current sales manager. Sue was hired.

The learning curve was almost flat for Sue as she skyrocketed into the job. In her second year, she won an all-expenses-paid trip to Barcelona for two and took Rosie. I wondered if Jeannie felt left out or jealous. After all, she was the one who had gotten Sue the job. But maybe Jeannie was asked and refused because of Sara.

Now, Jeannie's father is very charming. One of those

rare men who, motionless, I would disregard if it were not for his aura of physical strength. But once he starts moving, Jack is captivating. Like any good salesman, he focuses on whomever he's talking to. With women, he stares into their eyes, doesn't appear to be scanning their bodies or undressing them, and quickly discovers something important to them. He asks questions. He appears fully *there*, fascinated by the topic and compelled by the responses. Jack hunts for synchronistic passions.

What do women want? We want to be heard. And known. And appreciated. We want someone to see us — our lives and our bodies — as exciting. Jack exudes that. And as you talk with him, you first feel appreciated and then you realize how his lopsided grin lends a hint of the bad boy. Then you want to touch the smattering of freckles covered with soft reddish hair on his arms.

When she started working for him, Sue was newly single after ending a two-year relationship because the man was drinking too much. The problems started when this boyfriend began not showing up when he said he would, or arriving very late.

"This isn't enough for me. I don't think it's too much to expect to see my boyfriend more than once a week," Sue complained.

He was often out drinking with his buddies or working. He seemed jittery when they were together. Even disinterested in making love.

"Is there another woman? Just tell me."

"You're the only woman I want. I'm busy, that's all." He wiped his nose with the back of his hand.

"Something seems wrong. Like we've run out of steam."

"I don't have any problems with you, Sue." He pulled up his jeans and slid his hand in his pocket and then reached for his socks.

Out fell a small plastic bag. It lay shining on her green rug. At first, Sue thought it was a jewelry bag. When she picked it up, white powder shifted. "What's this?"

He looked at her and shrugged.

"This is why you've been so unavailable?"

He didn't answer.

Sue understood instantly that she couldn't have a relationship with someone using hard drugs. She wasn't the nurturing, rescuing type. Life was too short and she wasn't getting any younger. "I'm not dealing with this. You have a choice and you can make it now."

"Don't give me ultimatums."

"Please leave."

She spent the weekend crying. The next morning Jack noticed the red eyes and easily pulled the story from her.

You know the scenario: The workplace friendship that becomes too close, lunches that last a little longer each time. When Jack noticed how turquoise set off the green in her eyes and commented that he loved hair that was almost, but not quite, black, Sue bought turquoise jewelry and darkened her hair.

I heard all this later. Much later. Initially, Jeannie was pleased that Sue fit in so well at the dealership. When employees were new, Jack transformed their loyalty and love for him into a commitment to the company. He spread his aura over the entire workforce. The sparkling cars built with no nonsense and easy care seemed to offer a promise of green energy, efficiency, and honesty in the smarmy backwaters of car sales.

Now, Jeannie and Sue's friendship had an additional shared arena. Once, I saw Rosie roll her eyes at a Friday-night gathering when they started talking about the new Astra. "Not work again. This is happy hour," she said and changed the subject.

I don't think that Jeannie's dad was ever a model of husbandly faithfulness. A man with his enticing charm has one woman after another hoping his exquisite attention is evoked solely and uniquely by her. But regardless of the competition for his attention, he stayed married to Jeannie's mom. And the women, one at a time, drifted away.

But Sue was different. Twenty years younger just as he was entering the last gasp of his own virility. A woman who shared his work zeal. A work wife.

Sue and Jack spent hours in his office, the door closed.

"You need some help?" Jeannie asked her.

"Help?"

"Hey, if you're having some problems getting the hang of things, come to me." Jeannie squeezed her arm. "I can show you the ropes. I mean, I've worked here forever."

"Your dad say something to you?" Sue brought her eyebrows together.

"No. Not at all."

"I'm doin' okay, I think." Sue smiled glossy red, revealing perfect whitened teeth. She looked, always looked, as though she had spent a week in the sun. She complemented her dark hair with silver chains around her neck, her wrists, her ankles. Her eagerness and determination were softened by her petite size. And these days she dressed in shades of turquoise and navy, bringing out the richness of her dark hair.

But the meetings continued.

When I asked Jeannie how it was going, she said, "I don't know, but I always felt good being with Rosie and Sue. Now I feel almost excluded from my own family."

"What do you mean?"

"Oh, it's just work. My dad always spends a lot of time with new employees."

But unease crept around the edges of her words. A year later there weren't long lunches anymore. Then one time Jeannie needed to ask her dad a question and couldn't reach him. He wasn't in the office. He wasn't at home. He didn't answer his cell phone. She thought maybe Sue would know the answer but couldn't reach her either. Jeannie shrugged it off. A month later it happened again.

One night Sue wasn't at the Friday happy hour. "Where's Sue?" I asked.

"Who knows?" Jeannie looked away and wrapped her fingers around the stem of her wineglass.

"Probably selling a Vue," Rosie added. "She's become so, so work obsessed." And then she glanced at Jeannie. But it was a fleeting look followed by a flush that only I observed.

"Hey, that's not my fault," Jeannie said.

"I know," Rosie almost whispered.

Prickles walked up my spine.

AND THEN EIGHT or nine months later, I got a call at seven A.M. At first, it was incorporated in a dream, the ring a mewling kitten accidentally locked in a closet. Before I could open the door, I realized it was the phone.

"Marnie?" Jeannie's voice was thick, her nose clogged.

"Jeannie?"

"I'm sorry. I know this is early, but could we have breakfast?"

"Come on over."

"Okay. I'll drop Sara at school and be right there."

I pulled out frozen ginger muffins and brewed coffee. Wrapped myself in my lavender bathrobe. It was early fall and the flowers had faded. Only the chrysanthemums bloomed yellow and purple. Their brightness was softened by a silvery rain while the birds warned of winter right around the corner.

Jeannie wore a cap pulled over her hair, a sure sign it was in need of washing. Her eyes were puffy.

"Here's some coffee." I set a mug before her on the coffee table.

She pulled a box of Kleenex from her purse and sat there looking as if she didn't know where to begin. Disney lay on the floor beside her, watching her with sorrowful eyes, his monkey dropped at Jeannie's feet.

I pushed the muffins across to her and sat cross-legged on the other end of the sofa.

"What happened?"

"Sue's having an affair with my father. She's fucking my father."

"What?" I reached for her hands, but she slid one away, grabbed a Kleenex, and blew her nose.

"She says Dad's going to leave Mom."

"Sue told you this?"

Jeannie shook her head and sniffed. "I found out about the affair and called Rosie. 'What's going on with Sue and my dad and don't fucking tell me work.'" Jeannie put her head in her hands. "Rosie was finally straight with me. 'I can't lie to you,' she said. After acting as though everything is hunky-dory." Jeannie lifted her head and choked out the words. "For two years, they were behind my back knowing that Sue was having an affair with my father and Sue being so friendly, so perky, so cute Sue."

"Jeannie." I hugged her and now she cried into my bathrobe, my shoulder.

"How could they do that to me? My father? My friends? All of them. Lie to me? Betray me? How could my best friend fuck my father? Take him from my mom? How could my other best friend keep this secret from me? For at least two years they've been together. Maybe more. How long has she worked for him? Four? Who knows exactly when it started. Rosie is just as much to blame." Jeannie's sobs muffled her words.

"Rosie? I don't understand."

"She knew for two years. Sue and my dad have an apartment together where they meet. I've been living a lie. Thinking they're my friends when all this was happening behind my back."

I placed my fingers over my eyes, trying to grapple with the story.

"Ohmigod," she wailed. "One fucking my father. One conspiring to keep me from finding out."

"Tell me from the beginning."

She inhaled. And sat back on the sofa staring into the eye of the blank TV. "I've suspected something for a while. But you know my father. Always the salesman. Always wooing his force into a mentorship of adoration. I figured—hoped, I guess—that Sue was part of the usual pattern." Her fingers twisted the tissue. "But his attention continued long past the usual first year. And they disappeared at the same time." She shrugged. Her voice was monotone, as though she had told the narrative to herself to make sense of it while her hands continued working the Kleenex. "At first I thought it was coincidence. But." A sigh floated. "Then I switched my days of work, had to because of Sara's field hockey practice, and I realized they were both gone for two hours on those days. Didn't answer their phones. I wasn't hunting for anything, you know?" She turned to me. "I didn't want . . . it didn't occur to me, that my best friend would sleep with my dad. That my father would sleep with my best friend. Didn't occur to me."

"Jeannie," I whispered, filled with concern for her.

"But then I had an optometrist appointment and it was on my workday. The waiting room is a storefront with that tinted glass you can see out of but can't see in through. I saw Dad leave the apartment building across the street. Two minutes later, here comes Sue. I watch her. She looks both ways and then walks away happy. Her hair bouncing on her shoulders like it does."

Jeannie clicked her tongue against the roof of her mouth. "I thought I was going to be sick. I sat through the appointment. Don't know how. Just sat there 'cause I didn't know what else to do. Too frozen, confused to do anything but what was next on my list while my world crashed."

"How's your mom?"

Jeannie was pale, her cuticles picked at, and her nails striped in ridges. "She doesn't know any of this yet. She's all excited about the trip they're taking to Italy and study-ing Italian." Her sobs resumed and then she shook her head. "Marnie? What do you do when you lose your best friends and your father simultaneously?"

"You haven't lost your father." I sipped my coffee. "Have you talked with him?"

"I don't know how to even broach the subject. It's so creepy. Him sleeping with my best friend. Almost like me."

"Sue's not you."

Jeannie shook her head again. "I don't know how Rosie could do this."

"I guess she felt in the middle. Couldn't break a promise to Sue."

"That's what she said. She said they spent a year struggling with their feelings for each other before they slept together. God. Dad is madly in love with my best friend." Her eyes narrowed and she sat back, looking straight at me, her eyebrows lifted. "Did she tell you? Did you know?"

"No. I didn't know."

"Shit. Did we go to Cozumel before or after Sue started fucking my dad?"

I remembered trying to put together a new history when Stephen was unfaithful to me.

Jeannie sucked in her lips so they seemed thin and turned down at the corners. The circles under her eyes were dark. She hugged her knees and curled into a ball. "I think of Mom and my heart sinks."

I didn't know what to say, so I sipped my coffee and started in on a muffin. The sharpness of the ginger was the perfect accompaniment to the situation, the spice along with a sweetness that was almost cloying. Food is always a great distraction and a comfort, but Jeannie was beyond the solace food provided. She held herself together with her arms. "I don't even know how I'll go to work tomorrow. How do I pretend everything is okay?"

"How do you know he's leaving your mom?"

"I asked Rosie if there was anything else. And she said that he promised Sue he'd leave Mom after Italy."

I cleared my throat. "That may be one of those usual lies married men tell their mistresses. A promise to leave their wife one date after another." I'm thinking of Juliet, how Tom promised he'd leave after his son's high school graduation, and then after his daughter's graduation. Juliet waited for one date after the other.

"Do I tell my mom and break her heart? If I don't, then I'm as bad as Rosie. Do I confront my father? Do I just quit my job and run away? That's what I want to do." She turned to me and her pupils were very light, almost yellow, and she kept them trained on me. "I want to pick up Sara and just start driving to a coast. Any coast. Start a new life."

"You have too much at stake here. And what about your husband? You're going to leave Mark? Have you told him?"

My questions hung in the air until she said, "He's preparing for a trial next week. I can't disturb him. I always have to make way for his job. I keep busy with Sara, then Rosie and Sue. And now . . . Now what?"

I tried to help her think of her options. She could tell her mom. Confront her father. And Sue. She could quit her job. She could talk to her husband. She could do anything.

But instead she did nothing.

Except lose weight. And then found an early-morning yoga class.

After she did her asanas, after she showered, after she fed Sara, made her lunch, and dropped her off at school, she'd drop by for a breakfast she never ate. Her body became thinner and, I swear, longer. Her new slender self moved with a stunned grace.

"Maybe you should see a therapist?" I suggested. "So you can decide what you want to do."

"Rosie must have told Sue and she probably mentioned it to my dad, but he's been acting like usual, normal." She didn't look at me but stared at a space on the wall, her voice monotone. "I think Sue is avoiding being in the dealership when I'm there because I hardly see her. Mom keeps complaining about how much Dad is working. Meanwhile, I feel like I'm part of a play. My father's not quite my same father. Nothing is like it was, but we act like it's the same. Nothing feels real. I walk and talk underwater." She pulled apart the toast smeared with jam, watching her fingers play with the crumbs. "Floating through different layers of reality. The casual work, the old father-daughter, the fact that we both know we know he's sleeping with my best friend but never talk about it. We slide between lives in different dimensions. And when I'm with Mom and Dad it's like it always was but different. I'm in layers of gauze."

"Except you don't hang out with Sue and Rosie anymore. That's changed."

"When I see them, I . . ." She searched for a word and then continued, "I saw them walking down Main Street busy talking to each other. They didn't see me. I was invisible. I heard Sue laugh, you know, her loud belly laugh like the whole world is hilarious, and thought I was going to throw up right on the sidewalk. Broke out in a sweat. Ducked into a store to hide."

I put my hand on her arm.

"Me hiding. Actually hiding. And I know, I know I'm stuck. Can't figure out if I should tell my mom. She'd be heartbroken. Maybe he won't leave her. I can't figure it out."

"Maybe you're doing exactly what you're supposed to be doing. Let them work it out. Let your father make his decision and let it unwind."

She continued as though she hadn't heard me. "If my mom finds out I haven't told her, she'll hate me as much as I now hate Rosie. 'We were protecting you,' Rosie said. 'We love you. So we didn't want you hurt, or your mom. This just happened,'" Jeannie rasped in Rosie's voice.

That was a month ago. "How's this going to work out for the cookie party?"

"Ohmigod. Is Sue coming?"

"She resigned. Told me that she was so busy at work it was probably better that she drop out for a while. That was back in the spring or summer. She must have been feeling too awkward and guilty to come. She got off the phone almost as soon as she delivered her message. We got a new cookie virgin. Sissy. Tara's boyfriend's mother. My co-grandma. If there is such a word."

"You're not going to kick me out, are you?"

"Of course not!"

"I won't look at Rosie, I'll just be with everyone else."

I squinched up my face when I imagined the party that had always been simply girlfriends enjoying one another. "You look like you could use those cookies. You look too thin."

"Yeah. It's all the exercise."

"Maybe by then this will be resolved. Right? Why don't we go for drinks and mussels this Friday. We'll go together."

"Do they still go?" Jeannie asks.

"I haven't seen them there. I went two weeks ago."

She frowned and shook her head.

"How about shopping? It's so much fun to go with you and the sales are terrific."

"Maybe."

But we never went. She just came for breakfast after yoga and played with her food.

* * *

NOW HERE WE are. Nothing has changed in three months except that Rosie has lost her determination to resurrect the friendship and Jeannie's trap has become the fabric of her life along with a passion for yoga. I glance at her nestled in cushions that she hopes will protect her from the whirlwind, her cheekbones sharp in her face and her eyes alert.

She says again, "It's not about me. It's about them. It's their fault. They have to solve it."

I soften my voice and say quietly and as gently as I can, "They can't solve it for you. They're going to solve it for them. How you react, what you do is about you. You blame the messenger and are furious at Sue."

"And my father. And I'm scared for my mom. And I'm trying to figure out what to do next."

"You can only rescue yourself."

"Whether I should tell my mother," she says as though I had interrupted her. "Confront my father."

"Jeannie, there's no way to put this back the way it was. There's no way for this to resolve without people you love hurting. Even if you decide to let them do what they need to do and not interfere, you still have to *decide* that. Be comfortable with it. Stop going back and forth looking for a rescue for all of them that works for you, too."

"You sound like Allie."

I continue, "You. The wonderful buoyant, organized Jeannie you are."

At that moment Charlene and Sissy and Laurie return from the kitchen. Charlene senses the silence and stops, and then enters the room.

"Me? Buoyant?"

"And visually creative," adds Charlene.

"And hysterically funny," Juliet adds as she, Allie, and Taylor return.

Allie gives Jeannie a hug as she sits next to her.

"Look, Alice's cookies. What cute bags! So feminine," Laurie says.

"And delicious," Charlene adds.

"Hey, it's cookie time." Jeannie grins. Her smile is too bright and fizzles away as everyone returns to her seat. Rosie enters last and sits quietly.

Jeannie looks at Rosie's tightly folded hands and slightly downcast eyes and melancholy expression. When Rosie looks up, Jeannie's eyes dart away. She's testing the waters. It's fleeting, and foreign, but naked in the thickened air between them.

I relax into my chair as Jeannie stands, holding a Chinese takeout box decorated with hand-stenciled green and red hearts and trees. Ribbons are tied on the wire handles. It looks like a happy seasonal package.

I wonder if she'll be able to pull this off. I wonder if she'll be able to switch from pissed off and sad to cheerful, if she'll reach down inside herself and grab optimism. Allie and I both know about the situation. And Rosie, of course. Maybe that's why Allie sat next to her, as though her presence would be extra support. Allie looks up at her and grins. And winks.

"Okay. Well, I couldn't figure out what kind of cookie to do this year. It seems a year where the future is all up for grabs and anything can happen." Her eyes meet Charlene's and then mine. "I mean, there's so much big change going on for all of us. For the whole world, really."

She looks at each of us and says, "Marnie's going to be a grandmother, and now Laurie is leaving, and Alice is flying back and forth, and Taylor, well, the company closed its plant. Charlene, she's recovering from a tragedy. And who knows, who ever knows what's going to happen to any of us?" Her voice trembles a little.

I place my hand on my phone, but it remains quiet and still. I check my watch. It's almost nine-thirty. Sky should have called by now.

"I thought about making the lemon drops I made last year that everyone liked, but decided to try this instead."

Jeannie stops and meets my eyes, Charlene's, Vera's. "I love you guys." She spreads her arms wide. "My girl-friends."

My eyes moisten at her bravery, at how hard she tries in spite of the maelstrom.

"Like I said, I started thinking about the future, and you know how I've gotten into yoga. Before each class we chant, and I find myself thinking about the various phrases throughout the day. And I thought with every-thing that's going on, we all needed positive fortunes."

"Om," teases Juliet, her palms pressed together, her gold chain catching glimmers from the flickering can-dles.

"You're studying Sanskrit?" Laurie asks.

"No. Just the phrases. Like 'breathe through this.' And so I decided to make fortune cookies. And I wrote my fortunes."

"Now that's what I like. Let's write our own futures and make sure they come true," Vera says. "Money."

"I'll second that. And a meaningful job with benefits," shouts Taylor.

"No more war," Allie says.

"Now, I experimented with several recipes and decided upon the best one. The tricky thing is taking them out of the oven, flipping them over, and putting the fortune inside, curling it, and then letting it cool in a muffin tin. You have to do it while they're still warm, so you can only do a few at a time." Jeannie hands a box to Allie and Allie passes it to her left as it goes around the circle.

"I like how you stenciled the hearts and trees," Vera says.

"Trying to make fortune cookies kinda Christmasy." Jeannie turns her head back and forth as she hands off each box to Allie.

Rosie gingerly sets hers on her leg as though it might still be hot. The box teeters on her knee and then she draws it into her lap.

Charlene opens her box and pulls the crispy crescent out. "It's green."

"I dyed them red and green." Jeannie turns to me. "I wanted them to look seasonal."

"There're fortunes in here?" Vera asks.

"Yeah. What's a fortune cookie without a fortune?"

I wonder if she has managed to smuggle nasty fates and curses into Rosie's box. Fortunes like "May evil visit your door." "May your bed be like burning straw." "May all your children be born dead." I think of Rosie getting that one and am washed with sorrow. She looks into space, hugging the box into her. Perhaps it would be a curse that's subtle like "That which you send out will come back to you." Or "May all your wishes come true."

Would Jeannie plot such a nasty revenge?

No. Rosie could have received any box.

"'The wheel is turning. This is the dark time. What must you gain from the night?'" Charlene reads. "Oh. What a perfect fortune for me." Her eyes fill. "I'm getting goose bumps. That's exactly what I've been thinking about these days. How amazing."

Rosie rips open her box, looking for salvation and forgiveness. "'I cast this from me like an empty shell.'" She blinks. "So." She tilts her head, wondering at the meaning, and then she smiles as though it is Jeannie's wish, not her fortune.

Maybe it is.

"They're delicious, too!" Charlene exclaims. "Almond."

"You must have eaten a red one. The green are vanilla. And then some have both flavors." Jeannie reaches in her bag, but there are no boxes left. "Everyone got one, right? And the hospice?"

"Yep." Charlene pats the hospice bag. "And Tracy and Alice. You're all set."

"Is each cookie the same fortune?" Taylor asks.

"No. You each have twelve different fortunes. I made thirteen of each fortune I wrote."

"That makes sense. It's appropriate, you know," Juliet says. "We share our lives and go in and out of the same fortunes."

"Didn't think of it like that," Jeannie says. "it's not so easy thinking them up."

"'May holiday lights illuminate your path.' That's perfect," Sissy says. "I'm so looking forward to this season." Her eyes meet mine. "And to our new grandson." She stops and tastes her cookie. "Another person to love and bring joy."

Jeannie sits back down, pushes the cushions away, turns to me and then to Allie with an easy grin on her face.

She did it. She faked it. She got through.

VANILLA

Ah, the seductive, rich scent of vanilla. The stories surrounding it are as romantic and sexual as its scent. First to cultivate vanilla were the Totonac, who lived in what is now Veracruz, Mexico. They believed that Princess Xanat, forbidden by her father from marrying a mortal, fled to the forest with her lover. The star-crossed lovers were captured and beheaded. Where their blood touched the ground, the vine grew.

The vine has thick, fleshy green stems and long leathery leaves. Small greenish flowers, a kind of orchid, open early in the day, but only for eight hours. The distinctively flavored compounds are found in the fruit; the pollination of the precious and picky flower produces only one. Vanilla flowers are hermaphroditic: they carry both male and female organs; however, to avoid self-pollination, a membrane separates those organs. For centuries, people tried to grow vanilla in locations other than Veracruz. Spanish explorers brought the plant to Africa and Asia, but it would not bear fruit. The French also failed. Alas, the monogamous vanilla orchid was wedded to a local species of bee for pollination. They tried to move the bees to other areas, but the bees only thrived in Veracruz and artificial pollination seemed unworkable. So Mexico maintained a monopoly on vanilla for three hundred years. It was the highest-priced spice next to saffron.

The vine grew and flowered, but without the bee no fruit developed until Edmond Albius, a twelve-year-old slave who lived on Ile Bourbon, discovered how to hand-pollinate the flower. With a beveled sliver of bamboo, he tenderly lifted the membrane separating the anther and the stigma. He gently transferred the pollen from male to female with his thumb. Sure enough, it bore fruit and his procedure allowed vanilla to be planted in other tropical places. Because of the short-lived flower, growers inspect their plantations daily for open flowers and immediately pollinate them, a labor-intensive task. Now Madagascar is the main producer. Artificial vanilla, along with bumper crops, have brought the price down.

Used for perfume, for aromatherapy, and to entice us to eat desserts, it's mildly addictive because it increases adrenaline.

Our ancestors thought it was an aphrodisiac and that it cured impotence, making it our first Viagra.

Sometimes, I dab on vanilla extract as a perfume. Isn't that what Scarlet O'Hara used to entice Rhett Butler?

8

Allie

Hanukkah Fruit Candies

> 1 cup each raisins, dates, and prunes
> 1 cup walnuts or pecans
> $1/2$ cup crystallized ginger
> Confectioners' sugar sprinkled on a
> plate or bowl (Start with $1/2$ cup and
> add more as needed.)

Combine the fruits, nuts, and ginger in a food processor until a paste is formed. With dampened hands, form into walnut-size balls and roll in the confectioners' sugar.

Mahyoosa

> 1 pound pitted dates
> 1 tablespoon unsalted butter
> $1/2$ cup ghee (clarified butter)
> 1 cup whole wheat flour

$^1/_2$ teaspoon cardamom
$^1/_2$ cup chopped mixed nuts (such as
almonds and cashews)

Combine the dates and butter in a food
processor and pulse until the fruit is mashed
and resembles a paste. Set aside. In a medium
saucepan over medium heat, melt the ghee. As
it melts, sprinkle in the flour and cook, stirring
constantly, until it turns light brown, about
5 minutes.

Add the cardamom and date paste. Reduce the heat to low and cook, stirring fre-
quently, until the mixture is fully combined. Mix
in the nuts.

Remove from the heat and let stand until
cool enough to handle. Using your hands,
pinch off 1 tablespoon-size pieces and roll
them into balls. Place in paper muffin cups.

In an airtight container, the cookies will
keep for several weeks. Makes 36

$\mathcal{W}$HEN ALLIE STANDS TO get her bags, Taylor jumps up, her gauzy scarf floating behind her. "I'll help." She marches off. The two shopping bags can easily be carried by one person, but Taylor carries one.

There's something different in the relationship between them. Why didn't I see this before? Taylor seems to be inseparable from Allie even for the time it takes for Allie to get her cookies. Could Taylor be in love with Allie? That seems crazy. Does Taylor even realize it? Is it just Taylor's feelings of admiration and gratitude that account for the consistent doting and the melting gaze? But that isn't consistent with Allie, who is pretty clear about how much she likes men. Allie seems oblivious, but she is not an oblivious person. Quite the contrary. She spots slight cues from people and fits them like pieces of a puzzle to assemble a complete picture. Allie doesn't interpret, unless you ask. She never pries but is simply supremely interested, always fascinated by everything. And everyone. She is a consummate therapist who loves people but is disinterested in the power or the use of the professional relationship as a defense against an intimate one.

Her face is relaxed as she carries the bag and sits down at the end of the sofa. Taylor plops into the folding chair wedged next to her. She is energetic, which is surprising as she seemed almost lethargic for most of the evening. Maybe she's preoccupied and distressed about her job situation. Jeannie, on Allie's other side, sips from a glass of wine. Allie's hair is softly shoulder length, highlighted in golden tones. Sometime tonight she reapplied lipstick, hoping to enhance her thin lips. She told me that she's on an endless quest to find lipstick or gloss that appears to thicken her lips. Particularly her upper lip. She's the only one who notices. The rest of us notice her broad smile and aura of boundless youth. The oil that gave her pimples in her teenage years has redeemed itself by granting her unlined skin now that makes her look younger than her years. She's in her early sixties but is often seen as in her forties.

She has a lover in his early thirties. It's no secret. We all love T.J. He's smart but wild. A perfect combination for her. He cracks up at her jokes and his thrill at her offbeat sense of humor has made us appreciate her one-liners even more. They've been together for three years and have been splitting up for the last two, but she consistently allows him to pull her back. They may do this dance for the next decade unless Allie ends it once and for all.

Actually, he's not just a lover. He lived with her for over a year. They have so much fun and seem so happy, I don't know why they don't decide to stay together. I've told her that many times.

"Men can always have children. He wants children."

"There're other ways to get children."

"My daughters offered to be inseminated so we could have his child, but that was too strange for him."

"Adoption? Foster children?"

"He wants an ordinary family. With children. And

he's afraid I'll die when he's about fifty and that he'll be alone."

Men do it all the time," I said. "Why can't you?" Two years ago we were on her porch, trees surrounding us. A pitcher of iced tea and a bowl of cut cantaloupe and blueberries waited on her marble table. Allie wore a bright green T-shirt and a beach glass necklace that brought out the green of her eyes. See. I don't know why she thinks her features are bland.

"A widower in his fifties doesn't need to be alone. There're thousands of us who'll scoop him up."

Allie tilted her chin back and laughed.

"You guys are so good together, you should quit thinking about how to break up and figure out how to make it." The heavy musk scent of viburnum wafted in on the breeze.

"You promised I'd get bored."

I did. That's what I thought, in the beginning. Allie met T.J. over the Internet. He was searching for therapists to learn more about the field and there she was, grinning in her library, her shining eyes looking vibrant and enthusiastic. She must love being a therapist, he had thought as he perused her website. He searched to see if she was on-line and IM'ed her. And Allie, sensing he was looking for more than simply information and in one of her adventurous "why not" moods, answered.

That Friday, they met at the Cavern Club and danced to Lady Sunshine and the X Band. I was with her, and so were Tracy and Silver and Vera and Finn, as we danced to "Hold On, I'm Comin'." T.J. looked preppy, but danced uninhibitedly. Smoke from the bar clouded the dance floor. They closed down the bar and went to the Fleetwood for breakfast.

Her son was older than T.J. "Well, I'm not going to call him Dad."

"Do you think, Mom, that he's interested in you for your money? That he's conning you in some way?" one of her daughters asked.

"No, he's using me for sex. I'm using him for his money," Allie quipped, but her daughter didn't laugh.

Yep, T.J. was rich. Inherited money safely tucked away in dividend-paying stocks. At least they were safe then. Who knows now?

T.J. was a neuroscientist trying to figure out if he wanted to continue precise and overly careful surgery into rats' brains or move to the creative free flow of therapy.

"You're the more mature one. Don't let him make any neurotic decisions," a therapist friend told her.

Her friend was implying that *she* was the neurotic decision. Obviously, Allie was old enough to be his mother. In fact, she was actually older than his mother, who had him too young to be more than a berserk friend.

But I said, "You're gonna hurt him. You'll get bored and leave him."

So Allie, the one who usually gave the advice, was getting it. From all sides. Don't hurt him. Protect him from you.

Meanwhile, what started as a two-week fling turned into a full-blown love affair carried out on a road trip to California, and then a trip to New York City, where they dropped off her youngest daughter at college. And then he moved in with her. Allie was happier than I'd ever seen her. A restless agitation was erased.

"You know I'll always love you. You know you'll live on in my memories of everything we've done together." He promised her this immortality. But couldn't promise her himself. His eyes were pale blue, the color of a clouded sky when he told her this, and he said it while holding her hands.

"You keep reminding me of my death," she shot back and jerked her hands away.

"I thought I was reassuring you of my infinite love."

But never commitment. As though amorphous infinite love is a commitment.

Maybe it is.

And so they tried to unwind. She said, "This Hanukkah, that'll be it. After New Year's, Zoe and I are going to Antigua and you and I should move on."

She bought fifty sunblock and a new black bikini.

He sent her emails telling her he had just made the worst mistake of his life. How many soul mates do you get? How many chances for happiness? He had all the time in the world, she should start dating, and when she found someone else, he would exit. That way he'd have her a little bit longer.

Crazy. Impossible. They were stuck in a love that never became a pledge. Jammed in a relationship whose goal was to tear itself apart.

I heard about this as it unfolded, she told me on her porch, or at my house for dinner, or on one of our long walks.

But Allie is Allie, always excited about so much—

the art she does, the clients she sees, politics — that the drama of the situation never threatened to pull her under. So now he spends the night with her a couple of times a week. Whenever they're together, they're happy. And she halfheartedly, haphazardly, dates others. Takes swing dancing lessons, and ballroom dance, and works for the Democratic party, goes to Saturday morning physics lectures, and is enthralled by string theory, quarks, the infinite continually expanding universe, the physics of brain function and heart regeneration.

"I used to think that someone who sat on her butt all day listening to people's problems would be cautious."

She laughed. We were again on her porch, the bluejays circling, a hummingbird buzzing at her feeder. "Nope. I learned the reverse. Learned that even doing what you're supposed to do can go horribly wrong, so you might as well do what your authentic self wants."

I nodded and sighed as I thought about Alex and Sky.

"I do what I want within reasonable limits and my reasonable is pretty broad."

But the truth is, Allie is an adventurer with a sentimental loving heart who doesn't really care what people think or how to impress them, and that means freedom.

When Jim and I started dating, it was Allie I went to. If anyone knew about dating a younger man, she did. I must admit, Jim being twelve years younger made me hesitate. Twelve years! I noticed the crepey skin above my knees, the creases gathering on my hands, the age spots that I renamed as new freckles on my arms, the weathering of my chest from years of sunbathing. Would he see me over him, the flesh of my face pulled by gravity into new pouches and bags, the sag of my ass and the sway of my breasts, and have his lust interrupted by the predictive scent of old age? Maybe we would only make love in the dark.

How did Allie take off her clothes in front of such a young man?

What did she do about the cellulite on her ass? The wrinkly thighs and knees?

That day, we walked around Hudson Mills, Disney on his leash. Both of us were determined to lose weight, but neither of us were actually doing anything except getting into better shape. But that was okay. I've been trying for three years to lose ten pounds and Allie loses and gains back the same six or seven a year. "Doesn't matter if we actually get there and stay there," she said once. "The point is we keep working on it. And, hey, we're in better shape and healthier than if we stopped trying."

The day was surprisingly warm in the midst of winter, as though we were given a respite from blasting winds and a curdled gray sky.

"He didn't believe my age. He thought I was lying for some bizarre reason, but by then we had made love. When he told me he was thirty-two, I said, 'You've read my web page, do the math. I'm old enough to be your mother.'" Allie laughed. "He told me after we were lovers for six months or so that he figured, since I was post menopause, maybe we'd have sex two times a week. 'Two times a week? How 'bout two times a day!' I don't know why there's this myth that older women don't want sex. We just can't get it as much because of men's problems."

The sun melted snow that clung to pockets of earth

and the air had the scent of wet ground. Disney investigated the earth and leftover snow with his nose, looking for old friends.

"Yeah. I remember thirty-year-olds. They can do it all night and all day."

Allie shot me a look that said "Thank God." And then she said, "But it's not about that. You know? Sex is ultimately only sex even if it shakes the stars and turns the planet. There're all the other parts of the meeting between the two of you. That invisible space that's formed from the projections of your feelings and ideas of each other. Mirrors of each other and for each other. The hopes and fears and transferences."

We walked in silence for a few steps, our sneakers hitting the concrete path simultaneously. Then ice broke off a branch and cracked as it fell.

"But sex sure can be a great glue," Allie added.

"Men are so visually programmed. I just can't imagine doing a sexy dance for him."

"He'd love it. Hey, I have this great CD of old-fashioned burlesque music . . . we should hire a stripper to teach us how to do it. The hell with all this jazzercise and step aerobics. Let's learn how to strip and shake."

We both laughed. Allie would probably practice in her living room and spring it on T.J. one night.

"I tried to get those tassels on pasties to twirl, but never could." Allie shook her head and her hair swung under her knitted cap.

"Now I can do that! I was the hula hoop champ."

"I never could do that, either," she said. "It's funny, isn't it? Men our age either are so ashamed of their biological issues—what is it, 50 percent of men age fifty have the dreaded E.D.—and they fantasize a younger woman will perk up that old member. So they deal with their changing sexuality by avoidance of women our age. They're almost afraid of knowing women their own age. And we . . . we're still able to do the sex part, just not the baby part. You think men would get smart and realize the play and great fun in that. What we all want—men and women—is intimacy, and our sexuality defeats us, well, not defeat exactly, but throws up hurdles along the way." We walked a few more steps and she added, "But it's a great motivator whether it's pulling you together or pushing you apart."

About five minutes later, after we had hit the bathroom on the trail and were rounding toward the river, still frozen and unmoving, she said, "But the age thing will get us in the end. T.J. and me. There's the kid issue. And the fact I'm going to die and leave him. He thinks about it all the time. He'll probably be the one to finally quit our dance."

"He could get cancer or have a heart attack and die before you. He could marry a woman his own age and she could die. You can't predict death and disaster. Look at my life." We both think about Alex.

She just walks for a few steps. A cardinal flies in front of us. "Ah. But he's a statistician. He counts the probabilities. Maybe that's all you can bet on. The probabilities. And, like I said, there's the kid issue. You and Jim don't need to worry about that."

"Not in the we-can't-have-them way. Instead they determine the time we have together."

"In a few years, they'll be gone." She walked with her hands stuffed in her pockets, the hood of her sweatshirt pulled over her head, her eyes on the road.

I know she's right. But I know children always affect their parents, at any age. And even then, even way before Sky was pregnant with this baby and Tara was pregnant, I thought about how pervasive children are in our lives and how hard it is for a stepparent to make that much room. How hard it is for a couple to agree on parenting even with their own biological children.

"The irony is, everyone thinks that children will bring a couple closer, but the research indicates that childless couples are happier. At least if you look at the divorce rate."

Allie just addressed the questions in my mind. "I love your research."

"My promiscuous reading?" She laughed and the hood fell back, her hair catching a breeze, her face subtly but fully made up. And then Disney pulled me down the path.

And then a few weeks ago, the week before Thanksgiving, she asked me, "Have you told him you love him yet?"

I squirmed in my seat. Allie was over for dinner on a weeknight. I didn't feel like eating alone. She brought a salad with dried cherries, blue cheese, and walnuts. I got up for some more wine when she raised the subject.

"You haven't answered your own question yet. Is Jim another chance for intimacy, an attempt at a permanent relationship, or another dodge from commitment?"

"'I love you' seems so permanent when we don't

know if anything's permanent." While I was up, I pulled the apple crisp from the oven.

"Nothing is," she said, her eyes pinning me as I fussed in the kitchen and finally sat down again. "We're all just walks along the way. Some very long walks. Decades. But even if there's almost forever, there's always that death thing gonna happen to one of you sometime."

I stabbed a piece of chicken and then scooped up some rice to eat with it. "Tell me about it, that death thing. But those three words come with demands and burdens."

"Yep," Allie agreed, a brussels sprout on her fork. "After my marriage broke up, I felt the loss of the shared life. But being alone has a wonder to it, and a freedom. Also an engulfing loneliness. Tradeoffs. Never any free lunch. When you have a partner, your life is important to someone. You're each other's witnesses. You behold each other." She said "behold" slowly. "You're less alone for a while."

I felt, I must admit, sad. Sad about my aloneness, and sad about trusting someone to stay around without some disaster happening. Illness. Death. Infidelity. I guess I am like T.J., but don't have age as an excuse, just history. "He's away too much" was all I said to her.

But Allie watched me, watched me smooth my napkin, toy with my food, sip my wine, brush my hair away from my forehead. "Not from you," she said. "Because of his job. Because of his kids. And do you? Do you love him?"

"I'm still infatuated with him. It's his cute smile and way of flirting. How much fun we have doing all the things we love together. How good a father he is and how he doesn't control me. When we're together, it's seamless. I consider him all the time. I'd be desolate if he left."

"Well?"

Then the phone rang. A reprieve from her question.

NOW TAYLOR'S LIDS are at half-mast, the lashes luxuriously shadowing her cheeks as she watches Allie with sidelong glances. Allie is wearing a black tank top and a green tie-dyed wraparound sweater. Black jeans. There's always something a little unusual about how she dresses, a combination of designer and Target but also comfortable and cozy.

How does she read Taylor these days? Does she think it is the kind of crush that younger women sometimes develop for older ones that is mostly a result of mentoring or is it sexual attraction? Allie doesn't seem in the least bit uncomfortable, so perhaps there's something I don't know.

Everyone is in her place, talking and laughing. I check my cell phone, but it is quiet. No call. I imagine Sky's restlessness, her sense of growing worry as she waits for her doctor's news. And then I imagine her and Troy at dinner, toasting their healthy baby with glasses of sparkling water. I've been forgotten in the joy. I think about Allie's statistic — the higher rate of divorce for couples with children — and the trauma Sky and Troy have had to endure to have a child. Laurie and Olivia. T.J. and his desire for a biological child.

When I glance across the room, there's the teddy bear Jim brought today with its hearts and Christmas trees tucked under the tree as if he had been there last year and the year before. He fits in that well. One of his paws is raised ready to slap a high-five; the other is resting on Tara's bear, which is getting some love at last. We fall in love and push ourselves to see our love expressed in a new life. I find myself wondering what Jim's and my child would look like. What interests and talents he or she might possess. When we make love, I want to obliterate our skin and truly be one in an orgasm that wipes away our individuality. A child would be concrete evidence of fusion. And then would develop, escaping our desire for proof of our love, existing for his, or her, own purpose.

JEANNIE'S MOUTH IS relaxed and her brows even. The anxious, angry look has smoothed away. Her attention shifts as Allie stands. "Nothing much has changed for me this year, one of those too fast years with nothing really resolved with T.J. Still doing that back and forth dance. Next year will be different."

"Hear, hear." Rosie raises her glass, the pale white wine shifting in the goblet.

"Naomi will graduate. But she's already out of the house. I'm still seeing my patients and still playing with my paints. So this is one of those years that have been about the change of the seasons and the love of family and friends. It went by in a blur. As though time contracted and we're gearing up for light speed. And, I guess, I haven't faced head-on the challenge presented." She purses her lips together.

We all know she's talking about T.J.

Allie reaches in her sack and pulls out a red Christmas stocking.

"Oh, boy. I love it when the containers can be used as a decoration," Laurie says. "Or something practical."

Allie passes the red felt stocking to Taylor, who holds it before handing it off to Sissy.

"Hmm. Let me tell you about my cookies. A few months ago there was a recipe in the *Ann Arbor News* for cookies from Saudi Arabia to celebrate the end of Ramadan. When I read the recipe, I realized they sounded very much like the Hanukkah cookies my mom used to make. So I pinned the recipe on my bulletin board thinking about how similar even the foods are between the Arabs and the Jews. These two brother tribes that have been fighting for thousands of years."

Allie continues to pass out the red stockings. "In this year of unity and the hope of peace, I made both kinds. The Jewish ones have sugar on the outside. The Arab ones have flour. But they are made with almost the same ingredients. The Saudi ones required a new ingredient, ghee, which is clarified butter, and you cook the dough on top of the stove. But the cookies are about dried fruit. That's the main ingredient and flavoring. So similar. And the stockings? Well, I figured if I was doing Muslim and Jewish cookies, I'd wrap them in a Christmas theme. Three of the world's great religions. Goes along with hopes for peaceful change here and across the world."

After depositing one in the hospice bag, I open my stocking and taste one of the Hanukkah ones. "I bet these are healthy, too." A sweet confection with the hint of spice and ginger.

"They're made of dried fruit and nuts. But they're high calorie."

"You outdid yourself this year," Vera says. "Cookies with a peace theme."

Allie laughs. "I know this is schmaltzy, but in spite of the economy and the dark cold, I'm thinking about all our steps toward equality and world peace. And isn't this commemoration—whether it's Christmas or Hanukkah—the celebration of light's return in the midst of darkness? Just after the winter solstice, the shortest day of the year, we get increasing daylight and anticipate once again spring and renewal. Just like the cookies, so much more alike than different."

We're all quiet for a few seconds as we each pull out a cookie. "I have a Saudi one," Jeannie says.

"I have a Jewish one," Rosie says, and she stares at Jeannie, toasting the difference as though to say if we can hope these two countries can make peace, maybe we can. We all have our sins.

Jeannie nods to her as they eat their cookies, watching each other.

Wow, I think. Wow. Could I be seeing this? Could this be happening? I watch them from across the room, Rosie with the glints in her short hair and Jeannie with that look of a startled fawn still in her eyes.

We all hold up a cookie. "To peace," Charlene says as she pops hers in her mouth.

"And the return to prosperity," says Laurie.

"Hey. Let's keep going. How 'bout meaningful jobs for all."

"And health care."

"Taking care of mother earth."

"Accepting love," Allie says, and her arm sweeps the party of girlfriends.

"Small carbon footprints."

"Nonfossil fuels."

We all laugh.

THE PHONE VIBRATES and I clutch it to my side and dash for the bedroom. It's Jim.

"Hi."

"Hey, you. Have you heard from Sky?"

"I thought you were her."

"I'm sorry."

"I'm always happy to talk with you."

"How's the party?"

"Good. Fun."

"I wanted to tell you that the kids are going to be with their mother this Friday. That means we're definitely on."

I hold my breath. I hear the laughter from the party in the next room and I smell the carnation and rose aroma from the flowers next to my bed, which is now piled with everyone's coats. I know what I should do, what I need to do. One of my lace pillows has fallen to the floor. I pick it up and put it against the headboard and stand staring at the coats strewn on my bed.

"Did you make another date?" He laughs, but it's a nervous laugh.

"I love you."

There's dead silence on the phone.

He hasn't heard me.

"All I have to do is promise you a date on Friday and you love me?" He jokes to hide the sudden awkwardness. He doesn't say it back.

I'm too late. I should have told him earlier, back when he first told me. That was months ago. The momentum is lost. Too late. He's moved away from me, from us. My timing sucks. All I've done is make myself vulnerable.

Shit. My heart quickens.

His kids were excuses. His way to keep his distance. He doesn't want more than we have.

"I told you last Valentine's Day. Now it's almost Christmas," he says tenderly, almost in a whisper. "Since then I've been waiting for you. Giving you time in spite of my crazy life."

I exhale. "I love you." I say it again, wondering if it'll feel different the second time. This time my voice is low and each word carefully articulated. I. Love. You. This time I'm standing still, hearing how he said it months ago. Deep, with that hint of gentleness.

"Call me when the party is over, no matter how late. I'll be waiting. And, Marnie." He hesitates for a moment. "I love you. I love you, too."

DATES

Dates are one of my favorite fruits, a treat I give myself at the end of a meal when I'm yearning for something sweet. Sometimes I plunge an almond, pecan, or walnut in the cavity left by the pit.

My grandmother loved dates and told me they were the tree of life, a staple food of the desert of Africa and the Middle East and the essential plant on which human life depended. Since they've been in cultivation for so long, at least eight thousand years, it's hard to know exactly where they originated, but most probably from the oasis of northern Africa and the Persian Gulf, the famed fertile crescent. Dates, along with olives, figs, pomegranates, and grapes, were in the second wave of our planet's cultivated plants. The trees had the drawback of not yielding food for several years after planting, thus cultivation was possible only after people were committed to village life. Images of date palms grace carvings from the earliest period of Egyptian and Mesopotamian civilization.

Dates can grow from seed, but because the fruit may be smaller and the tree may be male, they are usually reproduced by cuttings so that the plant will produce as heavily as its parent. It takes four to seven years for a date to bear fruit and they are able to reproduce for seven to ten years. The fruit we usually buy has been allowed to sun-dry on the tree. Less ripe forms of the fruit are also eaten. In modern cultivation, dates are pollinated by hand; one male plant can pollinate one hundred female plants. Now, a vast spreading of seed is some men's idea of how things should work for all species. But these male plants need help, so skilled workers climb up on ladders or, in Iraq, use a special tool that is attached to the tree, to pollinate the female trees.

Dates are still a crucial crop in Iraq, Saudi Arabia, and North Africa west to Morocco. In Islamic countries, dates and yogurt or milk are the traditional first meal when the sun sets during Ramadan. Dates are also cultivated in southern California and Arizona after being introduced there in the mid 1700s. When we eat dates, we eat the gift from the tree of life.

9

Sissy

Cheeseburger Cookies

    2 12-ounce boxes Nilla wafers

    1 egg white

    $\frac{1}{4}$ cup sesame seeds

    4 to 5 tablespoons milk

    $\frac{1}{2}$ teaspoon almond extract

    4 cups confectioners' sugar

    Yellow food coloring

    Red food coloring

    1 cup coconut

    Green food coloring

    2 10-ounce packages grasshopper chocolate-covered cookies

Place the wafers on 2 trays—one should have all the wafers facing up (round side up) and the other should have all the wafers facing down. Each tray should have the same number of wafers, 35 to 40.

Brush the wafers facing up with a little egg white, then sprinkle with sesame seeds on top.

To make the frosting (cheese): Stir 4 tablespoons of milk and the almond extract into the confectioners' sugar. Add more milk if necessary. Add yellow and red food coloring until you get the color of American cheese.

To color the coconut (lettuce): Place the coconut in a lidded jar and add green food coloring. Shake until lettuce-colored.

To assemble: The frosting-cheese is the glue. Place the frosting on a facing-down cookie. Add a grasshopper cookie. Repeat for all wafers. Then put frosting on top of the grasshopper cookie and dip into the green coconut. Repeat for the entire tray. Then dip frosting on the flat side of the cookies you've sprinkled with seeds and place on top of coconut-lettuce. You've made a miniature cookie cheeseburger. Isn't it cute!

$\mathcal{S}$ ISSY INVITED ME TO a family barbecue last Labor Day. I suspected it was her way to get to know me on her own territory. By that point, Tara and Aaron were living down the block from her and our grandchild was visible in Tara's rounded abdomen. Not huge like she is now, but unmistakable. Across the street a boarded-up house was almost smothered by a trumpet vine. Bags of garbage waited for pickup. People Roller-bladed down the street. Special Intent, Aaron's stage name, Red Dog, and Tara were working hard on their demo CD. That day, Sissy, her neck wreathed with colorful beads, greeted me with a welcoming smile. Brown-skinned with voluptuous breasts, she opened her arms and gave me a hug and kiss. I smelled a perfume of roses and lemon. She wanted to show me Aaron's world, or maybe she just wanted a grandmother alliance. But she was the one confident enough and bold enough to reach out to me.

I like to think of myself as comfortable in circumstances without established custom, but, in truth, Tara was never easily compliant and always pushed at boundaries wanting to do things according to her own idea of how they should be. I didn't know whether her choice of Aaron—and he was certainly a choice and not a result of that shit-happens attitude that so many kids assume—was rebellion or a positive love. Now I know. But I didn't in the beginning.

I remember the exact day that Tara met Aaron. Tara had dyed her hair black the previous week.

"Makes you look old, takes away your innocence."

Tara rolled her eyes. "That's the point, Mom."

Two Saturdays a month Tara worked for the Youth Volunteer Corps at the Y and that day they were sent to Habitat for Humanity. She was fifteen. That night, at dinner, Tara announced that she had spent the day painting and had made a new friend.

"Good." A friend who volunteers for Habitat for Humanity must be a conscientious person, I thought.

"Yep. He's from Detroit. He's black. He's in training school."

"What?" Training school is a euphemism for prison for juveniles. "How could he be a volunteer?" I sensed bravado in the rush of her words as I served the salad.

"He's on a special work program, getting ready to be released, and we, like, spent the day painting this room white and talking about my school and music. He's a musician, too, Mom." Tara's eyes were the green they turn when she's happy. Even the black hair hadn't changed that. "He writes rap lyrics. You'd like him."

"Why's he in jail?" It was spring and the sun was just beginning to set, casting a pink glow over the table and her arm.

Tara shrugged. "Didn't ask him that, Mom. Aaron got my address and he'll write." The moment of accord was dashed.

"Maybe," I said.

But he did. A letter came with florid pencil calligraphy, swoops and swirls over the slender loops of each capital. Tara grabbed the envelope, grinned, said, "Told you he'd write," and ran up to her room. She spent the evening answering him in her round hand, decorated with circles dotting the *i*'s.

The letter writing intensified. I asked more questions. When's he getting out? How old is he? Where're his parents?

"He's seventeen."

Two years older than Tara. "Will he graduate from high school?"

"He's getting out next year. Yes, he'll graduate. They, like, make them go to school there. He's smart, Mom. Really smart. And I don't ask him about his parents." She stopped for a minute, searching her memory. "Oh, his mom's a nurse. He told me. Didn't say anything about his dad."

"What's he in for?" I asked.

"I don't know." Tara looked away.

"You don't know? You haven't asked?"

"He *said* he'd tell me when he sees me again." She turned to walk out of the room.

"Whoa. That can't be good, Tara," I called to her retreating back.

When Sky called, she grilled Tara about him. I could tell from Tara's answers that she was reticent but more open with Sky than she was with me. "We have so much in common. We're just alike in our souls," I heard her say.

By fall, they were still writing. Tara continued to volunteer at the Y, but Aaron never returned to Habitat. "I wanna invite Aaron to the homecoming dance."

"Homecoming? I thought he was in training school," I said. We were in the kitchen, making spaghetti.

"He is, but, like, he thinks he might be able to get a weekend visit. He hasn't gotten into any trouble since he's been there and they allow special privileges. Can he stay here?"

"With us?"

"Where else? Detroit would be too far away. You'll like him, Mom. His rap name is Special Intent, and he keeps writing me lyrics. Wanna hear 'em?"

I narrowed my eyes at my daughter. Was Tara naively assuming my acceptance, or was she testing me? A kid in juvenile jail who wanted to be a rap star? But I knew that censoring the relationship would only fuel Tara's curiosity.

"I'll think about it," I said, and then added, "You know, at your stage, boys're merely the flavor of the month." I sprinkled basil in the sauce. Our conversations always took place at dinner. The bribe of food meant Tara would be there and might talk to me. Funny how different my daughters are. Sky told me everything, Tara tells me as little as necessary.

Tara rolled her eyes and jerked her head away. "This has been, like, five months, Mom." She was tearing up lettuce for a salad.

"In a long-distance relationship, there's not enough time to get bored or annoyed," I warned her.

Tara had her hand on one hip, her mouth twisted in an expression of annoyance, and then said, "Besides, look at Sky and Troy."

She got me there. "I just don't want you to be disappointed," I said slowly while stirring the sauce. I didn't feel as casual about it as I was trying to sound. I had dated men of different races, but, for one reason or another, nothing major had come from those dates. I had grown up with my father's subtly racist comments and knew he'd be dismayed by Tara's boyfriend if he were alive. That wasn't how I felt when I was a kid. And certainly not now. Even my father may have changed his attitudes by now. But my concern increased because Aaron was in prison. It's the accumulation of difficulty. Race, class, the stigma of incarceration.

Tara interpreted my last comment as agreement. "Do you have a map? He, like, needs to know how to get here."

"What about computers and Mapquest?"

"If he could get it that way, he would have, Mom."

"In the car, Tara. Take the one from the car."

Homecoming was two months away. I didn't want to provide her with an excuse for rebellion. Things had been tenuous enough since Tara hit puberty and decided she wanted to live life on her own terms.

The letters kept coming. Two, sometimes three, a week, padded with pages. Tara read me some of his songs. At least they weren't the misogynistic lyrics filled with the "n word" that I hated. He seemed to be stretching for something.

"He sounds angry at the world."

"Guess he's got that right."

"You know"—I worked to keep my voice even and soft—"most people who've been to prison return. I think it's over 65 percent. Don't keep a blind eye to what it means. Prison doesn't even try to rehabilitate, it just teaches violence and how to be a better criminal."

"Not him. You don't know him. Besides, he's in a special program."

"I'm concerned about you. *You*, my darling daughter."

TARA ADDED BLUEBIRD-COLORED chunks to her black hair. She pierced three more holes in her ears, one in her eyebrow, and one in her lip and filled them with silver hoops.

When I saw her, I said, "That looks like shit. Like you want to be garbage."

"All the kids are doing it."

"Not all."

"All the artists and musicians."

She's just trying her wings, I told myself. Always pushing at the margins of everything. At least she hadn't started putting plugs in her lobes. Her grades were straight As and she spent most of her time at the piano practicing, composing music, and singing. It hadn't been easy with Stephen's and my divorce and he hardly saw her.

A few weeks later, I asked. "When's that Aaron kid coming?"

Tara shrugged. "They read the letters, and when they saw the map, they thought he was planning an escape and so he lost his minimum-security status, was removed from the special program, and now there's no way he'll be here for homecoming."

"That's too bad, honey."

My voice was so monotone that Tara checked my expression to see if I were sarcastic or relieved. I felt genuinely sad for Aaron but had hoped that when they saw each other again the passion and fascination would have dissipated.

"Aaron says it's the stupid institution. I shouldn't feel bad," Tara said.

"Did he tell you why he's there?"

"I haven't seen him, Mom. Don't you, like, ever listen to my answers?"

"What are you going to do about homecoming?" I wiped the kitchen counter.

"Me and Jennie and Robin are going with Shorty, Ted, and Kevin. No dates. Just friends. Going to rent a limo and go out to eat at Macaroni Grill. They're all disappointed they won't get to meet Aaron."

"How're you going to afford that?"

"Mom. I saved it from my birthday money this summer. Aaron and I knew we wanted to go."

She surprised me. She switched from the annoyed, seemingly impetuous teen to a young woman who planned and made sacrifices to achieve her goals.

I was wrong about Aaron. He didn't peter out like a teenage romance. Instead Tara became a twenty-first-century hip-hop statistic. Unwed pregnant eighteen-year-old white girl and black, fresh-out-of-prison, wanna-be rap star. Single mom. A patchwork of jobs barely supporting them. Dreams of fame and money. It would be funny if it weren't so sad. Meanwhile, my daughter and her boyfriend met in a space of their own creation.

Tara had always been passionate about music. It was as though she took Stephen's unrealized dream—to be a rock star—and made it hers. Whether it was his genetics or encouragement or an *x* factor in her, her zeal for music and a preternatural dedication to it were apparent when she was a toddler. "Doesn't this sound like rain, Mommy?" She played two notes on a toy xylophone very softly. By the time she was six, she made up melodies copying a bird's song, her dangling feet unable to reach the pedals of the piano.

So Aaron came along and they wrapped each other in the same dream. And then he was out and living in Detroit with his family and they saw each other whenever they could get the time, a car, and the gas money for the trip.

"So what was he in for, anyway?"

"It's a crazy story, Mom." Tara avoided my eyes.

"I'll listen as long as it takes." I closed the novel I'd been reading.

Tara sat across from me and pleated the crease in her jeans, the blue chunks in her hair iridescent.

I waited.

"You can ask Special, you know, he'll tell you. He's not a closed person. He talks about stuff." Tara's fingertips pressed her jeans as though smoothing out my concerns.

"You're here. You tell me."

"Well, like, he and some friends stopped to get pizza. He was sitting in the backseat of the car, didn't even go into the pizza place. He's not sure if it, like, was spur of the moment or if his friends planned the robbery of the pizza place from the beginning. An off-duty cop was picking up a pizza for his family. He pulled out his gun and arrested them. Saw Aaron in the backseat of the car and arrested him, too."

"He was guilty by association?"

Tara looked beyond me. "Aaron had five dime bags of weed on him that he got as a deal for thirty bucks."

"He got time for that? For thirty bucks of pot?"

"Essentially. And being in the wrong place at the wrong time."

I squinted at her. There was something more here. "Was he going to sell it? Was that the deal?"

Tara shrugged.

"He's a small-time dealer?"

"That was then."

"Is he?"

"No."

"Was he then?"

She shook her head.

"Harv and Kim's kid, what's her name?"

"Katie . . ."

"Got probation and community service for a lot more pot than that. What did she have? A quarter ounce. Is that the whole story? Had he already been in trouble?"

"Nope. First arrest. But, Mom." Tara's voice had an exasperated tone, as if she were the adult and I was the teenager. "Katie's white and had a lawyer. Katie lives in Ann Arbor, not Detroit."

I tilted my head up and said, as much to myself as to her, "Unfortunate circumstances. Careless actions. Bad luck. Bad decisions." When I turned to her, she was watching me while her fingers worked her jean crease. "Don't want you caught up in that."

"Aaron coulda cut a deal. He would have had to testify against his friends. Be a snitch. He couldn't do that. They, like, gave him the max."

"You think that's honorable and virtuous?"

"Don't you?"

"Depends on how you look at it. What effect did his time have on his own future? What effect did it have on his family?"

Tara pushed her shoulders back and raised her chin. "I think loyalty and caring about others more than yourself are good character traits."

"Sometimes." I nod. "Were they loyal to him? If he really didn't know the robbery was going to happen, why didn't they protect him? And now he has a record."

Tara thought for a moment. "Like a juvie record. But yeah. He was, like, stupid to himself, but good to his homies." Her shoulders relaxed. "Got his GED in jail and worked on his music. He says sometimes good comes out of bad, and bad comes out of good."

The Labor Day barbecue was the first time I heard him sing. And the first time I met Sissy and was welcomed by her smile. She wore glossy purple lipstick that day, a color I vowed to try.

We were outside. Someone had pulled out an old sofa, card tables, plastic chairs. Sissy wore a V-neck blouse that showed off her cleavage. Her arms were adorned with sliding bracelets. Large hoops were in her ears. Sissy's friend Darling was there, in a pink T-shirt and a Pistons hat, helping Sissy turn the ribs. Cooking sauce and sizzling fat from the grill scented the air. Neighboring families brought chicken, macaroni and cheese, and cake and more chairs and blankets. Then, as dusk fell, they pushed Aaron to sing.

Red Dog nodded to Sonny, a kid about ten. "You

gotta help. You say, 'Jail, what is it good for? Absolutely nothing,' when I point to ya."

"Come on, Dog. We do it." Aaron stood beside Red Dog. Tara turned on her keyboard.

> *If you heard doin' time*
> *was some cool shit.*
> *Tell you with this rhyme*
> *that's some bullshit.*
> *Doing 23 in*
> *1 out*
> *stuck in a 9 x 6*
> *nothing but a concrete crypt.*

Red Dog points to Sonny.

> *Jail! What is it good for?*

Tara helped him out.

> *Absolutely nothing.*

The rest of us spat back.

> *Wondering each day*
> *how much sun you'll get*
> *eatin', drinkin', sleepin'*
> *in the same space you shit.*
> *Reminiscin' and missin'*
> *all that's near and dear to ya.*
> *When the prohibitions of prison*

Become real to ya.
Jail! Huh, uh. Good God, y'all

Sissy grunts.

What is it good for?

Everybody shouts.

Absolutely nothing.

"You the dude! Rap and been to jail." Sonny cleared his throat.

"What?" his mother shouted.

"Not cool going to jail," Aaron said and sat down next to Tara, who was now lounging on a blue blanket, her hand, decorated with black nails, cradling the mound that was her baby.

"Hear what he says? Going to jail ain't cool."

"That's what the song's about. Waste of time and hard. I learned I didn't wanna go back. Learned that you gotta know who you loyal to. Can't be loyal to homies ain't loyal to you and you don't know that till life plays them hard, till push comes to shove." Aaron leaned back on one elbow. "Learned, I guess, free air too sweet to forfeit. This my life, my one and only, and I don't wanna waste a bit of my time locked in a nine-by-six." He looked at Tara lying on the blanket, her belly announcing her pregnancy. "I want to be around to take care of my mini-me and see where my music goes."

I didn't know what to think. No question Aaron

seemed to be serious about his life and devoted to Tara.
No question he was focused. I could feel the love, affection, and respect between them.

"Look, Momma." Sonny's face tilted up. Imperceptibly, night became complete. Stars lavishly spangled the
black sky. A hush fell over us as we gazed at the Milky
Way, its diamonds exaggerated in their brilliance.

"People used to see figures in the stars—like kings
and mermaids, gods and goddesses—and make up stories about them," I said.

"I don't see no people up there," Sonny said. "I see a
car." He pointed to the sky, tracing the outline of a car.
"See? And look. There's a gun, think it a machine gun."

"Yeah, looks like a semiautomatic." Red Dog chuckled.

"What they doin' up in that sky?" Sonny wondered.

"That's Big Mickey's BMW SUV up there and he
ridin' round looking for the dude that kill him, his lady,
and his baby las' year," Red Dog suggested.

"That's his Uzi, aimin' at the city waitin' for Big D,"
Sonny added. "Gonna get him for the homies he smoked.
Mickey's still protectin' his 'hood."

"Protecting? Honey, none of them protecting a thing
but their own banks. Look over there." Sissy pointed to
a star, turning her purple nail into an amethyst. "Know
what I see? I see Martin Luther King giving his speech
in 1963 right here in Detroit. See his hand held high?
That's the bright star right there." Sissy's finger jerked
to another star. "What did he say? 'We gonna march
and bring a new day of freedom into being. Make the
American dream a reality.' He said that right here when
I was a little girl. Momma took me to hear him, and

there he is, up in our sky. Making sure it come true. And maybe, just maybe, it will."

Everyone looked at the protective stars.

"That's who's up there. Martin Luther King, not no Big Mickey still fighting over who's gonna sell drugs to what 'burb." Sissy nodded.

"There's Tupac and Biggie up there inspiring us with their words," Red Dog said. "The twinklin' stars are the backgrounds."

Aaron lay on his back, hands behind his head, gazing at the sky. "Yep, and over there, right there"—Aaron pointed to a cluster of stars edging toward the zenith—"is Pops. See him? See his two eyes? That milky area above them is his afro and the star right there is his mustache. He up there sayin', 'You doin' all right, boy. Just love, just love.' 'Member how he usta say that, Momma? 'Just love, just love each other and it be all, all right?'"

"Yep. That's what Garvey say all right. Instead of I love you, he say, 'Just love. Just love.' That and 'Be sweet to each other' on his way out." Sissy leaned back in her chair, face tilted to the stars, a can of Budweiser in one hand.

"'Member that guitar he bought me? Traded his ol' watch for the guitar, didn't have no strings, at Diamonds 2?"

"Man was generous in his own way," Sissy said. "That's the good part, his easy love. I'd forgotten that. Just remembering he always be leaving for somewhere, didn't ever know quite where. Till he finally left for good and forever."

"Girlfriend, he didn't leave. Garvey died." Darling picked up a Nutter Butter cookie.

"Easier to be angry than boo hoo 'bout it." Sissy drank from her can. "Forgotten the lovingness in all that leaving. More consistent with the rest of my life."

"We make up stories all the time," Tara said. "We don't even *see* continuously, but in Polaroids and then our mind strings them together to make a movie. Even when we dream, it's really one-shot pictures and we make a narrative out of it so it makes sense."

"Maybe we revise our own histories in light of what we know now to make sense of what's going on," I added. "Maybe our lives finally exist in the stories we tell ourselves about them. When we're in the drama, we don't know anything except what we experience. The people in our lives change as our understanding changes." I sipped on my beer.

Sissy leaned back and looked at me. "You got that right. We always perchin' on jerky steps of our own knowing. Tryin' to make sense. And tryin' to figure out what to do next."

Tara and Aaron cuddled on the blanket.

I leaned back and examined the stars. "Well, I better start going home. Tomorrow is a workday."

As I walked up the stairs to Aaron and Tara's apartment to gather my things, I heard Sissy laugh and Sonny asked for another song.

> *When I remember what I lack*
> *How I was unable to love you back*
> *So many times I lied*
> *Yet you kept me on track*
> *How many times you cried*

For that I apologize
I saw through the obstacle
Of concrete and steel confusion
Your love for me
Was no optical illusion
Like an angel
You have stepped in
From an unguarded angle
In my heart
Your love crept in

Red Dog harmonized with Aaron's melody as they sang his words.

I thought then about the love between Aaron and Tara, the shared dream and passions, the obvious closeness of Sissy and her friends. The barbecue had accomplished what Sissy wished: I was less anxious about Tara and Aaron's love. I saw that he wanted to be with her and be good to her. But there's a long way from wish to a reality that lasts years. Especially starting out so young and from such different backgrounds. Well, maybe not so different. Sissy and I are both single mothers with children from different men. Neither Sissy nor I trust that we won't be left for one reason or another. How will that play out between these two? Maybe they'll cling to each other extra hard. Maybe they'll let each other go more easily.

As I gathered my purse and bag of now-empty pie pans, I thought about the easy love that flowed between them all. Jim was with his children at his mother's house that night. I wondered if we could make a life filled with as much love and acceptance. Being lonely in a marriage is worse than being alone.

A verse floated through the night.

> *Believe in me*
> *And this I guarantee*
> *You can be certain of one thang*
> *I'm gonna love you past*
> *Your hurt*
> *Your pain.*

Even then, even four months ago, I remember thinking if only someone could do that. I haven't let anyone even try since Stephen. Maybe Jim could love me past my pain. Maybe I took the first step tonight by telling him I love him. Just maybe.

Now here we are and fall has become winter. Sissy has brought her bags of cookies.

"Time for the cookie virgin to lose her virginity," Rosie joked.

"Don't worry. We'll be gentle," Juliet said, and Jeannie started laughing.

"Ohmigod. Give her a break," Vera said. "I remember when I lost my cookie virginity. I worried that my cookies wouldn't be good enough to meet all the rules and the packages wouldn't be cute enough. That I wouldn't be acceptable. It was like junior high all over again."

"Like you won't measure up. The cookie bitch will cut you out," said Taylor.

"Now, now. I've never kicked anyone out. Unless they didn't come or send cookies. I just let them know the cookies they made didn't work."

"Yeah, like those lemon bars that were delicious but melted into each other."

"And the year five of us made chocolate chip cookies."

Sissy's eyes check out each one of us. Her brightly colored scarf brings out orange tones in her hair.

"Besides, we want the story," Charlene says.

"Okay." Sissy spreads her hands wide. There's no nervousness to her gestures, she seems as comfortable tonight as she did at her Labor Day barbecue. "Been getting a kick at being a virgin at anything by this point in my life. Time to devirginize me in this one last thing." She nods her head quickly, as though drawing an exclamation point, and we all laugh. "I have to tell a story about my cookies, so here it is. It's a story about Aaron, Tara's baby's father. My littlest one. Words was what he was about." She sits down, then leans forward and turns toward me, as though I'm the only one in the room and this tale is for me. "Aaron, he's the smartest of my five. Gotta say that. Don't know why, but he is. He's the one always saw the world differently, things other people don't pay attention to. Hearing rhythm. Even the honking horn." Sissy clicks her tongue. "When he wasn't nothing but a baby, if a horn would honk beep beep-beep, he would pound out that same beat on the table or floor." Her hand makes the motion of drumming.

Like Tara and her xylophone, I think.

"And wondering about words." She expels some air and shakes her head. "Got words in his mind and got on my last nerve with questions. 'Who decides the words, Momma?' he asked me. 'Who decides? Who gets to name everything?'

"I told him, 'Adam. God let Adam name everything.'" Sissy narrows her eyes as though trying to see Aaron as a boy. A cluster of small moles on her cheek dances. "Strangest little boy. As though the power of things was in the word for them. He walked around asking me for the word for everything like he was collecting them in a box." She stops.

I sit back and her eyes move to Juliet and then to Allie, the two women with whom she has spent most of her time tonight. "When he discovered two names for the same thing . . . like rain-sprinkle-shower-drizzle he asked why Adam gave it so many names. I tried to explain how each one's a little different. Then he realized there was one word for two things. Like nail. He went, 'Why only one word for metal you hit with a hammer and the thing on the end of your finger? Why Adam cheat those two things?'"

"'Honey, you jealous of Adam.'

"He looked at me, closed his eyes thinking hard, so hard, and went, 'Yes, ma'am, believe I am.'

"'Don't you be jealous of what God decided.'" Sissy shakes her finger as though little boy Aaron standing in front of her, at the cookie party with us.

"'Think I'll make up my own words,' he goes.

"What a mess that was. For a while he mashed words and no one understood him. School called, telling me, 'Miz Peoples, Aaron need speech therapy.' He didn't need speech therapy, he needed knocked upside his head for being jealous of Adam, I tell 'em."

We chuckle.

"I stopped talking to him unless he said it in regular words. I wouldn't even feed him 'less he asked for it in English words." Sissy sips her wine. "Got hungry, he sure did. 'Milk. Hot dogs. Spaghetti. Burger. Chicken,' he said.

"I gave it to him. 'Regular words gets you somewhere, see, son. See, honey.'

"He looked like he lost his best friend. So I try to make things better. 'Don't you know you naming by how you put words together? Then you being a little bit Adam. You adding to God's words that way. Not inventing stuff no one understand.'"

His intoxication started so early and expanded. Just like Tara. Funny how both my daughters met partners young and formed relationships that have lasted for years. Maybe it's a rebellion against my constant hunt and search.

"You think that be enough." Sissy's hands are on her knees as her voice trails off. She sits on the edge of the chair, talking into the coffee table. "But that little man get something in his mind he don't let go. Struggles till it's solved. The next year in school he found the dictionary. Oh, boy. Here we go again. 'See, no Adam named everything. This book, dictionary named everything.'

" 'It's like this,' I say. 'Adam named everything and then some Englishman put all Adam's names in that book and called it a dictionary. And if you hear a word Adam made up and you don't know what it means, you look it up in that book.'

"Aaron looked at me with those eyes of his that go on forever like children have and I know he's not believing me, so I go, 'Boy, you better soften those eyes and don't come at me with that attitude.' He look down and I say, 'Go ahead and ask me something. Go ahead. Think of a word.' He blink at me and say, 'Nothing. I'm thinking nothing.'

"I look it up in the book. Point to it. *Nothing. No thing. Not anything. Lack of existence, nonexistence.*

" 'What's that, Momma? Nonexistence?' So I look that up, too.

" 'Oooooh. Momma. These words hold hands with each other . . . I want you to read me that book, Momma. I wanna know all those words.'

"I tell him that's one book he has to read to himself. Here. I stick it back at him. He's just in second grade or third grade but he sit and puzzle out those words. That boy and words. Should have named himself Word Serious."

Sissy leans back, sips on some red wine. Her eyes arc the room, judging our reaction to her story. We tilt toward her, waiting for her next words. "That's my son. Aaron Marcus Peoples. Special Intent." Sissy leans back and laughs. "Maybe that's his special intent, to help with his words to explain the world."

Sissy reaches in her sack and pulls out a McDonald's bag.

"It's a cookie party. Not a fast-food party," Rosie jokes.

Sissy passes the white bag to Laurie, who passes it to Vera, and it begins its circle. "Aaron's first made-up song was about a hamburger cookie. His two favorite things to eat. Forget now how it goes, but it was a little rap. And so I made these for him." She then reaches and retrieves a small hamburger. "Partly my way to encourage him to speak in the common language." She holds it up so we can see it. "See. It's a hamburger made with store-bought cookies. Orange-colored frosting pastes the layers together and looks like cheese."

"Oh, look. They even have sesame seeds on their little buns," Taylor exclaims.

Sissy distributes the McDonald's sacks. As soon as I get mine, after depositing one in the hospice bag, I open it up and pull out a miniature hamburger. "Amazing! It looks just like a hamburger." I taste the sweet-chocolate-mint crunch. "Tastes great."

"Wow." Juliet laughs. "You get the prize for the best-ever cookie virgin."

"These are terrific."

"They mostly an assembling trick. Like the auto in-dustry." Sissy laughs.

"How inventive."

"You're amazing," Charlene says. "Loved your story, too."

"Let's keep this cookie virgin." Jeannie grins. I haven't seen one of her spontaneous smiles in some time. Recently, she forces them at appropriate occasions but rarely otherwise.

"The hospice will love these hamburgers. Can't you see the little joy the surprise of them will bring?" Allie says.

"Ohmigod, so amazing!" Rosie exclaims.

"We're all creative. Each in her own way." Singling

out one girlfriend may make others feel inadequate or spread jealousy. I grew up with so many siblings that I always try to avoid any hint of favoritism or preference. "These are almost too charming to eat, but they're delicious."

"And so cute in their McDonald's bag. How did you get them?"

"I worried about the containers. Went to McDonald's with one of my grandbabies and saw the bags. So I just asked them for bags and told them what I was going to use them for. They gave me a bunch. They seemed happy to be part of this."

Sissy invited me to a Labor Day barbecue and I invited her to my cookie party. We were beginning to blend our lives. Our co-grandma relationship will last regardless of the vagaries of the years on Tara and Special Intent. The baby will certainly receive lots of family love. Sissy's face is wreathed with smiles and the candlelight catches her jewel-red studs. We both now know about friendship and love in our two different worlds as we execute the dance of getting to know each other.

Now Sissy says, "You know, I wasn't so sure 'bout this cookie bitches stuff, but you . . ." She nods at me and then stops, as though she's decided not to say what popped in her mind. "Well, I'm glad our little bit of genes is mixed together for infinity."

Sissy's words remind me of my grandmother. She held me on her lap and explained about the first woman who walked the earth. People everywhere in the world are from her, that long-ago evolutionary Eve who fed and protected her offspring and secured our existence.

And my children and their children will continue with what I've given them from my body and given them from my soul. That was my grandma's view of the meaning and purpose of sex and reproduction. Now it's as though Sissy with her talk of the infinity had eavesdropped on that conversation. Perhaps bridging past and future is the theme of grandparenthood. Straddling. Yes. That's the word.

SUGAR

Sugar used to be as expensive as gold. Slave labor in the Caribbean islands permitted the production of sugar to be cheap enough for ordinary use. We love sugar. Its sweetness provides a burst of energy now common in drinks, candy, and desserts. But we don't take it for granted because we know, by the time we're in middle school, that too much makes us fat and gives us cavities. Excessive consumption is also correlated with type 2 diabetes. So sugar has a dark side—the historical toll it has taken on the workers who produced it and the toll it takes from those of us who overconsume it.

Sugarcane grows in tropical climates and was originally from south Asia and southeast Asia. Ancient humans sucked on the cane to extract the sweet flavor. The juice was first turned into sugar in India about seventeen hundred years ago. Muslims refined the production. Alexander the Great sent some to Europe from India.

The 1390s saw the development of a better press, which doubled the juice obtained from the cane. Sugar plantations expanded to the Canary Islands and then the Portuguese brought sugar to Brazil. Columbus procured cane for the Caribbean and it soon became the chief crop, making the Caribbean the largest producer of sugarcane. Slave labor made cheap sugar possible, and by the eighteenth century, all levels of society consumed the former luxury product.

No crop has had such a formative influence on society. The production of sugar demands huge amounts of labor, first supplied by African slaves, then indentured workers, and then free laborers. The industry produced multiethnic populations. Now sugar is in oversupply, and dependency is keenly felt by the populations of the cane-growing countries.

In the late eighteenth century, Europeans began experimenting with sugar produced from crops other than cane. The beet-sugar industry took off during the Napoleonic Wars when France was cut off from Caribbean sugar. Today, thirty percent of sugar is produced from beets.

Granulated sugar comes in various crystal sizes from coarse-grained sugars, such as sanding sugar (also called "pearl sugar," "decorating sugar," nibbed sugar, or sugar nibs), which adds "sparkle" and is used to decorate pastries. Sugars for table use typically have a grain size of about 0.5 mm across. Powdered sugar, 10X sugar, confectioners' sugar (0.060 mm), or icing sugar (0.024 mm), is produced by grinding sugar to a fine powder.

Brown sugar is produced in the later stages of refining, when sugar forms fine crystals with significant molasses content, or from coating white refined sugar with cane molasses syrup. The color and taste strengthen with increasing molasses content, as do the moisture-retaining properties. Thus, brown sugars tend to harden if exposed to the atmosphere. Too many times I've banged hardened brown sugar with a hammer into pieces small enough to whirl in a food processor, trying to restore it to usable condition.

10

Vera

Double-Dipped Chocolate Peanut Butter Cookies

1 1/4 cup all-purpose flour

1/2 teaspoon baking powder

1/2 teaspoon baking soda

1/2 teaspoon salt

1/2 cup unsalted butter, softened

1/2 cup granulated sugar

1/2 cup packed light brown sugar

1/2 cup creamy or chunky peanut butter

1 egg

1 teaspoon vanilla

1 1/2 cup semisweet chocolate chips

3 teaspoons shortening, divided

1 1/2 cup milk chocolate chips

Preheat the oven to 350 degrees. Combine the flour, baking powder, baking soda, and salt in a small bowl. Beat the butter, granulated sugar, and brown sugar in a large bowl with an electric mixer at medium speed until light and fluffy. Beat in the peanut butter, egg, and vanilla. Gradually stir in the flour mixture, blending well.

Roll heaping tablespoons of dough into $1\frac{1}{2}$-inch balls. Place balls 2 inches apart on ungreased cookie sheets. (If the dough is too soft to roll into balls, refrigerate for 30 minutes.) Dip a fork into additional granulated sugar, then press it in criss-cross fashion onto each ball, flattening it to $\frac{1}{2}$-inch thickness.

Bake for 12 minutes or until set. Let the cookies stand on cookie sheets 2 minutes. Remove the cookies to a wire rack; cool completely.

Melt the semisweet chocolate chips and $1\frac{1}{2}$ teaspoons shortening in the top of a double boiler over hot, not boiling, water. Dip one end of each cookie one-third of the way up; place on wax paper. Let stand until the chocolate is set, about 30 minutes.

Melt the milk chocolate chips with the remaining $1\frac{1}{2}$ teaspoons of shortening in the top of a double boiler over hot, not boiling, water. Dip the opposite end of each cookie one-third of the way up; place on wax paper. Let stand until the chocolate is set, about 30 minutes.

Store the cookies between sheets of wax paper at cool room temperature or freeze up to 3 months. Makes about 2 dozen (3-inch) cookies

*A*FTER SISSY FINISHES HER story there's silence. We don't often consider our bodies as part of the evolutionary process. We focus on our individual, particular selves and ignore the universal. The message from my grandmother is forgotten in our daily lives. Occasionally, when one of us is complaining, we might say, "Oh, what am I bitching about? Everyone goes through this." Or, "I should count my blessings. I have two healthy children and Joannie's having chemotherapy today and people in New Orleans still don't have homes." We're so thrilled with our unique and particular babies that we forget when we give birth we are contributing to evolution. Now I'm about to become my own evolutionary Eve.

I check my phone, but no calls.

I check my watch. It's 9:45 P.M. Almost seven in California. You'd think that the doctor would have called by now.

Softly, so softly at first that I can hardly hear it, Al Green starts singing from my iPod player. I had forgotten it was on, it was turned down that low and we were so immersed in passing out cookies and one another.

"Hey, is that what I think it is?" Juliet trills. "That's my song and perfect timing for our seventh-inning stretch!"

Allie walks to the stereo and turns it up and we hear him promise to make it all right. Juliet sings with him and begins revolving her hips, moving her shoulders as she grabs my hand to pull me toward her. Her palms are on my back as her eyes look into mine, the smell of Addict perfume now replacing the Charlie.

"Remember?" she asks. "It was so long ago that day at the jazz festival." She shakes her head and spins me away to turn me under her arm. "No. It was just yesterday."

The rest of us follow Juliet's and my example. In the corner, Taylor's hand is on Allie's back as they rock to the music, Allie pulls back and Taylor swings her and then moves toward her, hips swaying until they return to each other's arms.

Sissy rocks her hips, sways her shoulders, and catches the subtlety of the beat. Vera rises.

And the horns blare.

Disney bounces between us, mouth grinning and tail wagging. "Look, Disney is dancing, too." Taylor laughs at Disney's excitement. His Christmas tie shakes with his movement. "He's doing the two-step." Her grin lingers and her fire has returned.

Vera's hips revolve in circles, her eyes half closed. Now Vera used to be a stripper back in the day, back when she was strung out on cocaine and trying to get her head straight over a miserable childhood and continued abuse by one man after another. But beyond that, regardless of the association of dancing with stripping, she loves to dance. Now, she lifts her arms high, moves to the beat, and a smile spreads across her face. No one else knows about Vera's past, not in this group anyway. I know because she used to wait tables as a bridge to a more square life and I trained her. Once, I suggested she tell the group and give us lessons. "I don't want to even think about those days. I simply enjoy the movement, the music, the transportation it promises, and I'm doing it for me. Not men."

"Now that's a lie," she says about the lyrics that imply that love, regardless, is always right. Her torso snakes with the words. "It can be the greatest wrong you do." She closes her lids and slides into a slow, very slow, jerk, her arms and hips twitching into each other and then flexing straight. "Well, not the love. The choice of who you put it on." Disney bounces in front of her.

I grab her hand and start dancing with her.

"Now that's love," she says when the lyrics suggest that love is about being good to each other. "It's not about regardless. And nothing wrong with being in love with someone unless it's the wrong someone."

"That's the truth," Sissy says. "And half the time they're wrong." Her head is high; the scarf doesn't diminish the elegance of her long neck. She brings out a syncopated beat with her hips, subtle as her small foot movements and the slide of her shoulders.

"And the other half they're the best thing in the world," Laurie says.

"Hear, hear," echo Rosie and Jeanette.

Gradually washing over me like a tide, I realize I'm scared that I told Jim I love him.

How do I know? How do I ever know?

Juliet's eyes are closed, and Allie's arms pump the air, her hips swaying as though T.J. is right before her and she's moving with him. It's amazing, all of us dancing together. We're freer with one another than we are when we're dancing in public. And then Allie is back in Taylor's arms and Taylor places her hand on the back of Allie's head and presses it into her shoulder. Allie meets my eyes and her expression is one of peace and belonging.

Then in a flick of the shuffle program, the beat picks up and we're suddenly swing dancing, twisting, trying to do the mashed potatoes on my carpet, jerking to the dances of our youth. Each of us without a partner, we dance as a group. The songs and vigorous movements last long enough that I break out in a sweat.

Several of us leave for more wine, water, soda.

And here comes a slow beat and again the women couple up and sway together. Sissy with Juliet. Taylor with Allie. I turn the music a little lower.

And then, unbelievably, Rosie extends her hand to Jeannie.

Jeannie reaches out her arm. Their fingertips touch.

I'm dancing with Charlene and turn her around so that we can watch this happen.

Jeannie glances at the ground.

Rosie's hand remains extended. Her mouth is open, her lips curving up at the ends in the beginning of a slight smile.

Jeannie perceives the expectancy and hope. She stares at the entertainment center, away from Rosie.

Rosie presses her lips together and shakes her head sadly, but her arm remains outstretched.

Then Jeannie touches Rosie's shoulder.

Rosie begins to lead the slow dance and then somehow, they're in each other's arms crying.

Allie sees this, too, and we, Allie and I with Charlene in tow, encircle them, so the five of us stand swaying while Jeannie's head goes onto Rosie's shoulder and she smoothes clinging hair away from Jeannie's forehead.

"It's been hard for me, too. Differently hard, but nonetheless. So. So?" Rosie leans back a bit and wipes another strand of hair from Jeannie's face.

Jeannie doesn't answer.

"So we're going to be okay. Somehow. And I'll be here for you," Rosie continues as if almost-whispered words will ease Jeannie into happy compliance.

"But you'll be there for Sue, too, and our interests are opposite. You'll be wanting something for her that'll hurt me and wanting something for me that'll hurt her."

"That's right. But you both know that." Jeannie nods. "And Sue's well aware, has been aware from the beginning of her . . ." Rosie can't find the right word and starts over. "She knows the pain that she and your father are causing you and your mom. Even if you never found out. And the pain they're causing each other."

I remember the push and pull from the horror and ecstasy of Stephen, where you think you're teetering on the edge of the world and you're convinced you can't survive the abandonment, the loss. And then you gain the heaven of belonging, of being one, when you're together. Then fear settles in as part of you. That craziness still reverberates in my love for Jim. "That pain increases the bliss," I say.

None of us know what to say to that and we listen to the music.

Then Rosie gasps a great breath and in a rush of words says, "Your father will resolve it because Sue has already thrown herself to the wind for him. That regardless love beyond herself or anyone else. Beyond her pain and her guilt or my pain or yours. Or even her own."

The music switches to lyrics bemoaning the addiction of love.

We back away and Charlene says, "Are our minds controlling the random button or something? It's as though it's the sound track for our conversation."

"Shit. It's the sound track for our lives."

Disney now dances in front of Charlene, his monkey in his mouth.

"Yeah. That's Sue," Rosie says. "Stuck in love. Or lust. Guess that's been me, too."

"And me. More times than I want to remember." Charlene laughs.

"And me. Me now, even," Allie says.

"Love." That's all I say.

And then damn if the random button doesn't move from the compulsion of love to the dependence on drugs.

Vera hears this and goes into high gear. She's been dancing while we were discussing Sue's irrevocable destructive passion and now says, loud enough so we can all hear, "Addictions. Drugs. Sex. Work. Money. Love." And then she twirls away. "Thinking they're the answer to life. Now that's the biggest lie."

And then she sways up to us and grabs Charlene's hand and swings her out and under her arm and we're all dancing again. This time there's a smile on Jeannie's face as she and Rosie dance. The happy rock comes on and brings in Laurie, Taylor, and Sissy, who were scarfing up food and drink.

And we all sing the lyrics together.

Allie's hands are curled as she pumps the air. Taylor grins and she punches her arms and shakes her hair. Her hair flows from her head, waving with her motions. Vera twists her hips and spins. Vera, ah, Vera, she loves to dance. So the ten of us dance and sing as one. "Everybody is dancin' tonight."

The spirit of our youth is thick as we laugh and move together. I catch Juliet's eyes. "Remember this?"

"Like it better now than I did then," she says.

"Brings me right back."

And she dances over to me and hugs me. "What would I do without you?" she whispers. "My best friend. Myself. My witness."

My eyes fill. Girlfriends.

IT'S LAURIE WHO switches this. "Everybody? Can we finish with the cookies? I need to go home to Olivia."

Vera says, "My cookies are waiting." And sure enough two Trader Joe's plastic shopping bags are on her chair.

"Cookie time," Allie shouts, then slides into the kitchen for more wine.

I turn down the player just as a song about the insecurities of our vanished youth begins.

"We still don't know what we're doing and it's forty years later," Juliet says. We're making a slow transition back to the business of the cookie party. Juliet closes her eyes. "More things change, the more they stay the same." And she automatically touches her chain as though for reassurance.

Vera says, "Uh, got that right." She has an uncanny way of reading people's secrets and accepting them as she accommodates her own. She expects each of us to have them.

Secrets.

Sometimes, like Juliet, entire secret lives. Sometimes, like Vera, secret pasts. Then there're things we only tell very few, or maybe only one other person. Juliet meets my eyes and winks. Sometimes, like for Charlene, there are things we simply can't communicate. Sometimes secrets are simply events that we aren't yet close enough to each other to tell.

"Hey, the cookies!" Laurie nags.

"So. You should be a boss, someone's boss," Rosie says.

"I am. Olivia's."

We all laugh except for Vera, who stands beside her Trader Joe's bags in her professional clothes. She always dresses with flair. The beiges and russets of her blouse complement her short blond hair. The most glamorous of us still, a Marilyn Monroe look-alike with implanted boobs done during her dancing days and eyes the blue of a cloudless sky. Unlike Marilyn's, Vera's smile is enthusiastic without timidity or childlike reticence. She told me once that she was shy when she was a kid. Beaten down by extreme poverty and an abusive father. But now Vera, professional Vera, is my best salesperson. She is expert at long-term care, gentle with people concerned about their future health. Warm, able to listen carefully to her clients and tailor a program for them, reassure them through the process and the anxiety of being accepted if they have health issues, Vera makes the most sales. Her confidence has been hard-won. And tonight she brought in a client that I predicted would walk. A salesperson is a salesperson and just like she teased the sale of herself — the tease being the hook for the continued interest — she's able to sell insurance.

I remember when I met her. Rough years for both of us. Both of us single moms. She didn't have the confidence then that she exudes now. Her childhood shyness was shellacked with bravado to hide her vulnerability. When the Gandy Dancer hired her as a waitress and asked me to train her, she wasn't sure of anything.

"You ever do this before?"

"What? Work in a bar?"

"No. Wait tables."

She giggled. And shook her head.

"How'd you get this job? Usually they start people as bussers."

She shrugged and I suddenly noticed her figure. "Oh." Carl, the manager, had a weakness for women with big breasts and Vera had obviously charmed her way into the job.

"Lucky it's just lunch. Not dinner. You're not scheduled for evening, are you?"

"I have another job nights."

"Follow me and watch. Ask questions later. And take home a menu and memorize it."

She was a fast and desperate learner. Her other job was stripping. Back in those days, the seventies, there was no Internet. There were more bars and more meeting people at bars. More flirting, much more flirting at work.

People weren't as worried about sexual harassment or the complications of workplace romances. In fact, I met Stephen waiting on him.

Vera made sixty thousand dollars stripping but had gotten addicted to cocaine. Chased powder with Dilaudid so she could steal sleep. She supported her son, Peter, and a man named Mickey, who took her to work, drove her home, and made sure she was safe. Mickey told her that she was the most beautiful woman in the club and reminded her daily how lucky she was to have him watch her back. He loved her like he never loved anyone, would die without her. You can imagine the con while he pocketed her tips so he could "take care of her." When she did something on the side he got a lick of that, too. And he beat her regularly just to remind her of his control and his love. She made him do these things when he was frightened he would lose her. Being beaten was love. After all, her father had loved her.

Then protective services received a complaint from a neighbor who heard the unmistakable sound of someone being slapped and punched, heard yelling and swearing through the walls. The call made her confront a hard fact: She could have her son, Peter, or she could have Mickey. She let Mickey take extra Dilaudid. When he passed out, she clutched a few clothes, Peter's favorite truck and blanket, and jammed the lot in the car. Grabbed her son and drove to a motel. Got a job stripping in a club on the outskirts of Ann Arbor. Left her furniture, dishes, sheets, most of her clothes, and everything she had managed to scrounge from a childhood almost as mean as her adulthood was threatening to become. A necklace her mom had given her for her sixteenth birthday. A baby doll missing one arm. A picture of her and her father and mother, the only picture she had of herself as a child. Left it all and drove away.

I don't remember where she was from or where she was before she was here. I don't know if I ever knew.

Cocaine made the pain go away. She didn't miss Mickey. And men's staring eyes were no longer a sacrifice but a score. The dancing was once again for her. They were irrelevant. She was good. And beautiful. She danced all night. Snatched a few hours' sleep. Read books to Peter, took him for walks, watched *Sesame Street*, slept when he napped. The cocaine helped her stay awake for her time with him. Then the babysitter would arrive and Vera would put Peter to bed and go to work.

One morning she fell asleep on the couch and woke up to see Peter dusting the coffee table with cocaine. "Look, Mama. I found some sugar." He licked his finger to pick some up and taste it.

Vera bolted upright. "That's not sugar. That's bad." She whipped the cocaine away. "That's bad. Bad for you."

"Why you have it?" Peter asked. He had one crossed eye and it drifted toward the sofa.

She shook her head, still struggling with pieces of a dream, a dream in which a cat got in a fight and her side split. In the still flickering image, Vera could see into the body cavity of the cat as it lay with its inner lids covering the eyes, gruffly moaning.

Vera clenched her eyes, pushed away the image of the red muscles and curved ribs glazed with blood. She gazed at smears of white dust, rinsed a dishrag with water, swabbed the table, and then threw the cocaine and water-soaked rag into the garbage.

That next afternoon she went to an NA meeting. And two days later, I met her at the Gandy Dancer Restaurant.

When people ask how we met, I tell them I trained her at the Gandy. Period. I know she told Charlene about the abuse from Mickey, but not that he was her pimp and not that she was stripping. Not that he was a heroin addict and that she occasionally used with him when she was out of Dilaudid. And when she's asked where she met Finn, her current husband, she never says in NA. Instead, without a beat, without a downward glance, without a smile or a shift of weight, she says, "At some meeting. Parents without Partners, I think."

Now he's a contractor and she is my best salesperson. Peter repairs computers and is married with a son. All the remnants of drugs and the debasement they caused seem erased.

Sometimes I think the past is gone, as though a book has been closed and a new one opened. But then I watch Vera dance and see that transported but yet wise expression flit across her face. I see the same old motions and I know the past is here again in a new guise. Once again she's thirty and struggling to stay alive and figuring out how to convey herself into her own place-world-space where no one, no man, can touch her. And when I see her persistence at making a sale, I know that it's driven by her fear of poverty.

I know, too, that no matter what Jeannie decides, no matter how much Rosie or me or Allie help her deal with this tangled triangle, her life has been altered. Her relationship with her father is permanently changed. Someday, perhaps, it'll be stronger and more honest. But the betrayal, the knowledge of it, exists in her present and into each and every day of her future . . . each and every one.

The past gets carried with us. It's always there.

The song about teenage anxiety plays softly. We're nineteen again with all our insecurities and hopes back in the age when decisions seemed without consequence because there was so much time to redeem them. Now everything is crucial. Or nothing is because so much of our lives are already played out.

Vera says, "These cookies are the ones you all love so much and want every year. The double-dipped peanut butter and chocolate."

"I was hoping," Rosie said, "Those are Kevin's favorite."

"But I did something different with the packaging. What I did is recycle the containers from previous years." She reaches into one bag and pulls out a red canister with familiar Christmas balls on them.

"I brought that two years ago!" Allie says. Disney has wedged beside her on the couch, his chin on her thigh.

Vera hands it to me and I hand it to Charlene. Vera reaches into the bag again and pulls out a green tin with white holly leaves on it.

"I haven't seen that in ages," Rosie says. "So. You've been saving these all these years?"

"Yep. And this year I'm into recycling." Vera hands over a large cup stuffed with tissue.

"Oh, I want the cup to match the other one that we got last year," Allie says. "Jeannie brought that."

"I remember when you used those velvet purses as containers. I used mine on New Year's Eve," Vera says as she passes a box decorated with red and gold squares and festooned with a gold bow and red bells.

"It's like revisiting all our old parties."

"All our old Christmases."

"God. This must go back twelve years." Charlene holds a merrily patterned box.

"Yep. Just think, we've gotten a hundred and forty-four different containers in the last twelve years."

Vera hands off a green felt bag.

"That's from Pat."

"Pat. Jeez. She hasn't been here for six or seven years."

"How long have we been meeting?"

"Sixteen years," I say. "Since Tara was a toddler."

"I was here from the beginning," Jeannie says.

"And me," Charlene adds.

"I came a few years later." Vera hands me a plastic green pail decorated with grinning Santas and then a red oven mitt with white snowflakes.

"That was Laurie's."

"From two years ago. How do you remember?" Laurie says.

"You always want to do something practical. Or simple. Like those elegant white boxes this year."

"We're gonna miss you," Charlene says. And we realize, truly realize—not just to make polite, everything-will-be-okay conversation—that this is her last cookie party with us. She will not be here next year.

A hush follows. We've been appreciating the passage of time as we pass along, touch, examine, and review

containers from years gone by, previous parties. Maybe
it's the time of night, the fact that we know we're more
than halfway through the party. And one of us is leaving
and one of us is struggling with everyone's worst fear, the
death of a child. And each of us has endured disappointment, sorrow, self-disgust, addiction. And loss.

Vera stands holding a small bag printed with candy
canes and holly and she passes it to me and looks into
her shopping bag with a downturned mouth. "That's it.
'All gone,' as Peter used to say." She shrugs, her palms on
her hips.

"That one's for the hospice," I say and put it in the
bag.

"Why a hospice?" Sissy asks. "Why not a safe house
or the homeless shelter?"

"We used to give them to a safe house," Juliet says.

"That was a while ago."

"This is why we give them to a hospice. Ten years
ago Tracy's mom was dying at Christmastime. And Tracy
visited her whenever she could and stayed as long as she
could."

I think of my own mother dying and remember the
pain that Tracy was going through and my eyes fill.
Almost as a reflex, I grab a piece of peanut brittle, my
mom's recipe.

"And then one night, at two in the morning, her mom
was sleeping that heavy-breathing, almost-stopping sleep
and Tracy went into the family lounge looking for something. She wanted a cookie. Just something sweet. Something good in all the dismal sadness of waiting for the
next step, not wanting it to come and wanting it, wanting

her mother's pain to be over, at the same time. When she realized how much she wanted a cookie that night, she suggested the hospice for our future donations."

"So what do they think about the cookies?" Rosie asks.

"You can come with me this year. The first time I talked with the head of donations. I told her about Tracy and made it clear that the cookies were for the families who were visiting their loved ones during this season. She had me fill out a form and they gave me a Christmas tree ornament. Here." I stand up and unhook a silver-colored disk with the words "Tree of remembrance, 1998" from my Christmas tree. I pass it around so everyone can see it. "It's on my tree and here for each cookie party." I laugh as though the ornament knows it attended years of parties and celebrations between long sleeps in its dark box.

"Now they know me. I just hand the cookies every year to the person at the desk and she thanks me."

"I always imagine the people at the hospice eating them," Allie says. "I think about what they're going through. The sadness, the darkness, the weirdness of that happening at Christmas. My grandmother's youngest sister died in childbirth on Christmas Eve." Allie shakes her head. "Think of the joy of a new baby, the horrible tragedy of losing your favorite sister, and the craziness of everyone celebrating the holidays." Allie shrugs. "My grandmother adopted the baby and she became my favorite aunt. I think of that when I make my cookies. That and the anonymous people at the hospice for the last ten years."

"Ten years. I've been cancer free that long," Juliet

says. "It's my tenth year since my mastectomy, chemo, and radiation." Ten years ago, Tracy's mom dying and Juliet's cancer. Everyone was fighting for their lives.

"It's been five years for me," Vera says. "You never stop thinking about it." Vera had rectal colon cancer.

"Almost two years for me," Allie says. "They just keep taking little parts of me, always those precancerous moles, luckily no more melanoma."

"How many of us have had cancer?" I ask and raise my hand for the squamous cell carcinoma that was removed eight years ago and then some more three years ago. Six of us raise our hands.

"I had a rare form of bone cancer, back in my late twenties," Charlene says. "And Alice, she's had that basal cell carcinoma."

"Seven of us? Seven out of twelve? Unbelievable."

We're quiet. Then Charlene says, "It's the environment."

"And the sun," Allie adds. "The beaches we all love so much."

"But do you think this is representative? That this great a percentage—more than half—will get some form of cancer?" Laurie asks as if all her healthy cooking is useless.

No one answers.

"So," Rosie says. She stands and her motions are fast and her grin broad. She's uncomfortable with this serious turn. She leans over and fills the empty glasses with wine, and when she straightens she asks, "Tracy. What about Tracy? Where're her cookies?"

SALT

Juliet and Dan went to Thailand one year. When she returned, she showed me her pictures and several were of a salt mine. Pyramids of salt set in rows stretched to the horizon. Workers were scattered throughout the mine. Seawater flowed in and was then trapped by small dikes. Evaporation, aided by a blazing sun and a windmill, occurred and workers raked the salt into the waist-high pyramids. This salt mine stretched more than a quarter mile to the sea, a series of rectangles dotted with salt piles set in neat rows. When evaporation was complete, workers shoveled and scooped the islands of dried salt into wheelbarrows and pushed them through the shallow water for further processing. This is how salt has been mined for at least eight thousand years.

Salt is crucial to our very lives as it's one of our electrolytes and necessary to regulate the water content of our bodies. Ironically, it can also be a case of too much is a bad thing, because excess salt adds to high blood pressure. And even though it's crucial for animals, it's toxic to many land plants.

We're equipped to detect salt with the taste receptors in our mouths, which partly explains why it is our most popular seasoning. And, equally vital, particularly before refrigeration, canning, and freezing, was its use as a preservative, especially for meats.

Thus, since prehistoric times, people have devoted lots of time to obtaining this necessary and important chemical. It was used in ancient Egypt for embalming and also for salted fish and birds traded around the Mediterranean. Salt caravans crossing the Sahara were operated by the Tuareg from ancient times until 1960. Roman soldiers were sometimes paid in salt, giving rise to the words *salary* and *soldier*. And the word *salad* literally means salted, the culinary practice of salting leafy vegetables. Venice ushered in the Renaissance not because of its manufacture of salt but by trading it. Mahatma Gandhi led a protest march against taxes levied by British rulers on the export of salt. The march brought millions of people together as one and was pivotal to Indian independence.

Sea salt from different areas has varied flavors. Table salt comes from the mass production of salt, often from underground deposits, refined in small grains. Like the salt mine Juliet saw, the manufacture and production of salt is one of our earliest chemical industries. Iodine is added to salt because it's lacking in some diets. And salt is treated to pour easily in spite of moisture. I vividly remember as a little girl staring at the drawing of the little girl holding a box of salt that contained the same picture of a little girl holding a box of salt to an imperceptible miniaturized perpetuity. Above her head blazed the slogan, *When it rains, it pours*. The drawing allowed me to contemplate infinity as I wondered at the increasingly tiny pictures.

Salt is added to raw ingredients to draw out moisture. A small amount of salt can be used to enhance sweetness. My mother always put it on her melon, and others sprinkle pineapple and grapefruit with it. Salt makes sweetness more pronounced by contrast. This principle is why salt improves the flavor balance of baked goods such as cakes and cookies.

11

Tracy

From: Tracy Temple
Date: December 7, 2008 4:59:03 PM EST
To: marnie444@aol.com
Subject: Tracy's "Super Hard" Nut Clusters

This recipe is pretty daunting.
        Please proceed with extreme caution!

Peanut Clusters

    1 teaspoon vegetable oil
    4 ounces semisweet chocolate [I used Guittard]
    4 ounces milk chocolate [Same brand]
    2 cups peanuts, chopped [I've also used pecans, almonds, or cashews]

In a double boiler
oil first, then melt chocolate.

Here's the hard part . . .

Don't let any water bubble into the pan, geez, you could really blow the whole thing then!!!

Place on a baking sheet lined with wax paper by rounded teaspoons.

COOL!!!! Then place in lovely packaging.

I know, it was another tough one, but when the going gets tough, the tough go to Hawaii.

Happy Holidays to all of my favorite women.

I really miss seeing all of you!
Love and
Happiness,
xxoo TT

P.S. JEEZ. I forgot to tell you to stir in the nuts after the chocolate is melted. heeheehee

*L*ET ME GET 'EM, Tracy's cookies." I walk into my office. Behind me, my friends laugh and talk. Bitter balls of sleet hit the house. When I glance out the window, frozen rain slants white in the darkness. It isn't sticking, but it smacks the house with a mean sound. I bring back the sacks, and Taylor asks, "Where's Tracy again?"

"Hawaii. With Silver," I answer.

Tracy and Silver are one of those couples who've found the secret to true and lasting love. When I'm with them, I'm reminded of how good it is when it's good. Theirs is not just a marriage that has lasted, but one where you feel their love and caring when you're with them. Each of them wants to make the other happy and seamlessly accommodates or sacrifices.

They sure started off with the odds against them, though. Tracy was too soon out of a bad marriage. One of those marry in your early twenties and by mid to late twenties you realize you did it to end your dependence on your parents and prove you're an adult. Then you parent the other the rest of the way until it's unnecessary and you realize you're unsuited. So Tracy, straight blond hair down to her ass, lips that always looked as though they were about to pout or grin, and a laugh that made everyone who heard it jump in, hit the Gandy Dancer Restaurant.

I guess she had decided to use sex, drugs, and rock and roll as an antidote to the blues because she'd do a double shift waiting tables and then go party. It was the heyday of partying, in the midseventies, when we hadn't yet recovered from the fact that we, or our brothers or lovers, might have to go die in Vietnam. She met Silver at one of those parties. He was tall and well built, hair curly and long. He had come into the city to do the sound for Iggy Pop or Bob Seger, one of them or both.

Now, Silver was in a bad marriage, too, but no one had officially ended it. I don't even think they had acknowledged it. His wife lived in one of those little towns in north Michigan that survive on tourists and sports. Motorcross racing, hiking, boating, camping in the summer, hunting in the fall, snowmobiles, cross-country skiing, ice fishing in winter, the year-round inhabitants nourished by the natural beauty of the area in spite of the perennial hard economics and winters. Silver stayed on the road more and more and, at that moment in time, hadn't seen his wife for several months, giving her the excuse of work, but she didn't complain. She enjoyed the money he sent.

Then came a party at the remnants of a commune about a half hour from the city. It was late summer, early fall, daylight was still long and the commune's gardens were heavy with produce. Eggplants. Brussels sprouts. Cauliflower. An entire field of tomatoes, some still green, and bending down in spite of the branches tied to stakes. Oregano and thyme tangled as I walked between the rows. And at the edge the unmistakable scent of pot trained to grow on the ground like an out-of-control tomato plant. The scent was almost hidden in the licorice aroma of basil.

Silver arrived, roaring in on his motorcycle. His helmet flattened his long hair until he shook it out. Tracy tilted her chin and straightened her shoulders as soon as she saw him, flicked her fingers through her long blond hair, licked her mouth and fastened him with her eyes.

He felt her staring at him, standing there with her lips in between a pout and a grin.

"He's so hot, he needs some ice," I said.

She laughed.

He turned toward her chuckle, and that laugh of hers, so merry but with a guttural hint of much more, snared him. The keg of beer and the bowls of homemade pretzels the commune made seemed endless. As darkness fell, a bonfire was lit. Sparklers and pot were passed around. Silver and Tracy danced to Earth, Wind & Fire, fastened together as they swayed, staring into each other's eyes.

Uh-oh, I thought and shook my head.

Then they disappeared. Off for a walk among the tomatoes or into the aspen forest surrounding the field. I wasn't her keeper, simply her friend. I just enjoyed the party, dancing, drinking beer, and talking with Juliet and Alex, my first husband, who came with me to the party.

He was alive then. So alive.

Sky wasn't yet born.

We weren't married. Just in love.

So long ago.

We had gone canoeing that afternoon, floating down the Huron. Lazily, without any desire to get down the river, trusting the current to carry us the right way. We pulled over at the arboretum and ate salami and cheese sandwiches, drank the wine I had packed, watched ducks, with half-grown babies behind them, cruise the water.

As we danced, his gray eyes searched mine. I caught glints of them in the flickering bonfire. His hands were warm on my back, his breath tickled my ear, ruffled my hair. He smelled of musk, his T-shirt now slightly flavored with the harsh aroma of burning chokecherry. His erection prodded my navel and I pressed into him and slid down the length of him, encouraging his plea.

He moaned. "Let's go home."

I pressed closer to him and slithered my hand under his shirt, his flesh wrapped the hard muscles of his back. "I want you."

My hand pressed down his pants, cupping his ass. "Soon."

He laughed. His hardness rubbed my stomach and his beard rasped my forehead. "I love you."

"I love you, too." See, I said it. It was easy then. I love you. We were in agreement. We loved each other. We were a couple. I told him a million times because I assumed we'd last forever.

"We're so fucking good. My life is wonderful with you in it."

"Mine, too. Can't you imagine us sitting on a porch in rocking chairs thirty years from now? Our grandchildren playing around us." See how I assumed we'd last forever? Convinced our agreed-upon love would place our lives on a predictable trajectory, safe, accompanied, and witnessed? My life would follow a customary path. Married to one man. Children. Jobs. A house with a garden that I kept neat and attractive. Friends.

"That's what I want." He wrapped his arms tighter around me and then grabbed my hair, gently pulling it further down my back and tilting my head for a kiss. His mouth warmed my body and his erection promised bliss.

He was so alive. Flesh warm and eager. He opened the blinds each morning and sang, "Let the sun shine in."

Spun me around when he came home.

Excited each spring about pitching for the baseball rec league.

Difficult to consider that eight years later he passed. No. Not passed. He died. He fucking died. Like a snap of fingers. That fast. Out of the blue.

I wonder if the wayward cells that swamped his blood and killed him were growing even then. I wonder. Reproducing as he asked me to marry him and made love to me and we created Sky. Creeping through his veins as he passed his test for a contractor's license and laughed and sang to Sky when she took four teetering steps toward him.

I learned not to assume anything. I learned to fill my life up and try to live every moment. And I also learned that anyone could vanish at any time. And thought that love was useless if it wasn't forever and knew that nothing is forever except your children. And your girlfriends. See. Tracy is still in my life. And Juliet.

MY EYES FILL at the remembrance of Alex's death, even now, more than a quarter of a century later, as I carry Tracy's cookies toward my living room. I touch my cell phone, still quiet. Check my watch. Now 10:15. I stop in the hall and tell myself, Face it. They know by now. Sky is probably crying in Troy's arms and delaying dialing me until the party is over. Sorrow washes over me, sorrow for her, sorrow for Alex. I wondered, wondered since the first time Sky got pregnant, if her baby would have his gray eyes.

But that night, that fall night with the fruit still on the vine, Tracy danced with Silver and I danced with Alex. Alex saw them and said, "He's married."

Then Tracy came to me, eyes shining, mouth wet with Silver's kisses. "I'm going home with him." She held my hands when she said it. "With him." The *m* vibrated between her lips and dangled in the air. Tracy smelled of musk and now lemon, which came from Silver.

"He's married."

"He told me."

She winked at me, that just-between-us-girls wink, that I'm-just-so-fucking-happy wink. "I'll be okay. I know it." She squeezed my hands. Her palms were moist and her pupils expanded so that her eyes looked black.

"Call me tomorrow."

"I promise."

It doesn't usually start like that. A zipless fuck that turns into a forever. Maybe it's our greatest fantasy. Sex so fabulous that everything falls into place and everyone else is immediately cast away. Suddenly, life is laid out in a straightforward path. Simple and clear and certain. You know just what you're going to do and why.

Or maybe it's the reverse. Everything is already in place and the sex seals the deal. You're meant to be together, first passionate lovers, then companions. One of those rare one-night stands that is ceaseless as though the physical connection makes all the rest possible, when really the emotional, mental connection made the physical possible. Maybe they knew that from their first glance. A fall in love at first sight that transcends the hassles, and just as ziplessly moves through the decades. So the connection, the communication, and an instinctual awareness and appreciation of the other's space are present from the beginning. The intimacy nuances and the sweet domesticity made the routine a joy.

A few days later she called, a new ecstasy mixed with peace in her voice. "This was different. Oh, my God," she said with a sigh, "different than anything I've ever experienced."

"So he's really great?"

"Great, yeah, but that's not what I mean. The sex wasn't just sex. It was . . . We transported each other someplace else. Someplace I've never been. It was beyond sexual, it was . . . spiritual. Like we were part of the universe. Everything was one and we were part of it."

I laughed. "What were you two smoking?"

"Nothing. Just each other."

I didn't know what she meant. Not then. I learned later. Meanwhile, Tracy's love for him also made her fascinated by his interests, and she discovered her vocation. Silver was a sound technician for rock bands. Tracy's buoyancy and grin, energy and ability to organize, the many musicians and artists she met through the music scene, gave her the idea to become a rock producer. Now she and Silver go on tours together. He does the sound, she does the production. It seems glamorous from the outside: six months all over the world, a new family each year in the road crew of people working together. Tokyo, Chicago, Sydney, Montreal, Paris, Madrid, Seoul, Nairobi, Los Angeles, Rio. I get postcards from all over the world stamped with Tracy's lip prints as she presses a kiss to me. Sometimes that's all I receive. A picture of a naked David from Florence and her trademark pink glossy lips.

"So. You'd think they'd be tired of traveling and would stay here for the holidays," Rosie says.

"They're using up frequent flyer miles," I answer. "Besides, that's work. This is vacation."

"Well, let's start," Laurie says.

Everyone sits down, and I pass out Tracy's cookies. "Hmmm. Tracy wanted me to tell you how she wished she could be here. She made these before she left and put them in these canisters." The boxes are covered in paste paper with red swirls making a scarlet sea of ripples, flashed with bits of gold leaf.

"These are gorgeous." Vera lifts the lid and unfolds the tissue paper, which makes a fire-crackling sound. "The tags all have her kiss prints."

I smile when I see the hint of a grin along with the sexiness of her kiss. I continue to pass out her boxes of cookies and place one in my bag and the last one in the hospice bag. "She sent me this email to copy for all of you." I wave the papers I printed of her email and hand them out, too.

"Oh," Taylor says as she reads the email, "this is so her. I can almost hear her laugh."

"I love that laugh," Allie says. "Every time I hear it, it makes me happy."

"I miss her." Juliet's mouth turns down in a hyperbole of a sad face. "When're they getting back?"

"Right before Christmas. For the Townie Party."

Vera eats the chocolate candy. "Hmmm. She made these a few years ago, too."

"She knew everyone loved them. And they're easy and keep well."

"I still miss her."

"Hey, here's to Tracy's laugh." I raise my glass and everyone follows. "Here's to Tracy."

"And Alice," Vera adds.

I wonder if maybe we need a new rule. You can only miss one party in a three-year period. I want people who will actually be able to be here. It's not about the cookies, never was, it is always about being together and having fun. And each of us makes the party merrier.

I don't know if it's the reference to absent people that rouses Charlene, but she stands and announces, "I'll go next." And she brings back the bags we had packed earlier that day.

"I guess we're in the chocolate time, because my cookies, too, are essentially a chocolate candy. Truffles. You loved them a few years ago, and maybe I . . ." Charlene swallows as she recalls how easy everything seemed a year ago and how everything changed in May. "Wanted to do something automatic, or maybe I wanted to remember that time."

Her eyes are quiet as they move around our circle and

she moistens her lips. The brazen cheer of her jaguar-print jacket, which she wore a few years ago, seems a lie. "I don't, I guess, have much of a story to tell this year. Not about the cookies. I made these particular cookies because you liked them so much and last year one of you was disappointed I hadn't made them again. I wasn't able to do anything new. I've done enough new. I listened to Georgian chants while I baked them." Her soft hair falls into her face. Her hands quiver slightly as she reaches in her sack for the blue canisters. And then she forces a smile as if to remind herself that there is still the joy of life and that's why she's here.

"Oh. Those are so cute," says Jeannie about the containers.

"I love these truffles," Laurie says. "Brian and I fought over them. I made him some for his birthday as part of his present."

"Thank you." Charlene's eyes are wet, but her smile reveals even teeth and her gratitude. "Well, I wanted to thank you. All of you. Each and every one of you," she adds as if it's our concern and love that enabled her to keep from splintering apart. "Thank you for your support, the calls, the letters, the visits," she chokes, and then clearing her throat, "the love." She passes another canister to Rosie and continues. "You really helped me get through it. You know Luke was very spiritual. The last thing he said to me was that he'd always be with me." Her eyes shine and she looks happy; her voice is soft, almost a whisper.

We listen quietly.

"Well, I don't believe in angels, but I feel his aura.

When I think of him I feel him and he's there in my mind. He said, once, that love's immortal. Maybe he's right. It's at least as immortal as all the people you love." As she talks she continues to pass the canister. We rest them on our laps or place them in our bags and listen.

Is love immortal? Do I still love Alex? Yes. And Stephen, in spite of myself. The love for him is mixed still with dismay, anger, and disappointment. That's why it hurts so much. My love, my feelings and concern, for Jim will persist, too.

Charlene continues. "Each day I get through I learn something more. Tonight I'm reminded of you guys and how much you and this party are part of my life. And how much I love it. How much fun you are. That there's fun in life." She repeats it as though she taught herself something. "Fun in life."

She turns to Jeannie. "Your fortune cookie said 'The wheel is turning. This is the dark time. What must you gain from the night?' We don't often think of that, do we? What is it we learn from the night, the night as a symbol of hardship or" — her voice cracks — "tragedy."

She stops and narrows her eyes slightly, thinking. "I'm not sure yet, but somehow Luke's death has changed me and I'm just beginning to relearn myself. I know Luke's death didn't happen to teach me, it just does, inadvertently."

"That's because of your resilience. Other people could be mired in the pain," Allie says.

"The issue is what I gain, because the fortune cookie happens to be right. This much I knew immediately when I read it: Each death is a gift. I'm not sure what the gift is yet. Maybe discovering the gift is my mission. Maybe that's my unfinished business."

"I bet it's something spiritual," Juliet says. "You say Luke was spiritual . . . well, he got that from you."

"Hmmmm," Charlene considers.

"Maybe a psychic?" Laurie suggests.

"Damn. I didn't think my fortunes would have this kind of impact," Jeannie says.

"It came to me while Allie was talking."

Allie brought her eyebrows together. "Talking about peace?"

"About darkness and light. About anticipating spring's renewal. I know I'll never be the same. The gift is partly how I'll be different. Reborn."

"It's that you've survived," I say. "You endured and are still here and talking. And aware that there's still fun in life."

"And giving us something from your own hands that you know we love," Allie says. "I'm still thinking that love's immortal. T.J. always tells me that. You know, in the Jewish religion, you live on in the acts of goodness and mercy you perform, there really isn't a heaven or hell."

"Maybe love is another way to say goodness and mercy, maybe they both spring from love," Charlene says. "I'll figure it out as I go on."

"Be a minister." Sissy's head is slightly tilted and her eyes are on Charlene. "Lead others through the valley of the shadow. You have the knowledge."

We sit stunned by this suggestion. It doesn't seem to fit with the old Charlene and yet as she is now, her lips slightly parted, a wise but somber expression in her eyes, it seems to suit her completely.

"Yes," Allie says.

Charlene frowns slightly, but other than that small movement, she remains immobile as we watch her think. "I don't really believe in one denomination over another. Or even in one religion as having all the answers."

"Maybe ecumenical?" Allie says. "Maybe for a hospice?"

"Maybe for abused women, and people in jail." Vera meets Charlene's eyes and they nod at each other. Charlene's brows lift.

"Maybe," Charlene says slowly, her attitude one of completion.

"Wouldn't that be one helluva gift that Luke gave you? Being a minister?" I say.

"I sense it in you." Sissy hasn't moved: her head remains tilted, her palms rest on her knees. "I been thinking about it for myself, the next step in my nursing 'cause medicine is only a part of the healing."

"It's a good idea, Sissy. Thank you." Charlene sits down, leans against the back of the chair, her arms resting on the arms and her palms draping over the ends. She sits like a lioness or a sphinx, motionless, the jaguar-printed jacket now perfect for her pose.

I know it's my turn next. When I look outside, there's no wind. The snow has individual, fluffy flakes. Each one is the size of a nickel. They come straight down. Everything is still except for the snow falling to the ground.

But the women are restless, as though they need a break from this heavy exchange, and so first Rosie gets up and goes into the bathroom. Sissy has taken over my seat and talks with Charlene.

"We should get together and explore this," Sissy says. "I know the denomination I want to be, but not how to do it."

Allie talks quietly to Jeannie. I hear her say, "You should tell everybody," and Jeannie answer, "They wouldn't understand."

"They'd understand following your own dream."

Jeannie nods. And then Allie stands up and goes into the kitchen for some water.

I make coffee and lay out cups, milk, sugar, and Equal while Allie cruises the table. There're only cheese and crackers left. I add a plate of my peanut brittle and unwrap a rum cake that Vera brought. The ginger flower seems elegant on the almost empty table.

And just then the phone rings. Just then as I place the Bundt cake, with its softly rounded humps and a sweet, slightly tangy scent of rum mixed with confectioners' sugar, on the table, gently so it doesn't move on the plate, doesn't fall off or slide, I feel the tickle on my hip. Just as I withdraw my hand and let the plate with its bounty rest on its own. Just then it vibrates.

I straighten and pull my cell phone from my waist-band. Look at the window.

Sure enough there's the picture of Sky taken last summer when I went to visit her. We ate breakfast on a patio and she was wearing a tank top. Now her gray eyes smile at me. And her grin gives me hope for a positive outcome.

I walk into my bedroom.

I'll be alone if I need to cry for a minute or two by myself.

Disney follows. His tail doesn't wag; he senses my tension, my fear, my anticipation.

No one is there but Disney and me and the bed full of coats. A black shiny one with a fur collar and hood, a red one with a crazy-colored wool scarf, a brown one with an elegant bright green cashmere-blend scarf were laid out on my bed. Some placed neatly, their sleeves by their sides as though standing sedately, some with arms akimbo as though caught in a crazy dance step.

I close the door. And flip open the phone.

"Sky?"

"Mom?"

I try to sense from that one word the outcome of the test, but the connection crackles so I can't hear her clearly.

I inhale.

"Mom?"

"Yes. I'm here." My words tremble.

"It's okay. She's okay." Sky's voice trills, lifts at the end of the sentence, loud with excitement and happiness.

I exhale with such force that I sit down on the side of the bed. Sit on someone's coat.

"Oh, thank God."

"I was getting so scared. It took forever. I called the office and it was closed. And I thought, Oh God, I'll have to wait another day. I can't wait another day. I can't go through another night." Her words rush, tumble.

"And then she called me. I squeezed Troy's hand so hard, I think I broke some fingers." Sky giggles. "She apologized for calling late, but she had an emergency C-section of triplets. She had the test results along with my phone number, was going to call me when the emergency came in. And . . ." Sky stops and inhales.

"I was beginning to . . ." I let my voice trail off.

"I know. Me, too. I had lost all hope. But then she called. Troy and I were just holding each other. I was crying, trying, trying, trying to be positive but positive had worn away with the drip of each minute, each hour. The entire day. This has been the longest day. I just heard a minute ago. Long enough to laugh and cry with relief with Troy and then push speed dial to get you."

"Yyyeeeeaaahhhh," I sing it, almost yell it. And then I exhale. "I'm so happy for you. For me. For all of us." I stop for a minute. "What's next? Any more tests?"

"Nope. Just a normal pregnancy. The ultrasounds are perfect, she's developing just like she's supposed to and there's no genetic abnormality. A perfect little girl, so we just have to feed me to feed her and love her and wait four more months to see her. She and I, both of us, growing." Sky laughs.

A sense of relief, of holding myself together, of pressure I didn't even know was there, fills me up. I feel light, but I hadn't been aware that I felt heavy. I had lived with that fear, that mother's sense of something not going right for her child, for so long it had become part of me. It's a weight that I can now release.

What a joy.

What a night.

"I'm so happy, honey, I don't know what to say."

"Me either. My dream come true. She's okay." Sky screams out the "okay" as though it is still unbelievable. "We just have to wait now. We can start Lamaze. Yippeeee! You'll come, won't you, come and be with me through my delivery?"

"Of course!"

"And I'll see you in a few weeks. We'll do a baby pregnancy celebration."

"By then Tara's baby might be born."

"Maybe."

"Wouldn't it be great if he's born on Christmas?" Sky asks. "What a present." For the first time, she is happy for Tara's pregnancy. In the past, she had expressed happiness, but the words were rote and polite. Her eyes hadn't smiled with her mouth.

"All babies are fabulous presents."

"They'll be friends, I hope. Cousins almost the same age. How's the party?"

"Great. You know. Always fun, always lots of love."

"Troy and I were too nervous to eat dinner, so we're going out to celebrate. I'll talk to you tomorrow, Mom. Okay?"

"Sure." Disney's mouth opens to a grin while his tail slaps the floor. "Get a good night's sleep."

"Mom." Her voice is somber. "I know this is weird, but when I thought I couldn't have a baby, I thought of Dad. It was like a piece of him died again, like he ended in another way. You know? Like I disappointed him. Now, in a way, he continues. You know?"

"Yes, I do. I was thinking something like that myself."

"Mom, I love you. So much. And thanks."

"Thanks? For what?"

"For just being my mom."

"Ah, darling. You don't need to thank me for that. It's been my pleasure. And more. I love you."

"Me, too. Bye," she says and hangs up.

CHOCOLATE

Chocolate. How we love it. It's the dessert of love and celebration. The Aztecs considered it the drink of the gods. Chocolate contains a substance that mimics being in love, and has a mild marijuana-like effect in producing euphoria and decreasing stress. It also contains caffeine. Yet the story of chocolate is tied to colonization, trade struggles, slavery, smuggling, black-markets, and finally, huge worldwide acclaim and modern industrialization.

The tree that produces the chocolate bean, the cacao tree, is native to Central and South America. It's a fussy tree, needing exact temperatures, constant moisture, and a canopy of larger trees, usually banana and rubber, to protect it from too much sun. It is also subject to fungus and pests. The flower, which is fertilized by a particular species of fly, grows right on the trunk. Only a few flowers become the fruit that's the size and shape of an American football. The pod contains the beans,

which are split open, fermented, and then
dried. One tree produces only a pound or
two of beans a year.

The Aztecs and the Mayans drank
chocolate mixed with honey, vanilla, and
chile three thousand five hundred years
ago. Try some coffee, cocoa powder, and a
smidgen of cayenne pepper. It's fabulous.
Chocolate was the drink of soldiers and the
elite, but it was also common at large festi-
vals and celebrations. Drinking chocolate,
like smoking tobacco, followed the meal
and had some connection with blood, perhaps because of its ritual use during human
sacrifice. The beans themselves were used
as money, so literally, money was growing on trees. When Columbus discovered
a canoe laden with cacao beans, he knew
their use as coins but did not realize they
contained far greater potential riches as a
drink and confection.

The Spanish brought chocolate to Europe and the food became a story of struggle, laws, horticultural development, and
smuggling. A second type of cacao tree was
discovered in Ecuador and the Amazon
basin, which was more easily cultivated
and is now, along with a hybrid from the
original type, grown in West Africa and
Asia. Meanwhile, Venezuela developed
cacao plantations. As native populations

disappeared, decimated by war and European diseases, African slaves were brought in to work plantations, some containing a quarter of a million trees. The Spanish crown, alarmed that trade developing between South America and Mexico set a precedent and threatened its control of European goods, banned the trade. The Dutch captured Curaçao, in 1634 and sent large cargoes of smuggled chocolate into Amsterdam; contraband and fraud flourished as Amsterdam became the hub of the cacao market by the mid-1600s.

The drinking of chocolate spread throughout Europe in special chocolate houses, which rivaled cafés. By the 1800s other drinks had become more popular, especially tea in England, which led to increased consumption of tea from their Asian colonies. Coffee also became more popular as a stimulant. Chocolate by then was heavily sugared and consumed mostly by children and invalids. Just in time to prevent chocolate from falling into disuse was the development of chocolate into a confection. This, too, began in Amsterdam when Coenraad van Houten extracted the cacao "butter," allowing the creation of chocolate bars. Cadbury meanwhile marketed chocolate with flowers and it became a token of romance with the implication of aphrodisiac powers. Then Lindt, in 1879, created a process that produced smoother bars. Hershey, following Ford's example, saw a way to mechanize production and built a workers' town in Pennsylvania surrounded by enormous dairy farms that supplied 60,000 gallons of milk every day. Hershey owned vast sugarcane plantations in Cuba complete with railroads and port terminals, all of which were nationalized by Fidel Castro.

By then chocolate was crucial to the celebrations of Christmas, Valentine's Day, and Easter. The production of chocolate has grown from 100,000 tons in the 1900s to 2,500,000 tons in the 1990s.

Chocolate has come full circle. I notice chocolate grown from specific world locations extolling specific flavors. Next to that on store shelves are carefully processed locally manufactured truffles and candy. The eating of chocolate containing more than 65% cacao, like other dark fruits and red wine, keeps your blood pressure down, your blood flowing by lowering cholesterol, and your heart healthy. It has the additional blessing of creating a mild euphoria. So the food of the gods, first accessible from only one species of tree confined to a single area, is now a pleasure and popular benefit for the entire world.

12

Taylor

Molasses-Ginger Crisps

> 1 cup softened butter
> 1 $\frac{1}{2}$ cups sugar
> Beat butter & sugar together 2 minutes.
> Add 1 egg + 1 yolk, $\frac{3}{4}$ teaspoon salt, 1 tea-
> spoon fresh ginger (finely chopped)
> 2 tablespoons chopped crystallized ginger

Use whisk to blend 2 cups + 2 tablespoons
flour, 1 $\frac{1}{2}$ teaspoons powdered ginger, 1 teaspoon baking powder and add to mixture.

Add $\frac{1}{3}$ cup dark molasses.

Make into 2-inch rolls and roll in
coarse sugar and chill a couple of hours (or
freeze for a few days if you want). Preheat
oven to 350 degrees. Cut the rolls into $\frac{1}{8}$
slices and sprinkle with more coarse sugar.

Bake for 12 minutes. Makes about 6 $\frac{1}{2}$
dozen cookies

*A*UTOMATICALLY I REACH DOWN to pat Disney's soft ears. Excited by my attention, he puts his paws on the edge of my bed, his tail circling rapidly. I lean down to hug him and then rise.

I remember a conversation I had with Allie when I learned of Sky's first pregnancy four years ago. We were at the Zingerman's Roadhouse restaurant. Summer was just beginning and we were on the patio, sharing a salad.

"Jeez. A grandmother. Here I just realized I was an all-grown-up adult." I shook my head in wonderment. "How did this happen so quickly, so soon?"

Allie laughed. "Hey, I was just reading that we, post-menopausal women, are crucial for evolution." She raised her Diet Coke as if to toast us. "We have a decade or two of life when we can't reproduce. Yet we can work our butts off and consume less calories than other workers."

"Well, we're supposed to, anyway." I took more bread and we both laughed.

Allie continued. "Turns out for the millions of years when we were hunters and gatherers, we kept our grandchildren fed until adulthood, especially when their moms were nursing new babies. We had to have grandmas in order for there to be childhoods, all those decades when kids learn from adults."

"Still. I'm excited for Sky and can't wait to hold my new baby, but I'm not old enough to be a grandma."

"I know. Me and my promiscuous reading."

She said it before me, but I love learning secondhand from her.

When I enter the living room, Charlene raises her eyebrows.

"Good news." My smile is huge. "Sky's going to have a girl, a healthy girl! Guess I'll be a grandmother twice." I laugh. "In a few weeks. And in the spring. A bounty of babies."

Charlene hugs me.

Sissy had moved to the chair next to Charlene, and they had been talking when I entered. "Great! I heard about Sky's pregnancy from Tara," Sissy says.

I shut my eyes to make all my former worry vanish. "I am so *relieved*."

"Hey. You hear from Sky?" Allie enters from the kitchen, rum cake on a plate and a cup of coffee.

"Yep."

"You don't need to tell me. You're glowing. Beaming."

"It's been a great day. Full of good news."

I pour a cup of decaf. Passing the table, I smell the rum sugar of Vera's cake and take a small slice. Laurie, Juliet, and Rosie are laughing in front of the sink. "Only two more people to go. You and Taylor." Rosie pouts to show how sad she is that the party's ending.

Laurie says, "Well, after all, tomorrow's a workday."

"And Olivia awaits." Rosie voice is light, but there's a tinge of jealousy.

I retrieve my bags and say, "Babies and husbands and lovers and jobs are waiting."

Everyone drifts in and takes her seat. At every party,

each of us picks a spot and it's ours for the night. During cookie hand-out time, we sit in that same seat as though it's been ours for years and we'll never relinquish it. The next year, we choose a different chair and guard it just as vigilantly.

"Good news. I just got a call from Sky and her baby is fine. A girl."

A chorus of "Yay," "Oh, I'm so glad," "Thank God," "What a relief," come so fast I can't distinguish them. "Hear, hear." Rosie holds her wineglass high. "To Sky's daughter."

"To healthy babies everywhere." Allie looks at Laurie and then at Taylor. "Ohmigod, that's schmaltzy."

"But a sincere and great wish," Rosie says.

We each sip whatever is in our glasses. I toast with my decaf.

I start. "This year I want to add two more rules. Here they are: If the first Monday in December occurs right after the Thanksgiving weekend, then the cookie party will be on the second Monday. Like I moved it this year."

"I remember how frantic everyone was a few years ago when that happened. Can't cook for Thanksgiving and then immediately bake for this," Vera says.

"Can't eat Thanksgiving and turn around four days later and come here either." Juliet has a piece of peanut brittle in her hand as she talks.

"Exactly. And the second one: Let's email the recipes to one another. That way, I won't have to type them all up and then email them. Simply email them to me or to all of us. That'll make things easier."

"That's how I did it this year anyway," Allie said.

"Well, I thought those were already rules," Laurie says.

"Enough business." I reach into the bag and pull out the animal-print makeup cases and start distributing them.

"These are so cool. So, so cool! I need a new makeup case anyway." Rosie hands a snakeskin case to Juliet and it begins its round. Rosie's attitude is breezy, maybe it's the wine, or maybe it's the hint of reconciliation with Jeannie.

"These cookies are my grandmother's pecan butter balls. To me they're the ultimate butter-nut-sugar treat. I've made them before, and you gave them your seal of approval." I pass a jaguar-printed case.

"Look. This matches my jacket!" Charlene says. "Think I'll keep this one." And sends on the zebra print that I pull out next.

By now Allie has opened her case and nibbles on a cookie. "Oh, I remember. I do love these."

"Did everyone get one?" So I place the last case in the hospice bag. "Why did I choose this particular cookie this year? It's my daughters' favorite. And, oh, this cookie is the one I remember most from my grandmother. In fact, I don't remember her making any other Christmas cookies. She made stollen, and fruitcake, and meringues, but only this cookie. And, I've been thinking a lot about her as I take on her role as a grandmother. She seems closer to me, even though she's been dead since before Tara was born." I stop myself and think, Amazing how the generations continue. How we repeat these ancient patterns if we want to, if we're lucky. "Grandchildren have been the theme of my year." And Jim. How startling that I should be becoming a grandmother the same year that

I've fallen in love, taken on a younger lover, and maybe even found my partner for the rest of my life. "I guess this cookie is a grandmother-grandchildren cookie." I laugh.

Then I see Tara's small hands roll the balls of dough. Sky reaches into the bowl. In the memory, I observe only their hands as they roll the balls. Chipped pink-pearl polish decorates Sky's nails. Tara, about four, smears the dough on her fingers and licks them. Sky carefully dusts her palms in flour and concentrates on forming round mounds with the same focus she employs for every task.

I clear my throat. "I remember helping my grandmother make pecan balls, and when they were little, Tara and Sky helped me. I was on the phone with Sky while I made these." I place my index finger over my bruised cheek. "That's how I got this. Multitasking." Before I began speaking I hadn't realized how these cookies were echoes of previous generations. In a few years, I vow, I'll make them with Sky's daughter and Tara's son. Chuckling to myself as I remember how the kitchen looked when Tara and Sky finished cooking, half the batter in their stomachs, the rest on their hands and the floor. Even then, the joy and fun outweighed the mess.

People in the kitchen cooking together. Almost as much fun as people eating together. Almost right up there with sex.

"Now, it's Taylor's turn." I fold the shopping bags and place them in the recycling.

"Oh," Juliet says, "I always hate it when the last one starts. It means the party's almost over."

"Doesn't have to be. Charlene is spending the night. Stay as long as you want."

Taylor brings out her bags. The added bags make the corner where she wedged herself next to Allie extremely crowded. I met Taylor through Tracy at one of the parties that Tracy loves to throw. She rented out an empty barn and hired local bands. Or maybe the bands did it as a favor, a rock and roll professional courtesy, since they knew her and Silver from work. Stephen and I had just recently broken up. Taylor and I started dancing when the band played "Honky-Tonk Woman." We were both on the floor, moving to the music, couples and other singles dancing around us. Rick, Taylor's husband, didn't dance and so the two of us spent most of the party together while Rick drank beer and watched. Sensing his eyes on us, I tried to wave at him to join us, but he looked away, a handsome man with a sour expression that some women would find an enticing challenge. He'd evoke the need to make him smile at any cost. A woman who thinks her mission is to make a man happy might turn herself into a pretzel to accomplish that task. That night, Taylor was pregnant with her second child. It wasn't perceivable then.

"You seem familiar to me," I said.

She shrugged and looked away. "I used to have bright red hair. Used to be twenty pounds thinner, too." She moved away and kicked back in a perfect swing dance move.

I tried to remember where I'd seen her before. I knew it wasn't at a party. "Maybe I've just seen you around town."

When the lead guitarist asked if she'd like to take the mic and she shook her head, I suddenly remembered.

"You were with that band . . . what was it called? Crazy Alligator."

"But that was another life. That was . . . what? . . . fifteen years ago. I can't believe you even remember!"

In between sets, she told me that she was now in Internet technology, working for Pfizer. Rick also worked there, in the research labs. Rick had played keyboards to Taylor's singing in Crazy Alligator Band. A blues singer, but without enough growl and pain in her voice, she was an okay local headliner, but could never be a star. Her sound was just too wispy. She held onto the mic like it was salvation, like it grounded her to the stage so she couldn't escape. That singer needs to reach down and let loose, I had thought. I hadn't paid any attention to the keyboardist. He was a journeyman, but without any pop. He had possessed a mathematical understanding of the music, but not the emotion behind it.

Rick and Taylor got tired of late smoky nights with little recognition and less money. Rick had a degree in science and finished his master's and started working for Pfizer. It might have been Parke-Davis then. And Taylor, who had a degree in education, took classes in computer science and began training people in pharmaceutical software applications.

Taylor, neither the one with the bright red hair, skinny jeans, and the swinging breezy style who I saw sing, nor the dancing Taylor with the highlighted hair and billowing colorful tunic who I met at Tracy's party, is Taylor now. Her hair is brown, showing a little gray at the roots. She hasn't gained any weight, though. In fact, it looks like she's lost some. Dark circles around her eyes make her look ethereal and somewhat frail. Her scarf hides more than it shows off. She wears no lipstick.

I don't know if the cause of Taylor's appearance is related to being in love with Allie, raising her family, or struggling to find a new job since Pfizer abandoned its Ann Arbor location. Maybe it's a combination of all three.

Now she stands before her bags. She waits patiently for her audience to sit down and be silent. But we don't quiet. We talk to one another. Jeannie and Juliet laugh.

Taylor clears her throat. And waits. She does it again and we behave.

"First I want to say, I love this party. I look forward to it all year, each and every year, probably starting in summer. Then I start looking for cookie recipes and browsing stores for clever containers. To me, it launches the holiday season. We know that it's going to be at your house." She turns to me. "Marnie, when I walk in here, the cinnamon and pine greet me. I see your decorations, the tree with macramé ornaments, lit candles everywhere. I feel the love of friends.

"This is my favorite time of year. The parties. The sparkling lights on Christmas trees, downtown, stores, houses. The joy and celebration lasts from this party through January 1. And then there's the beautiful snow. Sledding, snowmen, snowmobiling, ice skating outside. I love it. And your party starts it off and is the best of it." Her voice diffuses. And she stands as though at a loss.

"Our party. We *all* make this party work," I say.

"But you're the organizer. You set the stage."

Taylor shifts her weight from one foot to another.

"This year I thought I'd have to quit. Things have been so bad." She closes her eyes and swallows.

We are quiet, aware of the trembling in her voice.

"I was heartbroken. 'Cause I know the rule. If I didn't bring cookies I'd be axed."

Her eyes fix on Allie. And then fill. She inhales and holds her breath and turns her gaze toward all of us. "Not many of you know, but my life crashed." She presses her lips together. "Rick had been having an affair with someone at work. I suspected it, and confronted him, but, of course, he lied. When Pfizer shut down he kept disappearing. Some research-oriented job search through HR, he said. But that was a lie. Meanwhile, Rick wasn't asked to move to Connecticut, and I haven't been able to find another job. So two jobless people, two kids, two cars, a mortgage, a dog, and a cat."

She glances at Laurie. "You never think it'll be you." She shakes her head. "You do everything right, work hard, but it can still happen. You guys are smart not to wait for disaster."

"We don't know what'll happen next."

"But you have each other. And you're working together. I . . ." She stops and starts again. "I . . . Well. Rick left four weeks ago, left with that other woman who did move to Connecticut. He took his Pfizer packet with him. Left me what was left of mine."

"Bastard," Rosie says.

"Turned out he hadn't been paying the mortgage since it ballooned. I tried to keep the house, but then, just before Thanksgiving, we had to leave." Her eyes are shadowed. "It's been hard. Fuck. It's been hell."

"Oh, Taylor," Laurie says, "why didn't you say something?" She shook her head. "I know. You want to take care of it yourself. You think you're supposed to. Like somehow it's your fault. My husband and I felt we just weren't working hard enough for the longest time."

"I couldn't find a job and there wasn't enough money to pay the bills and feed us. I was frying sardines and making a chicken last for three days. Peanut butter and beans were my refuge. My unemployment was up and the separation package all spent. Then . . ." She wraps her arms around herself.

"They foreclosed on the house. Just two weeks ago. Right before Thanksgiving. Rick must have known because he left two weeks before the final notice. I couldn't believe it. But it happened and there was nothing I could do." She pauses and closes her eyes. "No one would buy the house; besides, it's worth less than the money I owed. I went to the courts to get help and to the bank, but things were too far gone by that point. Rick had kept how dire everything was secret from me."

"Rick'll have to pay eventually, you know," Rosie says. "He'll have to pay child support, spousal support, and arrears. He can't get off scot-free. I know a lawyer who can help you." She's referring to her husband.

"Me, too," Jeannie says. "We may be able to do something with the mortgage company."

"I was too . . ." Taylor stops. "Startled and stunned like a deer in headlights. Ashamed. Overwhelmed."

"Is it too late?"

"Too late for the house. Too late for Rick." Taylor pushes her shoulders back.

"But not too late for you and your kids." Charlene's and Sissy's words are on top of each other.

"But that's not the only story. I didn't think I could come here, couldn't take money needed to feed my kids to use for cookies or packaging, even from the dollar store. I struggled to figure out where we'd go — my mom's? Rick's parents? My sister's?" She reaches for a glass of water.

I knew she had lost her job. She called me months ago and I suggested she consider moving into sales — it was rough, but it would be something. She wanted to stay in teaching and training. She needed a job with benefits to take care of her children. I suggested she try the U, but they had a hiring freeze. She had tried there already. I invited her to networking breakfasts, but no luck. Everyone had pounded every inch of pavement and pulled in each favor.

"I should move to India," she joked.

I didn't know Rick was having an affair. Didn't know he had cleaned her out and abandoned her and their kids. I remember his eyes while we were dancing all those years ago, looking slantwise from the corner. At every gathering, he kept himself separate and just watched as we drank and laughed. The downward curve of his lips lent him an aura of disapproval and scorn. I told myself it was just the way his mouth was formed. The last few years, he seldom joined us at all, too busy finishing up experiments, working in the lab. Everyone I knew who worked for Pfizer put in sixty hours a week, so I didn't question it. All those long hours made it difficult to keep a relationship alive.

I think of Jim's hectic work.

Taylor seemed like the spark in the marriage, the one with the added spice of flair and enthusiasm. Rick seemed the consumer of her energy, but maybe that matched her drive to feel needed. Two kids, though, swallow that energy. I know. I remember. And Rick's downturned mouth expressed not just smugness but dissatisfaction. Depression, I thought. People will do anything to distract themselves from it. Anything. Including abandoning a wife and kids. Anything.

"And then the day before Thanksgiving, Allie said that we could move to her basement. It's a separate apartment with a small bedroom, huge living room, and its own kitchen and bath."

"It's okay in a pinch and they can stay until Taylor gets a job and enough money to rent something else." Allie smiles at Taylor. And then I understand Taylor's adoring gaze.

"Allie saved my life," Taylor says.

"Bull. I'm a port in a storm. That's what we're for. Girlfriends. To help one another. And I have the space," Allie protests. She waves her hand as though to sweep Taylor's dependency away. Anyone would do this, her gesture says.

"I've been there. Couldn't have managed without Charlene when we were single moms and our kids were little. You pull together and get through it," I say.

Taylor continues, "Tracy helped, too, and Silver loaned us his truck for the move. Then right before she left, Tracy and I went shopping for the containers and she paid for them. Allie bought the groceries so I could make these cookies. And helped make the cookies." She grins at Allie.

"That was the fun part," Allie says.

"How come you didn't tell us?" I ask.

"This all just happened last week. And then I knew I wanted to tell everyone myself. Tonight. Here. Allie's keeping us from being, I don't know, homeless, I guess, but she and Tracy made it possible for me to be here." A gentle smile, tender and tentative, spreads over her face. "And it is so good to be here. This is food for my soul. Healing just being here. I love you all so much. This is one thing I didn't want to lose." Taylor reaches in her sack and brings out cheerful star-shaped boxes with Santa spreading across the lid and reindeer prancing along the sides. "Here they are." She gives the first box to Sissy, who passes it around.

"The cookie has three different types of ginger—fresh, powdered, and crystallized. I love that juxtaposition of spicy and sweet in crystallized ginger, so each flavor is crisp and exaggerates the other. But this year, with all the love that Allie and Tracy showed me, and Marnie trying to help me get a job, and all that love and caring from my girlfriends." Her eyes fill so she has to stop to wipe her cheeks. "Well, you're the sugar in the spice I've just been handed."

Silence lasts for several moments.

We each absorb her words.

"That's so touching," Jeannie says.

And then Taylor says, "My girlfriends. I love you all. And what would I do without you?" She hands off her final box. "That's why I wanted to go last. Because . . . I needed to be fortified by your love"—she raises her glass of white wine and chuckles—"to tell you what's been going on, but mostly how much I love this party and what it means to me . . . and how much you mean to me. And it's almost like, well, you saved our lives." She pushes her lips together, eyes wide as though she's said more than she's wanted and plops down.

"What would we do without one another?" It was a statement, not a question. Each of us knew the answer for herself.

"But that's what this party really is about. Girlfriends," Taylor says. Her somber mood is erased and glimmers of her spark have returned.

"Yep."

"Not cookies. Not even giving them to our friends and the hospice. But girlfriends," Vera says.

"Regardless of what other shit or joy, we have one another," Allie says.

"Regardless, we're always here," Taylor says.

"To girlfriends." And we raise our glasses once again.

ALLIE STARTS CLEANING the kitchen. Rosie takes her seat and Jeannie and Rosie cluster with Taylor. Rosie knows a lot about family law. "Believe me, he'll have to pay eventually," I hear her say.

"But that doesn't help now. Besides, you can't get blood out of a stone," Taylor replies.

"This'll get better," Jeannie says.

"It's a question of time." Their eyes meet as though they're talking to each other as much as to Taylor.

"I know that. This'll end. But the solution is a job with a livable wage and benefits." Taylor shrugs. "I've filled out at least two hundred applications. Gone on twenty-five interviews, only to be told I'm overqualified."

Laurie has her coat on, her purse thrown over her shoulder, and her cookies packed in a large shopping bag. "Well, I gotta get to Olivia," she says and kisses me. "Let's get together after the holidays."

"Give lots of sugar to that baby," Sissy says.

"Bye, everybody." Laurie pauses at the door, staring at us.

The tremble in her voice halts me. This is her last party. "I love you all." Laurie is engulfed by hugs, wrapped in I love yous, Goodbyes, Drive safes, Merry Christmases, and Happy New Years, covered with wishes warmer than her coat.

The open door reveals that the snow has stopped. I hope there's no ice under the snow now blanketing limbs of the trees, roofs, streets, and cars.

Vera says, "I'll give her a goodbye party."

"I was thinking the same thing."

Disney bounds for the door in a wild flurry of tail and bouncing, his monkey in his mouth.

Tara has returned.

"How're the roads?" I hear Laurie ask as they pass in my driveway.

"Okay, but drive slowly. Slippery in spots," Tara calls back as she enters the house.

"Like perfect timing, huh?" Tara says.

"We just finished." I hug Tara and feel the hard wedge between us.

"Hear from Sky?" Tara's eyebrows lift as she whispers the words.

"Yep." I grin.

"I'm so glad! Relieved. It would have been terrible, I would have felt so guilty or something, you know?"

"The awful irony you talked about last summer."

"Exactly," Tara says. "But now, it's, like, all good."

"A girl. She's having a healthy girl."

"You'll have one of each. And my baby will have a cousin about his own age." She grins. "Perfect. I tried to get here earlier, wanted to scoop up a bit of the party, but my friends and I were like . . . My time ran away." Tara shrugs.

"Here's some cookies for you." I hand her an extra dozen of the pecan balls.

Sissy is still talking with Charlene when Tara enters. "Here's my ride," Sissy says and stands.

Charlene retrieves paper and a pen from her purse and begins writing. "Let's get together," she says. "Here's my number."

Juliet gives Sissy a hug. "So good meeting you." And then hugs Tara.

Jeannie asks, "Have you started contractions yet? Those Braxton Hicks?"

"Maybe the baby'll be born on Christmas day," Taylor says as I follow Sissy into my bedroom to help her with her coat.

Sissy pulls her coat from under another one and I hold it for her so she can easily slide her arms into the sleeves.

"Thank you, Marnie. This was a wonderful party."

"I'm so glad you could come. And glad that Tara has you for her baby's grandmother."

Sissy laughs. "Not sure about Aaron yet, huh?"

I'm impressed with her straightforwardness.

"I guess neither one of us could be completely sure about any man." She shakes her head, her short dreads dancing all over her head.

I laugh, because she's right. Unfortunately, right for all of us. "I'm working on it with Jim."

"Aaron's okay for a young dude." Her words minimize the gleam of pride on her face.

"I think he's sincere and they sure have passion for music in common." I look at her, seriously look at her, and say, "He loves Tara. I know that. Thank you for showing him to me tonight."

"That was all for you. Well, mostly for you."

We're feeling our way to each other, making an alliance from the serendipity of being tossed together by our children.

"I figure, if they love each other and share so much, some of that's got to be in us," she says. "You and me." And she points to each of us.

Her candor is never abrasive. "I appreciate how you put things on the table. You don't allow invisible elephants to be covered by the rug in the middle of the room."

She laughs. "This is new for both of us. I never expected a half-white grandchild."

"Me either." And we both laugh. "It wasn't really the racial difference, though, but the fact he'd been to training school."

Nodding her head and then raising those fine brows, she says, "I didn't like that, either. Not one bit. But Aaron is on the other side of all that, wiser from the struggle."

"He seems to be, and we'll see if they can provide each other security and comfort. That's not easy regardless of what decisions we make. Especially right now."

"Life"—she shrugs—"just does its thing without worrying about our silly selves." She buttons up her coat.

"Our baby will have us and we form a coalition."

"He'll have us. And them. That's a lot," Sissy says.

"Next time we see each other it'll be in the delivery room."

"I told everyone to be on the lookout and to call me instantly so we can pace together." Sissy laughs. She retrieves a floppy red hat from her coat pocket.

Vera comes into the bedroom. "Oh," She grabs her coat and leaves, calling, "See you, Marnie. Nice meeting you, Sissy."

"I'm leaving, too," Sissy says as she checks her watch. "Nice meeting you," she calls as she walks out.

Vera kisses me goodbye before she leaves.

I hug Tara and say, "See you Christmas Eve, you and Aaron."

"If you want, if you don't already have other plans, you can come to my place for Christmas night," Sissy says.

"Sky and Troy will be here."

"They can come, too."

"What a great idea, for us all to be together," I say.

Tara and Sissy move toward the door. "Goodbye, everyone," Sissy says.

"See you next year."

"We love your hamburgers."

"You're a great cookie virgin," sing back a mixture of voices.

And then, "Looking forward to seeing that baby, Tara," Rosie says.

"Remember to breathe. Always breathe," Jeannie says.

Allie and Taylor have finished the dishes while I talked with Sissy. They freshen up their glasses with water, or wine, and move into the living room. I revolve my shoulders and my neck. My upper back is tired. I add white wine to my glass and move into the living room.

Juliet has her coat on, a bag of cookies in one hand and her empty platter in the other. She waves as she leaves. "Bye. Love you guys. See you in a few weeks."

Six of us return to our seats, our same seats.

"I've made a decision," Jeannie says. "I'm leaving the car dealership."

"You've worked there since high school! You wanted to run it," I say.

"Now, it's excruciating. And who knows how this will play out? Maybe it'll be Sue's and I'll be working for her. Either way, nothing will be resolved soon, and when it is, whatever way it is, the dealership will never be the same. I'll remember Dad and Sue and their inconsiderateness."

"They considered you," Rosie says. "And your mom."

Jeannie drains her glass and sets it on the coffee table with sufficient insistence that the crystal sings.

"You have a right to be angry," I say.

She nods. "I won't be stuck anymore and I need to

do my own dream. I'm thinking of starting a yoga studio. Not quitting immediately, but getting further training and being certified and then opening up a studio. Moving emotionally out of the dealership."

"You could open one up now and hire people to teach. And meanwhile get your certification."

"Possibility."

"Rents are cheap. Might be a great time to get a good deal." Rosie loves to set things up.

"I'd love to help," Taylor says. "I've got the time. It would be fun to do something productive. And I sure could build you a web page."

"Okay," Jeannie says. "And I'm going to tell my father that his actions have made it untenable for me to also be working with him. That I'm extremely uncomfortable about having to keep this from my mother. I don't know what to do about that yet, but at least there's no reason to pretend to my dad. That's the difference. I'm not pretending anymore."

"Yoga has been a solace for you." I think about our morning breakfasts, Jeannie shiny with sweat.

"It's been life-changing," she says. "I'd like to give that to other people. A retreat where . . ." She hunts for the word. "Namaste exists in all its forms. Yoga. Maybe meditation. Maybe life coaching. Maybe something on nutrition and healthy foods. Green living. I don't know."

"Therapy?" Allie adds.

Taylor repeats, "Life coaching . . . that's like training. Hmmm."

"A women's retreat?"

"Men, too. Why exclude them?"

Charlene enters the living room wearing soft apricot pants and a tank top, wrapped in a periwinkle shawl. Her face is washed and she smells of lime and lavender. A glass of water is in her hand as she slides back down in her seat.

"I don't know what to do about Sue," Rosie says. "I'm stuck in the middle, too. Maybe the three of us should talk about this."

Jeannie shakes her head. "There's nothing for me to say to her."

"Maybe after Italy?"

"Then my father's hand will be forced. Or will Sue just wait endlessly?"

Rosie shrugs, closes her eyes, and presses her lips together.

"This'll eventually get worked out."

"Yeah. Like being unemployed and living on the kindness of Allie is temporary," Taylor says.

"But at a cost."

"Maybe not a cost, but a blessing. A strengthening," Charlene says. "Already you've discovered new things about yourself and a possible new path."

Allie retrieves her coat. Her cookies and empty plate are in her hands. "I've got an eight A.M. patient." Then Taylor is packed up and ready to go.

"So. Taylor, you get in touch with me. Tomorrow. I'm serious. I'll talk with Kevin and we'll see what we can do," Rosie says.

"Thank you. Thank you so much for just giving this party every year." She hugs me.

"Maybe we can work on the yoga studio together?" Jeannie says.

"We love you," Charlene says. She doesn't say you'll get through this. And she doesn't say I've been there and I know. I don't, either. We glance at each other, and the time we lived together dovetail babysitting, jobs, taking care of Sky, Luke, and each other is in that look.

Taylor sees this and says, "Yes, I know. It's like you said, get through it stronger and more me." She turns to Jeannie. "Maybe singing in that studio, too." And she laughs.

By the time I wave them goodbye, Rosie and Jeannie have their coats on. Rosie is always the first one to arrive and the last to leave. I hug them and watch as they walk out together. Jeannie says something to Rosie. I see Jeannie turn her head and watch her mouth move, but I don't know what she says. It provokes a hug from Rosie. They stand in the middle of the quiet street, hushed by the blanket of sparkling snow, the streetlights shining on their hair, and I watch them clasp each other before they part to brush off separate cars.

I TAKE OFF my clothes and wash my face. The bruise blooms purple with tinges of yellow around it as a flower on my cheek. I put on crazy-colored striped flannel pjs, the kind I'd never wear with Jim, and wrap myself in my lavender robe.

There's wine in my glass, which is still decorated with its Santa ornament. Charlene lies on the sofa, a pillow from my bed under her head and a blanket covering her. I sit in the chair she occupied all night.

"Another great party."

"Next year will be even better."

Charlene curls her hands under her chin. "Yes, it'll get easier, but it won't go away. And I'm thinking Sissy may be right."

I nod. "I could see you as a minister. Not twenty years ago, not ten years ago. But now." I revolve my shoulders back and then massage my neck. "I told Jim I love him."

Charlene raises her glass. "Quite a night for you. Good news from Sky. A major step with Jim. And you've opened yourself to *both* your new grandchildren." She stresses the word *both* to underscore my earlier concern and displeasure at Tara's situation.

"Sissy's amazing. If her son is half as fabulous as his mom, Tara found herself a prize. And me, I'm going to so enjoy adding to all that love."

"Maybe Luke is right and love is immortal. Maybe it's the ultimate ripple effect. The ultimate butterfly's wing."

"One of them, anyway." I can't help but think that negatives ripple, too. Wars create more wars. Hatreds escalate into monuments to revenge. But Charlene doesn't need to be reminded of harm. "And maybe love is, ultimately, the best we get. It doesn't solve everything, but in spite of it all, it's the most significant thing we have."

"Yes. The best we've got." She smoothes a strand of hair away from her cheek. "And we did it."

"Once again." We made our cookies, shared them with our friends, and got one another through the dark time.

We rejoiced and celebrated another year.

"Yay, for us."

Yes.

GINGER

Before chocolate became the taste of dessert, ginger was considered the luxurious flavoring by Europeans. Native to Asia, where its use as a culinary spice spans at least forty-four hundred years, ginger grows in fertile, moist, tropical soil. The plant produces clusters of white and pink flower buds that bloom into yellow flowers. It is the underground root that becomes the spice.

Ginger is at least as well known for its medical uses as it is for its dietary delights. Important in Chinese medicine for many centuries, it's mentioned in the writings of Confucius and named in the Koran, indicating it was familiar to Arab countries as far back as A.D. 650. Ginger is a known diaphoretic, meaning it causes one to sweat. Henry VIII instructed the mayor of London to use ginger as plague medicine.

It is used to relieve acid indigestion and nausea from seasickness, morning sickness, and chemotherapy. My grandmother insisted on ginger ale when anyone's stomach was upset. And, for me, it makes great tea. Just grate it, put it in a tea ball, and add some honey. It's an everyday medicine without taking pills. Great if your stomach is upset. There is some evidence it reduces joint pain and arthritis, and may have both blood-thinning and cholesterol-lowering effects. It is effective against diarrhea, especially a form that is the leading cause of infant death in developing nations.

Ginger has long been used as an aphrodisiac, taken either internally or externally. It is mentioned in the Kama Sutra, and in the Melanesian islands of the South Pacific, employed to gain the interest of a woman since eating ginger increases the flow of blood to the groin. Conversely, in the Philippines it is chewed to expel evil spirits.

In Asia, it is used in pickles, chutneys, and curry pastes as the ground dried root is an ingredient of curry powders. Pickled ginger accompanies satays and sushi and is a garnish to many Chinese dishes.

Ginger was one of the earliest spices and, during Roman times, the most highly prized import from the East. Known in Europe since the ninth century, it became so popular that it was included, like salt and pepper, at every table setting. By the twelfth century, at least for the well-to-do, dried ginger was used in desserts, including cakes, cookies—especially gingersnaps— and gingerbread. In English pubs and taverns in the nineteenth century, barkeepers put out small containers of ground ginger for people to sprinkle into their beer—the origin of ginger ale. Ginger flavors puddings, jams, preserves, and drinks like ginger beer, ginger wine, and tea. Preserved ginger is also eaten as a candy, chopped up for cakes and puddings, and is sometimes used as an ice cream ingredient. My grandmother introduced me to crystallized ginger, a treat at holiday time.

All of these ingredients add richness to our lives. One of the blessings of living in modern times is that we benefit from the collaboration of Mother Nature, human ingenuity, and civilization. Just think. Sugar, ginger, and cinnamon from the East. Chocolate and vanilla from Mexico. Dates and flour from the Middle East. Nuts from all corners of the world. An array of foods from our earth and its history in thrilling diversity to whet our appetites and imaginations.

People are mixes of ingredients, too.

Each one is a combination of sugar and salt, of spiciness combined with sweetness that enhances both flavors. Our love and support is leavened with the nutrition of nuts and wheat, the sharpness of ginger and the opulence of vanilla, the headiness of chocolate—all plants, like people, which are rare and sometimes tricky to pollinate!

Next year we will gather again, laden with new cookies, filled with excited cheer and drawing on even greater wisdom. Who knows exactly where we will be? We will open our circle for a new cookie virgin. I suspect Sissy and I will become closer allies. But will Rosie have her baby and Taylor a new job? Will Jeannie have moved beyond her dilemma of twisted triangles to focus on her own life and career? Will Allie have made a definitive move one way or another in the relationship with T.J.? And me?

And me?

Maybe, just maybe, Jim and I will be together, loving each other. Maybe, just maybe, I will recognize and believe it.

I'll have two grandchildren. Two babies. I'll once again witness the world through the fresh eyes of a child. And I know that whatever happens, whatever wonders or hurdles life presents, my family and friends and I will journey together.

13

Beyond the Cookie Party,

2010

FOOD AND COMMUNITY ARE essential to our very survival, and women, especially, appreciate and rely on friends for support in tough times and celebration of great occasions. *The Christmas Cookie Club* and the cookie exchanges that inspired the novel celebrate both—and maybe that is part of the reason the book has had such a national and even international appeal. I must confess that I was blind to this when I conceived and started writing the novel. The gathering numbers of cookie clubs and people who receive joy, comfort, and merriment through them took me totally by surprise. I only knew how much I loved the cookie club I joined, which has become one of the highlights of each year. Yes, we look forward to the excitement of sharing wonderful treats in beautiful packages, the accompanying stories, and donating part of our labor of love. But most of all, we're drawn by the great cheer and support of dear friends as we gather to celebrate the end of a year and buoy each other through another harsh winter.

As I toured with the book, I felt I had given voice to a movement that I did not even know existed. Cookies, simple to make and small enough not to be a diet buster (if you stick to just a few!), solve the need for a flavorful sweet or crunchy treat. And through cookie clubs, we have invented a community ritual to share the work of holiday baking and gift giving. They are, in fact, a contemporary extension of women planting, harvesting, and preparing food together from earliest times. To lend my readings the feeling of a cookie club exchange, I brought cookies whose recipes were included in Marybeth Bayer's and my *The Christmas Cookie Cookbook: All the Rules and Delicious Recipes to Start Your Own Holiday Club.*

Some of my happiest childhood memories involve cooking with my family; for me, the smell of home is often the smell of yeast, cinnamon, nuts, and sugar. When I was an adult, Lala, my grandmother, taught me how to bake these molasses cookies and suggested that I maintain a canister of homemade treats for my children as a symbol of love and welcome. A great idea, but in these modern times, it was squashed by the constraints of my job; being a soccer, football, ice skating, and field hockey mom; music lessons; and playdates. I love the strong molasses taste and nuts in this recipe and, it resonates with my fond memories of Lala. The origins of my family's grand tradition of women sharing their life stories lie with her. We would gather in her kitchen to cook, bake, and talk. Lala always told the perfect tale from our own family history to elucidate her point. Now, I share her recipe with you as I did with the attendees of my readings.

Lala's Molasses Cookies

    1 cup (2 sticks) unsalted butter, softened

    ¾ cup sugar

    1 egg

    1 ½ cups all-purpose flour

    ¾ teaspoon baking soda

    Pinch salt

    ⅓ cup molasses

    ¾ cup chopped walnuts

Preheat the oven to 350 degrees.

In a large bowl, cream the butter and sugar until light. Beat the egg.

In a medium bowl, sift flour, baking soda, and salt.

Add flour to butter and sugar alternately with molasses. Add walnuts.

Drop the dough by teaspoonful on a parchment paper–lined cookie sheet 2 inches apart.

Bake for about 15 minutes.

Makes 4 dozen

I tested several almond cookie recipes, hunting for the perfect one, before choosing this as my 2009 cookie party contribution because of its robust almond taste and crunchy texture. My Dutch publisher had created darling tins, whose lids were embossed covers of my book, as a marketing tool and sent me some so I could nestle the cookies in those special containers. My friends and my readers loved this recipe.

Almond Cookies

2 ¾ cups all-purpose flour
1 ¼ cups sugar
½ teaspoon baking soda
½ teaspoon salt
½ cup (1 stick) unsalted butter
½ cup butter-flavored Crisco
3 eggs
3 teaspoons almond extract
60 blanched roasted almonds

To blanch almonds, put them in boiling water until the skins crinkle. You can test this by taking one out, running it under cool water, and seeing if the nut will easily pop from its skin. Drain the almonds and let cool. Remove the skins and roast the almonds until light brown. I roast them at 350°F and watch them very closely so they do not burn.

Preheat the oven to 325 degrees.

Mix the dry ingredients in a bowl. Cut in the butter and Crisco with a pastry knife until the mixture resembles cornmeal. Add two eggs and the almond extract and mix.

Roll the dough into one inch balls. The mixture is crumbly. Set the balls on a cookie sheet covered with parchment paper. Press one blanched and toasted almond on top and press down to flatten. Beat the final egg with a little water and brush on top of each cookie. Bake for 15 to 18 minutes. Cool. They are even yummier the next day. Makes 60 cookies

The following recipe also uses almonds, but the dough is easier to shape and mold because it is less crumbly than the one above. This is one of Marybeth's recipes, and they are so much fun to make as they give the baker a chance to be creative. You can try caramel instead of chocolate. Fill them with any kind of preserves you love. I tried raspberry and they were delicious!

Chocolate Thumbprints

Almond Cookie Dough

½ cup granulated sugar
½ teaspoon salt
¾ cup (4 ounces) whole almonds

1 ½ cups (3 sticks) unsalted butter, cut in large
    chunks and slightly softened
4 teaspoons pure vanilla extract
¼ teaspoon pure almond extract
3 cups (13 ½ ounces) bleached all-purpose flour

⅓ of a batch (10 ½ to 11 ounces or 1 ¼ cups)
    freshly made Almond Cookie dough (above)
¼ cup coarse sugar, such as turbinado, demer-
    ara, or sanding sugar
2 ½ ounce bittersweet or semisweet chocolate,
    coarsely chopped
5 teaspoons unsalted butter

Process the granulated sugar and salt in a food
processor until it looks powdery and a little
finer, 30 to 60 seconds. Add the almonds and
process until they are finely chopped, about
20 seconds. Add the butter and the vanilla
and almond extracts. Pulse until the butter is
smooth, scraping the bowl as necessary. Add
the flour and pulse until soft dough begins to
form around the blade. Transfer the dough
to a large bowl and stir briefly with a rubber
spatula to be sure it is evenly mixed. Portion
the dough into equal thirds. If you have a scale,
weigh each third; each should weigh 10 ½ to
11 ounces.

Make the thumbprints before chilling the dough. Scoop up a generous teaspoonful (2 level teaspoons) of the dough and shape it into a one-inch ball with your hands. Roll the ball in the coarse sugar and set it on a tray lined with waxed paper. Repeat with the rest of the dough, setting the balls slightly apart. Press a thumb or forefinger, dipped in flour, into each ball to create a depression. Cover and refrigerate the cookies for at least two hours, but preferably overnight.

Remove the cookies from the refrigerator and arrange them one inch apart on an ungreased or foil-lined cookie sheet. Position a rack in the center of the oven and heat the oven to 325 degrees. Let the cookies sit at room temperature while the oven heats. Bake the cookies for 10 minutes. Gently redefine the depressions with your thumb or the tip of a wooden spoon's handle, if necessary. Rotate the sheet and continue to bake until the tops are lightly colored and the bottoms are golden brown, another 8 to 12 minutes. Transfer the cookies to a rack and let cool completely.

While the cookies cool, prepare the filling. Put the chocolate and butter in a heatproof bowl set in a wide skillet of almost simmering water, or in the top of a double boiler.

(Or microwave on medium power for 1 to 2
minutes, stirring after the first minute.) When
the chocolate is almost completely melted,
remove the bowl from the heat and stir until
completely melted and smooth. Spoon the filling into each depression. If the filling hardens
while using, reheat it in the pan of hot water.
Yields about 24 cookies

My novel about the importance of friendships has
enlarged my own. I traded cookies for tales about the
importance of cookie clubs to their members. In South
Carolina, a cookie exchange is in its thirtieth year and includes grandchildren of the original members. A mother,
now using a walker, asked her daughter to obtain a signed
book for her at my reading in St. Joseph, Michigan. Fans,
inspired to start their own cookie club, showed me pictures of smiling partiers, told me wonderful stories, and
handed me many recipes.

Through Facebook, Twitter, and the blog on my own
webpage, I learned about clubs baking cookies for the
troops in Iraq and Afghanistan, and churches in Chicago committed to donating fresh cookies to the homeless, echoing our club's donation of cookies to charity.
Cookie exchanges posted photos on my Facebook wall
and exchanged recipes. In 2010, I had a cookie contest on
my Facebook fan page and received enough wonderful
recipes for many more years of cookie parties! I asked my
readers to vote for their favorites and here, from Florida,
Missouri, and North Carolina, are the prizewinning reci-

pes in three different categories, presented in their own words:

The Yummiest: La Quinta Blackmon's Chunky Peanut Butter Cookies

1 cup (2 sticks) unsalted butter, softened
2 cups all-purpose flour
1 teaspoon vanilla
1 cup pecans, chopped
2 cups peanut butter
2 eggs
1 cup brown sugar

Preheat the oven to 350 degrees.

In a large bowl, mix all ingredients until smooth.

Scoop the dough onto ungreased cookie sheets (I use a small ice cream scoop). Bake until brown.

This makes a lot.

The Most Creative: Ina Esquivel Konieczny's Semi-Homemade Chocolate Cookies

These are easy to make, no mess, and everyone loves them!

> 1 box devil's food cake mix
> 2 large eggs
> 1 teaspoon vanilla
> ½ cup (1 stick) butter, softened
> 1 12-ounce package white chocolate chips or peanut butter chips

Place a rack in the center of the oven and preheat the oven to 350 degrees. Line cookie sheets with parchment paper or use ungreased cookie sheets.

Mix first 4 ingredients until moistened. Cookie dough will be thick. Fold in chips until well distributed.

Drop heaping teaspoons of the dough 2 inches apart on prepared cookie sheets. Bake for 10 to 12 minutes or until cookies have set but are still a little soft in the center. Remove pans from the oven. Let cookies rest on the cookie sheets for about 1 minute. Remove cookies from the sheets with a metal spatula and transfer to wire racks to cool.

The Most Traditional: Paula Broshar's Old Fashioned Gingerbread Cookies

1 teaspoon baking soda

¼ cup hot water

4 ½ cup sifted all-purpose flour

2 teaspoons ginger

2 teaspoons cinnamon

½ teaspoon salt

1 cup shortening (vegetable oil, butter, or mixed)

1 cup brown sugar, packed

1 egg

1 cup molasses

¾ cup cold black coffee

In a small bowl, dissolve soda in hot water and set aside to cool.

In a large bowl, mix and sift together the flour, spices, and salt.

In a large bowl, cream the shortening and sugar until light and fluffy. Stir in egg. Mix well. Add molasses. Mix well. Add sifted dry ingredients alternately with coffee, beating well after each addition.

Stir in baking soda and water mixture.

Refrigerate for dough 4 to 6 hours.

Preheat the oven to 350 degrees.

Using ⅓ of the dough at a time, roll out dough to ¼-inch thick and cut gingerbread

men or any cookie shape that you prefer.
Place on a cookie sheet and bake until golden.
Store in an airtight container. Freezes well.

LaQuinta, Ina, and Paula, I'm so glad you sent your favorites to us!! And that we could present them along with all the other great recipes, participate in the fun of a contest, and get bunches of new recipes. I put the three winners' names in a hat, picked one, and it was the gingerbread cookies I baked for the Christmas cookie club that year. Yes, I made thirteen dozen individually decorated and delicious gingerbread girls and posted pictures on my fan page. The advent of social media has allowed me to be much closer to my readers and now I have windows into the lives of many new friends.

Sharing food is one of the oldest means of connecting with others, and I love seeing that it's just as powerful in our post-millennium, technological world. The ripples have spread not only in the United States, but throughout the world, emphasizing once again the smallness of our planet.

The Christmas Cookie Club was reviewed in Germany and the reviewer Tweeted me a link. I used Google to translate her review. The next morning, I happened to appear on TV and mentioned to the anchor this amazing event. She, too, was struck by the ease of connection across oceans and continents and brought it up on air. I sent a link to my German reviewer so she could see me talking about her on a U.S. TV program. And all this happened in less than 24 hours!

In North Adelaide, South Australia, a new cookie

club was inspired by the novel to bring cookies to their local hospice. The manager of the facility e-mailed me to say how thrilled her residents were by the prettily wrapped and very delicious cookies. "I cannot even begin to tell you the impact this had on our patients," she wrote. Wonderful how such marvelous ripples spread.

The twentieth gathering of my home cookie club was in 2010. *The Christmas Cookie Cookbook: All the Rules and Delicious Recipes to Start Your Own Holiday Club* had hit the stands two months previously, and Marybeth was ready for our party, with appetizers waiting for our friends.

Because man cannot live by cookie alone, we always like to have some savory snacks on hand as well. Here are a few of my favorites from our cookbook.

Brie en Croûte

> 1 sheet frozen puff pastry
> 1 tablespoon unsalted butter
> ½ cup walnuts or pecans
> ⅛ teaspoon ground cinnamon
> 1 8-ounce wheel Brie
> ¼ cup brown sugar
> 1 egg, beaten

Preheat oven to 375 degrees.

Defrost puff pastry for 15 to 20 minutes and unfold.

In a saucepan, melt butter over medium heat. Sauté pecans/walnuts in the butter until golden brown, approximately 5 minutes. Add the cinnamon and stir until nuts are coated well. Place the nut mixture on top of the Brie and sprinkle brown sugar over the mixture. Lay the puff pastry on a flat surface and place Brie in the center. Gather up the edges of the pastry and press around the Brie, gathering it at the top. Gently squeeze together excess dough and tie together with a piece of kitchen twine. Brush the beaten egg over top and sides of the Brie. Place the Brie on a cookie sheet and bake for 20 minutes, until the pastry is golden brown.

Serve with a fresh, sliced baguette.

To give it a special look, cut extra pastry into heart or flower shapes, bake until golden brown, and place around edges of the Brie.

THE TANGY BITE of ginger cuts through the rich sweetness of carrot in this comforting and delicious soup. This wonderful recipe can be made vegetarian by substituting vegetable stock for the chicken broth. Roasting vegetables brings out their natural sugars and intensifies flavors. By baking all the ingredients together, you'll get the best-tasting soup.

Roasted Carrot Ginger Soup

1 ½ pounds carrots, peeled and halved lengthwise

1 pound parsnips, peeled and quartered lengthwise

1 large onion, sliced

3-inch piece fresh ginger, peeled and chopped

6 tablespoons unsalted butter

3 tablespoons packed dark brown sugar

8 cups rich chicken broth, more if needed

Salt to taste

Pinch of cayenne pepper

¼ cup crème fraîche for garnish

Snipped fresh chives for garnish

Preheat the oven to 350 degrees. Combine the carrots, parsnips, onion, and ginger in a shallow roasting pan. Dot with butter and sprinkle with brown sugar. Pour two cups of the broth into the pan. Cover well and bake until the vegetables are very tender, about 2 hours.

Transfer the vegetables and broth to a large soup pot. Add the remaining six cups of broth. Season with salt and cayenne pepper. Bring to a boil, reduce heat, and simmer partially covered for 10 minutes.

Purée the soup in a food processor, adding more broth if desired. Serve portions with a teaspoon of crème fraîche, and sprinkle with chives. Serves 10.

THIS SALAD IS a wonderful palate cleanser before we settle down to the serious work of dessert and storytelling. The cinnamon, toasted nuts, and even the red and green lettuces all say "Christmas" to me!

Mandarin Orange Salad

11-ounce can mandarin orange segments, drained
1 tablespoon honey
Cinnamon
Handful of walnuts (broken into large pieces)
Lettuce (romaine, red or green leaf or mixed)
Extra-virgin olive oil
Salt and pepper, to taste

Place the mandarin oranges in a small bowl. Add honey and sprinkle with cinnamon. Set aside for several hours (or longer).

Toast walnuts at 350° for 3 minutes, and let them cool.

Wash and tear lettuce into bite-size pieces. Add oranges. Add enough olive oil to wet greens and toss well. Sprinkle with a little salt and pepper and sprinkle with walnuts.

Note: If taking to a potluck, wait to toss with olive oil and keep walnuts in a small bag until ready to serve.

The flavor of oranges, cinnamon, and honey makes this recipe a perennial favorite in the dead of winter. I am repeatedly asked to bring this salad and it is extremely easy to make.

Mandarin Orange Salad and gingerbread cookies in hand, I walked into Marybeth's house in its customary Christmas club dress: lights twinkling, candles glowing, her table laden with plates of veggies and fruit, cheese and crackers, shrimp and sushi. Carrot soup simmered on the stove, the Brie en croûte was already half devoured. I placed the salad on the table. Marybeth and I planned to surprise all of the members with copies of our cookbook—but I soon discovered I had a surprise of my own.

In the living room was a new guest, a woman who resembled my friend Daphne in facial structure, smile, and aura. I was astounded to learn that this woman was my surprise: Daphne's long-lost sister, Melanie! A fantastic chain of events had resulted in this miracle. I used parts of Daphne's life in my character Charlene, and thanked her in the acknowledgments. Melanie's book club picked the novel as their selection. When she came to the acknowledgments she saw her sister's name, now hyphenated. Meanwhile, a reporter mentioned Daphne's name in an article and Melanie, who had searched for Daphne every holiday season, was at last able to find her on the Internet. Melanie reached one of her and Daphne's relatives, who passed her Melanie's number.

Melanie was driving when her cell phone rang. She immediately recognized Daphne's voice. Within minutes, the two were bawling, as Melanie described how losing Daphne meant living with an ache in her heart while Daphne spent her adult life aware she had siblings, but unable to find them. Each of them, one in New York State, the other in Oklahoma, pulled to the shoulder of their respective highways and talked and cried. My novel had reunited these two sisters after twenty-five years of separation, and tonight Melanie was here to enjoy the party and rejoice at being with her sister.

Since then, they've talked often, healing the quarter-century absence. They delighted in family reunions in New York and Texas, and now, with their children, in Michigan, where the entire cookie club witnessed their glorious sisterhood. Melanie presented me a framed picture of them hugging and grinning from ear to ear. "Thank you for making this possible, Ann. Without knowing it, you've reunited a family," Melanie said as she looked around Marybeth's twinkling living room. "And this is where it all started. Thank goodness for Christmas cookie clubs." Daphne said to me, "Your book reunited a family—amazing how things work. It's the mystery of life that's so wonderful and oftentimes overlooked. This is a Christmas miracle that came from a lovely Christmas book." Of all the wonderful things that have happened as a result of the novel, the fact that I was able to help a dear friend find her sister is at the top.

Of course, we have to end with sweets, and what better than those perennial holiday staples chocolate, toffee, and my personal favorite, nuts? Our cookie club allows and encourages candy, and I wanted to share some of my favorite recipes with you.

English Toffee

> 2 cups unsalted butter
> 2 cups sugar
> 2 tablespoons light corn syrup
> ⅓ cup water
> 11½ ounces milk chocolate chips
> 1 cup finely chopped, toasted nuts (almonds, pecans, or walnuts)

Line a 15x10x1-inch pan with foil, extending over the edges. In a 3-quart saucepan, melt the butter then stir in the sugar, corn syrup, and water. Cook over medium-high heat to boiling, stirring until the sugar is dissolved. Using a candy thermometer, cook over medium heat to soft crack (290 degrees—about

15 minutes. Soft crack is between 270 degrees and 290 degrees, and for this recipe I have found it best to stay at the higher temperature. At 270 degrees the toffee was too chewy and it will stick to your teeth!). Pour into prepared pan and spread evenly. Cool five minutes or until top is just set.

Sprinkle chocolate onto toffee. Spread evenly and top with nuts. Press the nuts into the chocolate and let cool for several hours. If necessary, place in the fridge.

Holding foil, lift candy out of pan. Break into pieces. To store, layer candy into airtight containers between sheets of waxed paper.

Marybeth made these for the cookie club in 2010 and I loved them.

Sugared Nuts

> 3 cups nuts (peanuts, whole almonds, pecan halves, etc.)
> 1 cup sugar
> ½ cup water

Preheat oven to 300 degrees.

In a 12-inch skillet over medium heat, bring

nuts, sugar, and water to a boil. Cook, stirring occasionally, until syrup has caramelized and the nuts are well coated, about 12 to 15 minutes.

Immediately spread coated nuts onto buttered large baking sheet. Bake for 10 minutes; stir. Bake 10 minutes more; stir. Cool on rack. Store in airtight container. Makes 4 cups

*For cinnamon sugared nuts: add ½ teaspoon ground cinnamon with sugar.

Truffles without Trouble

Basic Chocolate Recipe

> 20 ounces semisweet chocolate chips
> 2 tablespoons unsalted butter, softened
> 1 cup heavy cream

Make the Filling: Place 8 ounces of the chocolate chips and the butter in a large bowl. In a small saucepan over low heat, bring the cream to a simmer. Remove from heat and pour half the cream into the bowl. As the chocolate melts, slowly whisk the mixture together until smooth. Then gradually add the remaining cream until it is completely incorporated and is thick and shiny.

Form the Truffles: Pour the mixture into a 2-inch-deep baking pan, spread evenly, and place in the freezer for 30 minutes or until set (it should have the consistency of fudge). Using a melon baller or a small spoon, form rounds and place them on a baking sheet lined with parchment or wax paper. Let the truffles harden in the freezer for about 15 minutes. After removing from the freezer, roll truffles between your hands into marble-size spheres, squeezing slightly (try to do this quickly, otherwise they will become too soft). You can now dust the truffles with cocoa and serve them as is, but they will hold their shape better if you coat them with chocolate first.

Make the Coating: Place truffles in freezer while you make the chocolate glaze. Place the remaining 12 ounces of chocolate chips in a large bowl over a saucepan of simmering water and stir occasionally, until the chocolate is completely melted. Remove from heat and let cool at room temperature, stirring occasionally until the chocolate starts to set. Drop the truffles into the melted chocolate and retrieve them with a fork and hold until excess chocolate to drips off. Garnish immediately

Garnish: For a nut garnish, roll the freshly coated truffles in a shallow dish of chopped nuts. For a sugar or cocoa garnish, set the freshly coated truffles on a plate and sift the garnish over them. Turn the truffles and sift again to cover completely.

Storage: Place the truffles on the lined baking sheet and allow them to set in the refrigerator for five minutes. Truffles will keep for about two weeks, chilled or at room temperature, when stored in a tightly sealed container.

Peanut Butter Truffles

    1 cup peanut butter, chunky or creamy
    4 tablespoons unsalted butter, softened
    12 ounces semisweet chocolate, cut into small pieces (or semisweet chocolate chips)
    1 cup cocoa powder

In a large bowl, mix the peanut butter and butter well. Chill the peanut butter filling,

form the truffles, and coat them following
steps from the Basic Recipe.

The experience of *The Christmas Cookie Club*, born
from my appreciation and enjoyment of my great friends,
has broadened my circle beyond anything I imagined.
Friends and food can be honored in a thousand ways.
Cookie clubs are an expanding phenomenon and ritual
that unites us in celebration and generosity to our com-
munities. Our winter lessons can be carried with us. So
throughout the year, please, enjoy and honor the food
you cook, and the people who surround you.

Acknowledgments

*T*HERE REALLY IS A Christmas cookie club and I was the cookie virgin in 2000 and have been a member ever since. Even though there are twelve women who meet every year, the women described in these pages are not them. As far as I know, none of us has had a secret extramarital affair for more than a decade, or has a friend making love with her father, or has a home in foreclosure. We've had babies, adopted babies, moved out of town, had much younger lovers, been cheated on, gotten married and divorced, struggled with financial issues, been single moms, recovered from our parents' death, from our own cancer. Yes, seven out of twelve of us have survived cancer. Amazing!! Terrifying!!

There is a head cookie bitch, Marybeth Bayer, who started the cookie club. Her unbelievable social and organizational skills as well as her terrific hostessing and cooking are the soul of our club and the inspiration not only for the setting of this book but for other aspects of my life. The rules for this club are rules she devised and every year she keeps us anticipating the party as one of the highlights of the holiday season and the entire year. We start joking and thinking of our recipes and packaging at the height of summer. Really! I borrowed her brilliant white hair and blue eyes for Marnie as well as her home, which I envisioned for this fictional cookie party as it is for our actual one. Charlene is based on a real woman, Daphne Mead-Derbyshire, whose loving and peaceful spirit in spite of trauma is an example to us all. The real Charlene used the gift of her son's death to become an ordained interfaith minister. Tracy's email message was actually written by Karin Blazier and so captured her happy, funny spirit that I couldn't resist borrowing it as well as her penchant for using a lipstick kiss as her signature. Each one of us is amazing; luckily, some of us have not been tried as much as others to learn our own mettle.

Some of the incidents here are true; for example, one of us really did the stand-up comedy routine about the nuts. We really do give one-thirteenth of our labor to charity and for over a decade it has been a hospice. We're aware that giving to others is another way to give to ourselves. Especially in these times, generosity, one another, and an optimistic spirit will get us through.

The cookie recipes have been used in our club. And we have at least a hundred more. Yes, we repeat our favorite recipes. The recipes in this book were culled from grandmothers, friends, clients, the Internet, or various cookbooks and magazines too long ago to be remembered.

Writing about the various ingredients was inspired partly by Zingerman's Roadhouse and my daughters who worked there. My daughter Melina Hinton discussed the production of produce and meats, and increased my awareness of food production methods and animal care. At the encouragement of Ari Weinzweig, my daughter Elizabeth Hinton wrote the story of African American cooking during Reconstruction by following two cooks' lives. Recipes from their cookbooks and the tale of their lives were presented at a dinner that reminded me of the motivation of food as a determiner of our culture and evolution. After all, from the plants' point of view, if they have one, it's all about reproduction. And from ours, it's all about staying alive combined with our great lust for variety and pleasure, both responsible for the fact that we're able to walk into a grocery store and buy food that was native to far-flung parts of the world. Each food I studied pulled out a whole stream of history and provided a window into the forces and events that provoked our civilization and culture. After all, it was the cultivation of wheat that made settlements possible, and our lust for cinnamon that led to the discovery of the New World, and our addiction to sugar that was made possible only through slavery, crucial for the United States to be the great diverse country it is.

I need to acknowledge several books that I used: Bruce D. Smith's *The Emergence of Agriculture*; Richard Manning's *Against the Grain*; Jared Diamond's *Guns, Germs, and Steel*; *The Oxford Companion to Food*, Alan Davidson; and *The Cambridge World History of Food*, Kenneth F. Kiple and Kriemhild Coneè Ornelas. Natalie Angier's *Woman: an Intimate Geography* and Sarah Blaffer Hrdy's *Mother Nature: A History of Mothers, Infants, and Natural Selection* were helpful in honing my understanding of the importance of grandmothers to human evolution.

And this book would not have been written quite this way without Ruth Behar, Elizabeth Hinton, and Tim

Kornegay. Tim wrote the rap lyrics that Special Intent sang; particular gratitude to you, Tim, as well as thanks for your suggestions on the entire manuscript. Good lookin' out! Special thanks also to Ruth who read this, sometimes with only a few hours notice, as each chapter was finished. And Elizabeth, your ideas are here from the beginning, thanks again for reading this over your winter break. Kieron Hales, sous chef extraordinaire, helped me perfect the fortune cookie recipe while Bev Pearlman and Gail Farley made suggestions that are incorporated, and Mike De Simone and Jeff Jenssen graciously tested each recipe. Thanks so much. All their support, criticisms, love, and friendship were invaluable.

I can't thank Friday Jones enough for introducing me to Peter Miller and his staff, Amina Henry and Adrienne Rosado, who pushed me to finish this and then found a fabulous home for the book. The team at Atria Books, Emily Bestler, who honed the prose, and Judith Curr, Louise Burke, Carolyn Reidy, and Laura Stern, worked to create a launch that was smooth as silk.

And of course, to the cookie bitches who supported and encouraged and were excited for me as I wrote.

Yay to us!!!

the
Christmas Cookie Club

Ann Pearlman

A Readers Group Guide

QUESTIONS AND TOPICS FOR DISCUSSION

1. How does the present action of the narrative, as well as the way details are revealed about characters, affect your reading of the novel? In what ways does the story draw the reader in as a new member of the group?

2. As Marnie says, "The people in our lives change as our understanding changes." (p. 223) How does each character in the novel change for you as you learn more about them? How does Aaron change for Marnie after hearing Sissy's story?

3. How does the opening of *The Christmas Cookie Club* establish the themes of darkness and light that run through the novel? How do you feel about the choice of the hospice as the recipient of the group's generosity? Why do you think Marnie is so especially attuned to the pain her friends suffer and brave in facing the starkness of events such as Luke's death?

4. Marnie wonders, "Is Jim another chance for intimacy . . . or another dodge from commitment?" (p. 24) Why do you think Marnie is so conflicted about moving forward in her relationship with Jim? What gives her the courage to tell him that she loves him?

5. The book highlights the social histories of baking ingredients such as vanilla, sugar, and dates. Was there anything you learned that surprised you? Marnie also mentions her personal associations with these

common items. What are your associations with these ingredients and others in your kitchen?

6. Thinking about Rosie's quest for children, Marnie wonders, "When I see a friend heading down a difficult road, how much do I confront, and how much do I accept knowing I'll be there to pick up the pieces?" (p. 79) What do you think is the best approach to friendship: honest advice or unquestioning support? How do you think Marnie is able to stay so nonjudgmental when it comes to her friends' tangled lives?

7. "The past gets carried with us. It's always there," according to Marnie. (p. 252) How is the past evident in the current lives of the characters? For example, how does the past affect Marnie's relationship with her daughters and with Jim? How does Juliet's high school façade help to create a long-term double life?

8. Rosie confronts Jeannie by asking if Jeannie had told her mother about her father's infidelity. Do you think the situations are comparable—a friend hiding another friend's betrayal and a daughter hiding her father's? How are the two friends able to reconcile over the course of the party?

9. While all of Charlene's friends are supportive and healing in different ways, how is it that Sissy, the cookie virgin, is able to best advise her on a path forward? How can an outsider sometimes better see a person for who they are in the moment?

10. Marnie describes "the season's thrill" (p. 84) of the holidays in terms of the warmth and excitement that

her friends bring to the cookie club. What are the key elements that form the holidays for you?

ENHANCE YOUR BOOK CLUB

1. Turn your book club into a cookie club! Divide up the recipes in *The Christmas Cookie Club* and share them according to the rules of the group.

2. Compare the group of friends in the novel to your book club. Get closer by sharing stories about how everyone in your group first met.

3. Jeannie fills her fortune cookies with sayings drawn from her yoga practice and lifestyle. Come up with your own fortunes, or compare favorite fortunes you've received over the years.

4. Interested in learning more about the ingredients described in *The Christmas Cookie Club*? Check out one of the books Pearlman used, such as *The Cambridge World History of Food* and share your findings with the group.

A CONVERSATION WITH ANN PEARLMAN

What inspired you to write this novel, your first work of fiction?

I've been working on fiction for some years, and a few of my short stories have won literary awards. I imagined this novel in 2000 when I first attended a cookie exchange and realized it would be a fabulous setting for a story about a party and the importance of women's friendships. I set it aside to write a nonfiction book. And when I got back to it, I wrote it with a complete sense of joy.

How different was the process of writing *The Christmas Cookie Club* from that of your nonfiction works?

You invent the characters and story when you write a novel. With nonfiction, I do a lot of research either to make sure my memory is correct or to gather information for added texture. In biography, there's an attempt to see the world from another person's eyes. So nonfiction contains more circling back. I use fictive techniques (dialogue, scene setting, etc.) in both.

Which do you prefer?

I like both. I particularly enjoy writing (and reading) books in which actual people, events, or places are mixed in with the fictional. Thus, I used Ann Arbor and its stores, restaurants, parks, and events as settings for scenes in *The Christmas Cookie Club*.

How did you choose the cookie recipes to include? Do they have a special meaning for you?

I chose my favorites. The pecan butter balls have special meaning because that is my grandmother's recipe and I remember baking them with her. A girlfriend mentioned that almost all of them contain nuts. I love nuts. I also picked cookies that carry the plot forward. The fortune cookies are an example of this and Allie's Hanukkah cookies and Ramadan cookies.

You mention that some characters were based on real women from your cookie club. How close are your depictions to your friends and how much of the characterizations came from your imagination?

The acknowledgments detail exactly what I borrowed from my real friends. For example, Marybeth (who is the hostess of the cookie party) does have gorgeous white hair but no daughters. I imagined all the rest.

Is there a character that you yourself particularly identify with in the novel?

I think I'm most like Allie, but my kids laugh when I say that and tell me there are elements of me in all the characters. That makes enormous sense to me because I think the narrative dream is similar to any other dream, and the characters are projections of various aspects of the writer/dreamer's unconscious. And so we all cannibalize our own lives, fantasies, and interests as we write. I do yoga, for example.

Infidelity is one of the recurring elements in the lives of your characters in *The Christmas Cookie*

Club. How has your own experience, as well as the experience of writing *Infidelity: A Love Story,* affected your perspective on how marital betrayal affects others?

I'm aware of how very common and how very scarring infidelity is both in my own life and the lives of people I know. Most marriages will struggle with it and it's implicated in the majority of divorces. I'm aware of what a challenge it presents to the couple and how much the entire family is impacted.

How do you think your writing is affected by your work as a psychotherapist?

I read somewhere that writers and therapists are very similar. The difference is that therapists believe they can help people change. As a therapist I am involved in transformation and am continually impressed with resilience and people's eagerness for life and happiness. What helps people to have the courage to change and the determination to struggle is a fascinating topic to me. The gift of being a therapist is that we hear and witness lives and histories. We see the elements and the stories that coalesce to form personality. I understand the complications of people's lives. It seems to me, none of us get out unscathed. All of us have problems at some point, and it's how we survive, interpret, and deal with them that define us. That struggle, along with my interest in transformation and maintaining joy in life, is a major theme in my books.

Are there any authors who have been inspirational to your work? Do you have any suggestions for future book club picks?

E. L. Doctorow because he was the first person to mix the real with the imagined. Truman Capote for using fictive techniques in nonfiction and changing the face of nonfiction. Jodi Picoult because you fall in love with her characters even though they're flawed, and you can't stop reading. Philip Roth because of his examination of sexuality and his amazing growth in his perception and understanding and portrayal of America. Margaret Atwood because of her interweaving of story and politics.

Do you have any advice for aspiring novelists hoping to also draw from real life experiences?

We're told to write what we know and we know our own lives best, yet distilling what the *story* is in our lives that may be interesting to others is not easy. So much of what we experience is exquisite because it's ours: our baby's first smile, falling in love, the death of a dear friend. Making that particular have universal appeal requires digging deep and ferreting telling detail and language.

Can you tell us about any other projects?

Marybeth Bayer and I recently finished writing *The Christmas Cookie Cookbook*, a workbook chock full of recipes and ideas for cookie exchanges. It was published in November 2010. I'm writing *A Gift for My Sister*, the sequel to *The Christmas Cookie Club*. Sky and Tara are the main characters; it's been a joy to write.

Want to know what happens next?

Read on for a sneak peek at Sky and Tara's story, the
next heartfelt novel from Ann Pearlman

A Gift for My Sister

Coming from Atria Books in Spring 2012

Sky

*E*VERY DAY WE WALK a razor thin line between
the ordinary and the tragic.

That thought bolts me awake.

3:42. The green numbers on my clock blare. The
rest of the room is dark. The numbers are a beacon in
the black. Why do I wake at the same exact time every
morning? 3:42. As though Mia's death had implanted an
internal alarm.

Troy is curled around his folded hands.

No sounds come from Rachel's room.

The air-conditioning snaps on.

Some of us tiptoe anxious about chasms on either side of the path we walk and some of us skip along ignoring them. And me? I thought if I walked a direct line with a firm destination in view, fulfilling each goal along the way, I'd be safe. Having a safety net was my plan to thwart lurking misfortune.

I felt as though it were my father's fault for dying. What else does a child think when parents seem all powerful?

My father's death came at me from out of the blue like a peculiar and deadly snap of the fingers. One day he pulled me high on the swing, his arms stretched so I was above his head, singing, "Fly, Sky. Fly," and pushed hard so I could reach for a cloud with my toes. I saw the glint of the sun on his hair, the flash of red and yellow leaves in trees blurred by my speed. Or have I nourished it so much, this last memory of my still-healthy father, that I added the trees I know so well from the park, when all there was, really, was the sight of the sky and the feel of the wind licking me as I soared?

The next day, he entered the hospital.

A week later, he was dead.

I was seven.

He was thirty-four.

Mom tried to explain that he was around me, and loving me. I watched her tongue tap her teeth and her lips move, but it didn't make sense then.

It still doesn't.

I was the only child in my class whose father was dead. The other kids ignored me as though it were contagious. I was the only kid I knew with a dead father until my freshman year of high school. Then, a kid's dad died from a heart attack. He was absent from my algebra class for a week, which had the other kids whispering, and when he returned, he laughed at a joke as though things were ordinary. I knew that game because even as a seven-year-old I had played it. If you pretend things are ordinary, maybe for a few minutes they will be. And sometimes, sometimes, and this is both scary and exhilarating, it works.

And for a few minutes you forget you have a dead father. 3:45.

Anyway, I digress. I don't know why I think about him every morning. I guess because his death was a startling change that twirled my life so it skipped to another path. Some things happen suddenly, and some you know are coming. Like death from cancer after a long battle. But for me, I didn't even get to prepare myself, I didn't have the time to be scared. It just happened.

Bang.

I wonder how my life would have been different if my father had lived.

Number one way: Tara wouldn't be my sister.

I'd probably have a different sister. Or a brother.

Tara was an embarrassing kid and then a rebellious teenager. She was so different from me. I guess that partly comes from having different fathers.

But what I really wonder about is Troy. I met Troy in eighth grade and we've been inseparable ever since. I read somewhere that girls without fathers are often sexual early and are promiscuous to fill a yearning for a man in their lives. I guess I was sexual early, but I've only been with one man. Troy. My best friend, soul mate, husband, and finally, at last, father of my baby.

I say at last because Troy and I, so perfect for each other, are actually even genetic matches. As a result, each conception has a fifty percent chance of a deadly genetic disease, which led to three miscarriages and a stillbirth. A lot of deaths. I would have traded everything for a healthy baby. Just please God, give me a healthy baby. Please. I begged as if you can make bargains with the future. I imagined parts of me I'd exchange, aspects of my life I'd cast away.

My pleas were answered. And I hadn't lost anything. Because then, finally, there was Rachel in spite of it all. Rachel with my father's gray eyes as though a piece of him were a part of her. I look in her eyes and see him loving and watching me. Just like Mom promised. His eyes and the rasp of his beard are my most vivid memories, and sometimes, just sometimes, Troy's face feels almost the same, but more gentle.

4:15.

Count your blessings. Troy turns toward me, pulling me to him, spooning me. I turn to him and, in the vague light from the window, I see his eyes shift and know he's dreaming. Soon, I'll hear the creak of Rachel's springs as she stands in her crib, holds on to the rails and begins bouncing and calling, "Mommymommymommymommy. Daddydaddydaddydaddy."

Since Mia died, I wake up early and try to make sense of it. The digital green lights flash on the clock. The house is quiet, as though I can figure out the answer to some question I haven't asked in Troy's and Rachel's systematic breathing.

I'm okay. Troy's okay. Rachel's okay. I'm sad. That's all. Life is unfair. So unfair.

But everyone knows that.

Lawyers especially. That's what we try to do, that's our mission. To make life fair. To even the playing field. To redress grievances.

THIS IS WHAT HAPPENED: Mia was my closest girl friend, my BFF. We met in a tort study group at law school. She tried to get pregnant and I tried not to have dead babies. We struggled over case law and fertility and trained for a breast cancer marathon together. Troy and I and she and Marc, her husband, went camping in the Rocky Mountains and gambling in Las Vegas. We talked about opening up a law firm together. Then she took drugs to stimulate ovulation and developed a cyst. While they were removing the cyst, she had a reaction to the anesthetic and went into a coma. She was brain dead. We watched appliances force air, and drip fluids and nutrients into her arms.

Four days later, Marc unplugged her equipment. We held each other's hands and cried.

There was an eerie silence when the machines stopped their breathing.

A lazy echo in the room. Then Mia was no more.

Twenty-six and dead.

That's worse than thirty-four.

That was two and a half weeks ago.

Since then, I wake up with a bolt and try to figure it all out.

4:30.

Why does my life revolve around tragedy when I have so many blessings? Rachel. Troy. A job that I love. A boss who allows me to work part-time until Rachel is in pre-school full-time.

When genetic testing results on Rachel were okay, I asked Mia, "You're not going to be so sad about this for yourself that we won't be friends anymore, are you?"

We had just finished running five miles on the beach. I was already slow from the extra weight of the pregnancy, and we were both breathless. She said, "I wish it were me, but if not me, I'm glad it's you." It was California winter. Not quite so many flowers. The impatiens sparse and pale. We had run along the beach, the breeze keeping us cool, and now we were walking through a marina that reflected the cloudless sky and a few palm trees.

"We can share her. You can come over anytime for a baby fix."

"I'll catch up to you. In a few months, these new drugs will work and we'll be pushing strollers while we run." I thought, *Tara's baby is six months older than Rachel, Mia's might be six months younger.* I like symmetry. That was more than two years ago.

It didn't work out that way.

A week ago, Rachel jumped in a swimming pool for the first time and I reached for the phone to call Mia.

Then I remembered she was dead, and my arm fell limply to my side. I saw a woman in Nordstroms with hair streaked like hers and I called, "Mia." And then blushed, embarrassed.

I miss her selfishly. I miss that she's not here for me.

But, mostly, I just miss her. It's as though I'm *her* missing her life. I try to explain it but even Troy looks at me blankly. I feel sad like I know Mia would feel at not getting to live the rest of her own life. But she doesn't know. She doesn't even know she died. I mourn Mia as though I'm Mia mourning her own life. There. Does that say it? I mourn the loss of her years with Marc, the unborn babies, the fascinating cases she'll never try, the great books she never read, the glorious food she didn't get to eat, the places she never visited, the love not made. All of it.

My thoughts ramble and always come back to this point. How unfair it is for her.

4:45.

And then I fall asleep.

"Mommymommymommymommy," Rachel calls.

6:01.

Rachel's arms are stretched for me to pick her up. She jumps up and down in her crib, her mouth open, laughing at the sight of me. I feel the sweetness of baby warmth as I inhale her aroma. Her hair, so silky and fine, tickles my cheek.

I hug her tight to me, so tight, as though I can squeeze extra life into her and protect her from all harm.

"I love you, Mommy," she says. "Eat granola?"

"Sure. With cherries and walnuts in it."

"Yipppeeee."

I stand her on her changing table and unbutton the crotch of her PJs. "Think you're old enough for big girl panties? Like Mommy wears? Want to try them?"

"Like Mommy?"

"Just like Mommy." We've been preparing for this day, and she's gone in her potty a few times.

"Yeah." Her eyes widen and I reach down to the shelf and grab the pull-ups that have been waiting for her. I put them on her and lift her from the changing table.

"Okay. Let's see you pull them down." I know she can do this and she does.

"See, Mommy, no problem."

"Okay, so when you have to go, tell Mommy and I'll help you. Or just go on your own."

"Eat now?"

She always wakes up starved. I carry her potty to the dining room with us. She walks down the stairs one foot at a time, holding on to the railing. Rachel thinks about each step before she makes it. Jumping into the swimming pool into my waiting arms was uncharacteristic of her, as she is usually so cautious.

"You're my little mermaid," I said, laughing.

I make my own granola, roasting oatmeal with flax seed, wheat germ, sunflower seeds drizzled with honey, or maple syrup, and cinnamon, mixed with water. Sometimes I add almond extract. Sometimes I add vanilla. I stir it every ten minutes for forty minutes while it roasts at 300. Before I eat it, I toss in fruits and nuts. I add chopped walnuts and cherries to Rachel's bowl and then milk. On mine, I sprinkle slivered crystallized ginger and almonds.

I'm almost out of cherries and almonds. I add them to the grocery list in my iPhone notes. The note says: dishwashing detergent, eggs, coffee, fabric softener, olive oil, cherries, almonds.

I hear Troy taking a shower.

Rachel delicately picks out the cherries and walnuts, one at a time. She places one in her mouth, concentrating as she consumes the flavor.

I take the opportunity to run upstairs and steal a few minutes with Troy. He's just out of the shower, drying off. He looks up, surprised to see me.

I grab another towel from the rack and begin dabbing his back, slicked with water coursing around the bumps in his spine. When his back is dry, I stand on my tiptoes to kiss his shoulder. He turns me around and holds me close, his body warm and moist against me. The steamed mirror exposes a foggy image of us pressed together. Me in blue shorts and a yellow tee shirt, and his pinkish, beige length, the brown of his hair, like Rachel's, fragments of colors blurred by condensation. He's all one beautiful length and I fill with warmth every time I see him.

He gives me a kiss, slow and serious, enjoying the texture of my tongue and my lips. "I'll be home early tonight," he promises.

"I'll be here," I laugh.

I pull back to look at him, his face as dear and familiar as my own, as though he's my mirror, another version of me. I kiss his nose. One of his ears misses a piece at the tip, and his other ear has it. As though each ear is a puzzle of pieces that have been split. Rachel has that, too. I touch his ears, and circle the shell of each of them, like a nautilus. I shake my head slowly, aware having him in my life has been a miracle.

"Ah, darling," he says, and his eyes close. "Maybe tonight you could get a babysitter and we can just check into a motel. We can have the whole evening together."

"On this short notice?" I laugh.

"You've been so sad and preoccupied since Mia's death." He wraps his arms tightly around me.

"Still can't sleep." And then I notice a pimple, swollen and red, on his shoulder. "Hey. That looks painful." I point at it with my index finger.

He turns his head to see it, "It is. Been putting cortisone on it, but . . ." He shakes his head and shrugs.

"Might be turning into a boil. You want me to lance it?"

"Done that twice. I've had it for about two weeks." He turns his head toward the shoulder and glances at it in the mirror.

I lean closer. It's red with a pale yellowish top. Smaller bumps cluster around the edges, and the flesh around it is almost purple. "Since Mia's death?" I guess I haven't been paying attention. "Looks like a rash. Is it itchy?"

He shakes his head. "It used to look like a spider bite before I lanced it."

"How 'bout some antibiotic cream and a Band-Aid?"

"Tried that. And hydrogen peroxide, and iodine and mercurochrome."

I pull out a tube of triple antibiotic cream, twist off the lid. I wonder why he didn't say anything. I guess he hasn't wanted to bother me.

"I don't think it's a big deal. Just a pimple or insect bite." He shrugs. "When's everyone coming?"

"Next week. Mom and Allie arrive on Wednesday." I wash my hands.

"And when's the concert?"

"Saturday. Aaron's mom, Sissy, is coming Friday. Don't know when exactly Aaron and Tara and the rest of the band arrive."

"Crew. Rap bands are crews." He shakes his head, watching as I peel the paper protecting the bandage. "Imagine skinny hyper Tara a rap star."

"You still think of her as five. You're not fourteen anymore either. But they're not stars. This is just their first national tour." I smooth down the adhesive strips and rub the Band-Aid flat.

He winces.

"At least the pimple–boil–insect bite is covered."

"Larry says they're on their way." Larry is the entertainment attorney Troy and I introduced to Aaron. "That number seven single makes them practically stars. It's amazing that Tara and Aaron have pulled this off. Who'd have thought they'd still be together?"

The tenderness in his voice and his thrill at her success bothers me. "She used to have a crush on you."

"She helped me woo you." He rubs the mist from the mirror and combs his hair.

"Woo me? She wouldn't get off your lap whenever you came over. You were the only thing that distracted her from her obsession with music."

He pats the top of his head to get the few strands of his cowlick to lie flat. "That was because she wanted everything her older sister had. Besides, I didn't have the guts to ask you to sit on my lap. I hoped you might follow her lead. And eventually you did." He laughs.

Troy has forgotten what a difficult teenager Tara was, or maybe just forgiven her. Troy and I were just starting law school when Mom called late one night. It was three a.m. in Ann Arbor. "I don't know where your sister is," she said without even saying hello or asking how I was. "I've been frantic. I've called her cell a hundred times and it goes to voice mail. Texted over and over and over. I'm standing by the front door, looking out the window at every car that passes, hoping it'll stop and she'll get out."

"She's probably just at a party, hanging out with her friends."

"Probably getting high or drunk." Mom finished my thought. "I tell myself that, but I can't stop thinking about all the terrible things that could happen: She could have run away, or be in a car accident, in some hospital. Or worse. Dead. She could be drunk at a fraternity party. What if she gets gang raped."

"You know Tara. This is just Tara being Tara." I heard Mom's quick intake of air.

"She does what she wants with no concern for anyone but herself. Just like her father. Like he's come back to haunt me."

I didn't know what to say. But part of me was smugly pleased when Mom criticized Tara or her father.

"She's never been out this late without calling, even if it's with some lame excuse."

"Mom. She's probably just partying."

But Mom couldn't stop. "I tell her, 'Call and let me

know where you are, that you're okay. You have a cell phone,' but she doesn't even do that."

And then Tara walked in the door. "Mom. What are you doing up?" I heard her ask.

"Where the hell were you?"

"With *friends*!"

"I was worried." Mom stretched out "worried" so that Tara could sense her anxiety.

"I was fine." I could almost see Tara shrug.

"Why didn't you call?"

"I'm out of minutes, Mom. Why didn't you pay attention to my bill?"

Tara's voice was crisp. She wasn't screaming or angry. She was indifferent. That was it. A chilling indifference.

"I'm tired. Think I'll go to bed," Tara's voice got softer as she walked away from Mom.

"Well, she's home," Mom said to me.

"I heard."

"I'll talk to you tomorrow."

"She's just being a kid," Troy said that night, learning against the headboard reading a syllabus. "Tara works hard on her music. A nerd with a wild streak. She'll be okay. You watch."

By the time Tara was seventeen, she was pregnant. Piled on top of that was her boyfriend's prison time, for dealing drugs, their crazy dreams of rap stardom, and her refusal to get married. Now, four and a half years later, Aaron, Levy, and Sissy are part of our family. Mom and Sissy are friends. And in an ironic twist of fate, my wayward sister is on the road to being famous.

"YOUR T-SHIRT SEAM may be irritating that pimple. The Band-Aid should help."

"Hey. You want to play doctor with me?" Troy jokes, his cowlick stuck down for now.

"Mooooommmmyyyyyy," Rachel yells. "All gone!"

"Tonight." I wink and then take off down the stairs, to find Rachel's cereal bowl tipped over on the tray and the milk dribbling to the floor.

"Okay. Help me mop this up." I pull her from the high chair and hand her a paper towel. She squeezes milk and bits of granola on the floor and tries to make finger paintings in the glop. I quickly wipe away the mess, and hand her some spray cleaner, which she spritzes joyfully. Everything is fun to her.

Troy comes down soon after. "There's some granola," I offer.

"No time." He pours coffee and milk in a commuter cup and smears peanut butter and jelly on bread. "Gotta hit the traffic." He checks his watch, grabs his laptop, and kisses Rachel and me. At the door he turns, points a finger at me, and says, "Tonight." Turns to Rachel, "I'll see both of my beautiful ladies tonight."

The door kisses the jamb as it swings shut.

The sun slants in through a window and throws a rectangle on Rachel's hair, turning it into blazing spun gold.

I pick her up and swing her around. "The floor is clean and it's a beautiful day made just for us."

I can get through each day. It's the nights and early mornings that are hard. Maybe I've turned a corner. Maybe I've figured something out, but I don't know exactly what. The answers I look for each morning at 3:42 flicker in my head as if I know it, but can't recognize them.

"Hey. You wanna go to the potty?" I carry Rachel to her potty, and watch while she pulls down her pants and sits down.

I hand her a book and turn on the faucet. Don't know why, but Mom always did that and it seemed to encourage me to go.

Rachel's eyes get big. "I did it. I pee-peed in the potty!" She laughs, her little white teeth shining like pearls.

She stands up and points, her pull-ups sliding to her ankles. "I did it."

"You sure did," I say with disbelief. I take out the container to pour the urine down the toilet.

"You're going to throw it away? Throw my pee-pee away?" Rachel's eyes are wide, her mouth open in bald horror. How could I throw her amazing achievement away when just a moment ago we'd been so happy with it?

"We'll save it and show Daddy. Then you can put it in the toilet—how's that?"

Her smile returns.

LATER THAT AFTERNOON, before Troy gets home, before we have a chance to eat dinner, and talk about our day over a glass of wine, or sit on our balcony and watch the sea lap the sand, or finish the flirting that we started that morning, the telephone rings. It's Stuart, my mentor and one of the partners at my firm.

"Hey, I went over that case law for the Hanson case. Got decisions that'll búoy up our arguments," I tell him before he even says hello.

"Sky." His patient voice carries that tinge of bad news. My mind skitters to what it could be. We're being sued for malpractice? On one of the cases I worked on? Another member of the firm died?

"Sky, I have some, ah, unfortunate news."

"What?" I start pacing with the phone pressed to my ear. *Sesame Street* is on the TV and Rachel sits on the floor, teaching a line of stuffed animals.

"As you know, our billable hours have decreased and, really, I guess, we were able to let you work part-time because we didn't have much work, and now, well, we don't even have that. So we have to let you go." He pauses.

I know that they—the partners—are billing those hours for themselves, even though my fees are less than theirs.

"Please be reassured . . ."

I resent his formality, selfishly creating distance so that firing me is less painful for him.

"When things change we'll contact you, and if you're still available we would love to have you back. I'll help you find a position with another firm, though I wouldn't relish you being our competition." He forces a chuckle. "We're going to miss you." And then his voice warms, "I will miss you."

His words seem to echo. I replay them in my mind as soon as he says them. *We have to let you go. Please be reassured. Another position.* I'm trying to integrate them. "I loved the work. And I love working with you." I shouldn't have said that.

He sighs. "This is difficult for me, for all of us."

For a minute there's silence on the phone while I consider my options. Maybe I should start my own firm. If Mia were still alive, I would. Maybe Troy and I could start a firm, but we need the consistent paycheck and benefits that come with his job.

"When do you think you could clear out your desk? We'd all like to take you out to lunch, too."

I don't know if that would feel nice or like rubbing salt in my wound. "I don't know. I'll have to get back to you." Maybe I'll go get my things tonight, while everyone is asleep. I know they will have already changed the passwords on my computer and made sure their client list is unavailable to me.

If I can't trust Stuart, who can I trust?

"Well. Let me know. And I'll help you anyway I can, Sky. You've been invaluable to the firm."

Not so invaluable, I think. Even if you do a great job, work weekends and evenings to meet deadlines, you're expendable. Even though Stuart gave me wonderful ratings on work evaluations. *And* accompanied that A+ rating with maximum merit salary increases. But I guess at the end of the day, I wasn't all that important.

Now what? Another thing in my life just ended, out of the blue.

I'm walking along an abyss that threatens tragedy every day.